Praise for Girl Unmoored

"Infused with love and punctuated with wry good humor…
Apron may be adrift, but Hummer's debut is on track."
– *Publishers Weekly*

"*Girl Unmoored* by Jennifer Gooch Hummer may be the un-
discovered young-adult novel of the summer."
– *Entertainment Weekly*

"I simply cannot recommend this book highly enough—for
the story, for the incredibly good writing, for the adorable
heroine and the cast of supporting characters…"
– *Seattle Post-Intelligencer*

"*Girl Unmoored* helps moor us all."
– *Portland Press Herald*

"This book is smart, funny and quirky. It's also a poignant
coming-of-age story that continues to enjoy strong cross-
over appeal."
– SheKnows.com

"Don't you just love it when you discover a brilliant new
author? I was giddy with excitement after I read the irresistible
novel, *Girl Unmoored.*"
– Barnes & Noble Book Blog

"*Girl Unmoored* is on its way to becoming a classic
coming-of-age."
– The Divining Wand

"I think you should just trust me when I say read it. Put
down whatever mish-mash you're reading and find this
book."
– Anthology of a Girl

"Read this book. You will feel human and alive. It's the one
I'm going to be touting all year, declaring to others that this

is the book we should all be trying to write. And the one we should all want to read."
–Write Meg

"I laughed, I cried... I felt mad, I felt glad... I liked, loved and loathed, and this range of emotions was all thanks to the skilled storytelling ability of Jennifer Gooch Hummer."
– YA's The Word

"Poignant, candid, and heartbreakingly unique, *Girl Unmoored* is the best debut novel I've read in 2012."
– Reader Girls

"If you only read one teen novel this year, *Girl Unmoored* is the book to read."
– Roundtable Reviews

"Holy *Are You There God? It's Me, Margaret*, Batman! There is a new coming of age novel on the scene and it's awesome!"
– Well Read Wife

"With stunning emotional honesty, *Girl Unmoored* shaves away layers of innocence to reveal the true meaning of love, and the power we have to save one another. Effortlessly funny and poignant, Jennifer Gooch Hummer's masterful debut offers surprises until the very end. I am head over heels for this book, and will gladly scream its praises from the rafters—for sure a must-read!"
– Elise Allen, *New York Times* bestselling co-author of *Elixir* and author of *Populazzi*

"From the shadows of loss and uncertainty to the ultimate act of forgiveness, Girl Unmoored is a uniquely rendered and quirky coming-of-age tale that will break your heart one minute and have you laughing out loud the next."
– Beth Hoffman, *New York Times* bestselling author of *Saving CeeCee Honeycutt*

Girl Unmoored

by

Jennifer Gooch Hummer

**fiction
studio
books**

The Fiction Studio
P.O. Box 4613
Stamford, CT 06907

Print ISBN-13: 978-1-936558-30-8
E-book ISBN-13: 978-1-936558-31-5

Visit our website at www.fictionstudiobooks.com

First Fiction Studio Printing: March 2012

Printed in the United States of America

For Mike

As you ramble on through Life, Brother
Whatever be your goal
Keep your Eye upon the donut
And not upon the Hole
– Downyflake Doughnuts, Nantucket Mass.

1

Incipit.
Begin here.

Jesus was in his underwear. That was the first thing I noticed. He had long blond hair that looked like he forgot to rinse the conditioner out of it and every time it flew in front of his face, he whipped it back over his shoulder.

"Wow, Jesus is foxy," Rennie said with her gummy-bear breath. But I tightened my jaw. Loud music was banging everywhere and colored lights were blinking. I looked at Rennie and watched her cheeks flash from red to purple.

On the way to the theater, while Rennie was putting on her lip gloss for the thousandth time and Mr. Perry was driving and Mrs. Perry was throwing her arms up and yelling, "Slow *down*, Bill!" I sat there looking normal but thinking about how much I wished we were going to see the real Jesus. Everyone needed a miracle once in a while.

But my life slammed back into me when we got out of the car and Mrs. Perry handed us our tickets. *Jesus Christ Superstar, The Musical*, it said, clear as day.

It should have said *Jesus Christ Freak Show* because so far there was just him and his underwear walking around angry dancers with big hair and big belts singing "What's the buzz?" every second. Even the sweaty faith healings that Grandma Bramhall watched on TV were better than this. At least those people got out of their wheelchairs in the end.

I put my feet up to block it all out. Our seats were smack dab in the middle of everybody and everywhere I looked people and their flashing faces were following Jesus. Even the old lady sitting on the other side of me who smelled like baby powder tapped her foot, and she had an eye patch so clearly she could have used a miracle. Her hand was shaking too, but I couldn't tell if it was because of the music or because her arm was plugged in wrong like Grandma Bramhall's neck.

Rennie frowned at my feet and nudged me with her elbow. I frowned back and sat up again. Then I slipped my bracelet out from under my sleeve and turned it right side up so *Holly Bramh #08092* was flat on top and *Maine Med* was on the bottom. There were 08091 other people in the hospital that could have used a little help too.

After a few more songs, Jesus froze. Then he turned and walked off stage. I slipped one arm into my coat and started to stand until a bang happened and the lights got dimmer and the music got darker. Someone kicked my seat and said, "Hey, do you mind?" so I slid down again.

Next, two guys in black capes started singing like they were running out of batteries. I tried not to listen, but their voices were low enough to crawl up your back. Even with my eyes shut, I could see their whips. The music sped up and a crowd of dark-hooded people grabbed Jesus and begged for things. He *wanted* to fix them—you could tell by how slowly he touched their foreheads—but it wasn't going to happen and he knew it. Still, they kept on grabbing. Until finally when they were about to suffocate him, Jesus pushed them all away and yelled, "Save yourselves!"

That stopped everyone all right.

"All you have to do to conquer death," he sang slowly, like it hurt, "is to die."

Which was ridiculous.

I looked around. You can't conquer death if you're dead. But no one else looked confused, not even Mrs. Perry, who can't take in too much information at once or she'll check on her big curl and say, "You lost me, now. Start again?"

After the song, Jesus looked worse.

Mary made him lie down in the middle of the stage. Then she started singing, "Everything's all right, yes, everything's fine . . ." and rubbing something on his forehead, which wasn't going to help him. No one ever gets saved by a forehead rub. Ask Laura Ingalls Wilder if you don't believe me. But Mary kept doing it anyway, begging him to let the world turn without him tonight because everything was all right—which it wasn't, because even his best friend, Judas, was acting weird. I snuck a look at Rennie to see if she was thinking what I was thinking, but she had her same old face on, blinking away like Bambi. Finally, Jesus went to sleep and Judas found the black capes and told them where Jesus would be on Thursday.

Then the lights came on.

"Is that it?" I asked Rennie, who was looking through her fancy silk pocket book for her Cherry Fine lip gloss. "Can we leave?"

"It's intermission, Apron. You're so naïve," she said shaking her head and standing. "I don't know why my mom had to invite you, anyway."

But I did. I was there when Eeebs told his mom he wouldn't be caught dead watching a bunch of faggots dance around. "And besides," he said. "It's the JV trip to Funtown Splashtown," which Mrs. Perry had forgotten about when she bought the four tickets. I knew almost everything about the Perrys. So I put my *Playbill* down on my seat and filed out like everybody else.

In the aisles, things got hectic. Everyone pushed and someone stepped right onto the back of my flip-flop.

Eeeb's flip-flops actually. Mrs. Perry said, "Sorry, Apron," but that was my best bet because Rennie's shoes were too small and Mrs. Perry's shoes were too fancy, and what happened was: I forgot my high heels. Last night when Mrs. Perry called me I forgot to pay attention to the skirt thing and didn't remember it again until after my dad dropped me off. Rennie rolled her eyes at my Stride Rites and reminded me that you have to wear a skirt for the theater. Mrs. Perry had an ugly yellow one with green frogs on it that fit me as long as I wore her pink belt with seagulls on it, but no shoes. Which was why now, in line at the concession stand, I got stepped on twice. And by the time Rennie and I both got our DOTS, I got stepped on two more times. Mrs. Perry was one of the times, but I hadn't brought any money and she had given me two dollars and said, "Here, honey, get whatever you want," so I wasn't about to get mad at her for almost breaking my toes.

"There's Seth Chambers!" Rennie whispered, jumping behind me and grabbing my shoulder. It was true. There *was* Seth Chambers. He might be dumb as wood, but he was also as handsome as ever: his blond hair long enough to tuck back behind his ears, his perfect teeth flashing white. Something drilled into my bellybutton when I saw him, but I wasn't about to tell Rennie that. She had so many *Rennie Chambers* scribbled in her math book she had to buy a new one. "Do you think I should go talk to him?" she asked my underarm.

I tried to say no, but the DOTS had cemented my teeth together. So I groaned instead. Finally Seth left and Rennie let go, sighing and chewing on another DOTS, which, if I was lucky, might cement her teeth together forever.

Then the lights flickered. In Maine that usually meant there were thunderstorms coming, but in the theater it meant get back to your seat. Someone stepped on the back of my flip-flop again and this time one of the sides popped out. Without any more flip in that flop, I had to skate it. Mrs. Perry said, "That's okay, honey," when she saw Eeeb's shoe was broken, but her mad face looked the same as her glad one, so you never really knew what was going on in between that curl.

The old lady was there when I sat down. I had some DOTS leftover, but I didn't ask her if she wanted any because then she'd have to buy new eyes and new dentures. Mr. and Mrs. Perry sat down again, too. They never held hands. And never once had I seen them kiss. I used to catch my dad hugging my mom by the icebox, but now I catch him hugging M there instead. M used to be Nurse De Costa. I'm supposed to call her Margie. But M is as good as it's going to get.

Mrs. Perry leaned her perfect tight curl over Rennie's lap and said, "Do you like it so far, girls?" I said,

"Yes, thank you," but Rennie said, "Can I get some more candy after?"

When the lights went down again, I slumped as low as I could in my seat and got ready for another round. And then things went really wrong. The hippies were back up there dancing and the low batteries were still warning everyone, and now Jesus was sadder and more tired. He didn't dance anymore and he hardly ever sang, except to say he was sad and tired even though he used to be inspired. And it turned out Mary was wrong and I was right. Everything *wasn't* all right and Judas was a traitor and Jesus got dragged around to see some kings and one of them whipped him. Then Judas died and Jesus got beaten up some more and wouldn't even ask them to stop and when *that* barrel of laughs was over, Jesus got put on the cross. He flipped his head back and moaned and asked in one long yell why he had been forsaken.

That made me sit up.

The hooded people went back to clawing at him and then all of a sudden it got so quiet you could hear a pin drop and Jesus was dead. You could tell by the way his hair hung down all over his face and he didn't whip it back.

Then that was it. The curtains smashed together and everyone clapped and yelled and stood. The noise came too fast. I blinked and tried to stand but couldn't get my feet to work.

"It's a standing O," Rennie said pulling me up.

The hippies and low batteries were taking their bow and when Jesus came out he was smiling and whipping and waving, not looking so forsaken to me anymore.

Just fake.

My stomach cramped.

"Cut your hair!" I yelled.

"What's your problem, Apron? Shut up," Rennie said, looking at me with her face all crooked.

"Don't you think he looks a little too much like the *real* one? He shouldn't get people's hopes up like that."

Rennie pulled one side of her lip up. She wasn't the sharpest tool in the shed, but that wasn't why she didn't understand. I looked past her to Mr. and Mrs. Perry. Rennie probably didn't even know what *forsaken* meant. She didn't need to.

When I looked back up at the stage again, Jesus was gone.

In the lobby, Rennie grabbed her mother's elbow and told her she needed to go to the bathroom.

"Can't you wait, kiddo? Look at the line," Mr. Perry asked, his voice iced in hope. "The exit'll be gridlocked."

But Mrs. Perry gave him a glare and steered Rennie toward the line anyway. Her uncle somebody died trying not to go to the bathroom when he was a boy, he just exploded inside out at the Thanksgiving table because he was too shy to tell his parents. That's what her glare said. I looked over at Mr. Perry. If I'd heard this story a thousand times already, imagine how many times *he'd* heard it by now.

Instead of looking like he remembered, he turned and walked toward a black shiny wall, picking his way against the flow of people headed for the exit. I skated my flop behind him, both of us stopping every few steps not to break up a family.

The black wall turned out to be a waterfall with two small hoses sticking out from the marble. Big silver

letters spelling out SPRAGUE THEATER were staying nice and dry just below them.

Mr. Perry sat on a stone wall that came out in a
corner, the water splashing behind him. I sat down next
to him. On the other side of the corner, two mothers
were trying to bounce the boredom out of their crying
babies.

"You should pray for sons," Mr. Perry sighed.
"There's never a line for the men's room."

"Okay," I said, not really smiling back. The Perrys
were the kind of people who always warned kids about
stuff that happens to you when you get old. Which I
guess is all you have left to think about once you never
have homework again for the rest of your life.

Mr. Perry and I said nothing until everyone left and
things finally got quiet. I could hear the uneven splash-
es behind me.

"So. How are you holding up, Apron?" he glanced
at me.

"Okay," I said wondering for a moment if he meant
my broken shoe. But his face was more serious than a
flip-flop, so I looked away and added a shrug. "I guess."

"Six months seems like a minute and a lifetime ago,
doesn't it." Another stupid thing to say. All it seemed
like to me was a lifetime ago.

"Not really."

Mr. Perry shook his head at himself. "Oh gosh. Of
course it doesn't." Then he nodded at me with his eyes
dialed on full. "I'm sorry, Apron."

A few leftover people walked by us and Mr. Perry
stared down at his shoes. "Apron, I . . ." he hesitated,
his voice coming out in little jumps. "We all miss her.
Holly was a very beautiful woman."

"Who's beautiful?"

Rennie was standing over us with her arms crossed. Those bouncing mothers were nowhere to be seen now.

"*There* she is," Mr. Perry smiled, wiping his hands on his pants and standing.

Rennie dropped her arms. "Mom and I have been standing out there, *waiting*."

"Oops," he said, taking Rennie's arm and starting toward the door; the two of them ignoring me and my flop trying to keep up.

↗   ↗   ↗

"So what did you think, girls?" Mrs. Perry asked in the car after we pulled out of the lot. I looked at the back of Mr. Perry's head, waiting for Rennie to answer first. Mr. Perry had an empty spot the size of a golf ball, but my dad's head was still fully covered. People with red hair don't usually go bald.

"Girls?" Mrs. Perry asked again and this time I looked up, catching Mr. Perry's frown by mistake in the rearview mirror.

"Great," I lied.

Rennie had been staring out her window ever since we got into the car.

"Rennie," Mrs. Perry asked, shifting herself around so she could see her.

"That was the worst musical I've ever seen," Rennie said finally. "There wasn't even a happy ending. He just died. "

"Yes, but remember, he died so he could save us all," Mrs. Perry smiled. "You can talk to Reverend

Hunter about it in Sunday School." She looked at me. I didn't go to Sunday School and we both knew it.

"It's still a bad ending," Rennie whispered.

I nodded, but Rennie didn't see it.

"Well. I will say, *those* people certainly can sing," Mrs. Perry sighed, glancing at Mr. Perry as she faced forward again.

"What people?" Rennie asked.

Mr. Perry snapped, "No people" and gave Mrs. Perry a sideways look. "And you wonder where Eeebs gets it from, Sue."

Mrs. Perry huffed at her window. "Just an observation, Bill," she said. "Most of them can carry a tune, that's all."

Mr. Perry shook his head.

Usually when the Perrys fought, Rennie would roll her eyes at me and mimic them. But this time she turned her head toward her window again and said nothing. So I said nothing back.

When Mr. Perry turned on the radio, "Girls Just Want to Have Fun" blared out. Rennie and I turned to each other with sudden smiles. Mr. Perry had taken us to a Cyndi Lauper concert for Rennie's birthday last year. Mrs. Perry wouldn't come so my mom did instead and he bought all three of us a Cyndi Lauper backpack. But now, Mr. Perry tightened his jaw and flipped the station. Mrs. Perry didn't like that kind of music.

"Dad!" Rennie whined.

But he was done talking. He stopped on some piano playing.

I waited for Rennie to whine some more like she usually did, but she didn't. She just went back to her window. So I turned to mine and watched the streetlights whiz by in one long yellow streak until finally they started flashing and by the time we came to a red light they were just plain old streetlights again.

"And why was Jesus in his underwear, anyway?" Rennie asked.

"Those were shorts, dear," Mrs. Perry said, bothered about it.

"Well, they looked like underwear," Rennie smirked. And then I couldn't help it; I started laughing. Mr. Perry told us to tone it down, but it was too late and before we knew it we were laughing hard enough for it to feel like things were back to normal. Until Mr. Perry turned right and we started down our long dirt road where there weren't any streetlights at all and normal was a lifetime ago.

2

Si vis pacem, para bellum.
If you want peace, prepare for war.

My dad was staring down at me smelling like coffee not wine, so you knew it had to be morning. "Time to get up, Apron," he said.

He looked tired; his freckles were hanging too low on his face. He used to have brown ones like mine, but now those were graying too.

"And don't forget the tunics for the Meaningless Bowl. Twelve greens and eleven blues, unless," his voice faded, "Jesus H. Christ, that moron, Chambers, shows up again." I groaned, but my dad said, "Hurry up" or "Fire truck," I couldn't tell which, and walked out the door.

I blinked enough to window wash the sleep out of my eyes and twisted my bracelet around. It was going to be sunny today. Already a streak of yellow was sneaking in from under the window shade, lighting up the *Little House on the Prairie* books on my shelf. I had read every book in the series by the time I was eight, and a few hundred times over since then. I have to sneak them now, though, otherwise my dad says, "Aren't we a little past those, Apron? I mean really. How about some *Moby-Dick*?" But the truth was that Laura Ingalls Wilder was the nicest girl I'd ever not known. Rennie would throw me under a bus for a piece of chocolate.

M's chocolate anyway. M told her it was from Brazil, but you could find the same kind at Stop & Shop if you knew where to look.

I flung my covers into a triangle and rolled out of bed. I could hear M banging things down in the kitchen and voices coming up from *Hello Maine!* By the time I got home from the play last night, M was asleep. That was all she did these days. At first I thought maybe she was sleeping in the guest room until I put a marble on her pillow that never moved. "They're doing it," Rennie nodded. I wanted to punch her perfect Bambi face in when she said it, but I knew she was right.

I shuffled over to my closet. You could hear a dog barking outside, which was Betty, whose mother, Nutter, was dead, too. My mom used to put leftover food on the porch for her until Mrs. Weller came over and told her that Nutter was getting too fat. My mom said, "Never again, Mrs. Weller. I'm sorry." But Mrs. Weller stayed right there frowning in the doorway under her orange umbrella. It wasn't raining, but everything she owned was orange. After that, Nutter came over anyway and my mom said, "A few bites won't kill her," which it might have, because after she fed her leftover meatloaf one time, Nutter got hit by a truck and the only way you could tell it was her was by the orange collar.

I walked over to my mirror and pulled off my nightgown. Two miniature pyramids with nipples that looked like someone had poked them through from the other side with a pencil stared back at me. Half the girls in my class were already wearing bras, but not me. Or Rennie, who had even smaller pyramids than I did. We were going to get our first bras together, though.

"At least you have big brains," Rennie would say. But brains didn't need bras, so boys never noticed me.

I slipped on my long-sleeved T-shirt with *Portland Head Light* on it and stepped into my pants. Sometimes I went for days without changing my underwear.

Then I brushed down my red, sleepy head, trying to see what M saw when she looked at me: someone pointless and pale and always in the way.

Downstairs in the kitchen, M was standing at the stove stirring something bumpy. Her eyes were glued to *Hello Maine!* It was going to be sunny today: "Mid-70s and gorgeous, gorgeous." She looked bad, even for M. She had sick mood written all over her and her black hair was down, which meant she wasn't going to be a nurse until later and we would have to meet her at the hospital for dinner. She wasn't a real nurse, she was only a nurse's *aide*, so she got the worst shifts.

When I walked by, she pulled her eyes off the screen just long enough to look me up and down once before turning back to the weather. "Morning, Aprons."

There weren't two of me though; it was just her bad English. I was supposed to be named April after my great grandmother, but my dad found out that *April* in Latin meant "opening" and no way was his daughter going to be called that. My mom said Latin had nothing to do with the real world and my dad said it seemed to be paying for the real roof over her head. She put *April* on my birth certificate anyway, but in such tiny chicken scratch to hide it from my dad that some wizard thought it said *Apron*. "Apron?" my dad asked. "What kind of numbskull would write that?" But my mom said it served him right for being so stubborn. And then they never changed it.

"Morning," I told M.

I climbed onto the counter and got down my bowl and cereal. Outside the trees were busy growing. Little green buds popping up everywhere.

"There is oatmeal," M said. Well if you wanted to glue something together, then you needed M's oatmeal. So I jumped down and went straight to the icebox for the milk. "Better that you eat the oatmeals, Aprons. In Brazil the Mammas would never let their childrens eat that *ca-ca*."

I could feel that thing creeping up in my throat like it always did whenever M was close. Pretty soon even a Fruity Pebble wouldn't fit down it, so I knew I better start eating fast. I got a spoon, took everything over to the table and sat down in my spot. A little girl lobster was painted right onto the wood. My mom had painted lobsters for all three of us: one with starfish sunglasses, one reading Latin, and one tap dancing. She quit tap dancing classes when she got into karate, but kept the lobster. The other side of the table was empty. It was supposed to have a baby lobster on it someday. I wanted a sister, but my dad wanted a son. Now though, I just wanted it blank. If M thought she could paint a nurse lobster there she had another think coming.

I poured some cereal and put the box in front of me so I could read the *Do You Knows* on the back. You never wanted to talk to M if my dad wasn't around.

"You will get fat eating this," she said anyway, pointing to the box and walking toward me with her bowl of glue and one of her Portuguese romance novels. "The boys will never like you." I tried to look shocked that the yo-yo was the most popular toy in the world and took a bite of my cereal, which was the best thing you could ever taste unless you had something in your throat trying to kill you or M staring down at you. Then it tasted like cardboard.

The toilet flushed in the hall bathroom. My dad would be in for more coffee soon. Out the corner of my eye, I saw M put her bowl down on top of the tap-dancer's feelers. My skin caught fire. You weren't supposed to put anything hot directly on top of the lobsters. "Please move that," I said as smooth as silk. But she ignored me. So I picked it up myself and put it down on the empty side of the table.

"Hey, that's mines," she whined.

"Keep it off the lobsters, please." I slid a place-mat from the center of the table over to her. My blood banged too hard inside of me, but my dad still wasn't out of the bathroom so I took another bite of my cereal. M clucked her tongue and reached over for her oatmeal, her book dropping to the ground with a thud as she did. But before she could snatch it up I saw it: a folded piece of paper that had fallen out of her pages. "K-1 Visa: Marrying within the U.S.," it said at the top.

Just when you think the toilet is about to explode into a million pieces, it shuts off. But I didn't hear it this time because of my bowl hitting the floor, causing a flood of Fruity Pebbles all around my chair. The cereal box had knocked over my bowl when I stood.

"What's going on?" my dad growled from the kitchen door. I swallowed that sugary milk gone sour and looked up at him.

"Oh dears, just an accident, Dennis," M said, wiping cereal off her bathrobe. The paper was nowhere to be seen now. I was the only one who knew the real M and what she was after, and M planned on keeping it that way. "I'll get the mop," she smiled.

But my dad said, "No, Margie. Apron can clean it up," and turned toward the coffee. "You're not going to forget the tunics again, are you, Apron?"

"Nope," I said stepping away from M.

"What did you say?" *Nope* was a four-letter word around here.

"No, Dad," I said, picking up my bowl, which was plastic, not even scratched. "I will not forget the tunics."

He went back to his pouring and I scooped up as much of the soggy mess as I could. "It might finally be our *Dies Faustus*," he chuckled. M didn't know what that meant, but I did: Lucky Day. "Margie's never seen a touch football game, *American* football, the *real* kind. She's in for quite a show with all of us old-timers out there, isn't she?"

I shook my head.

When I opened the broom closet, something scurried. I froze. One time we found a raccoon in the corner. I couldn't see any raccoons anywhere, but the scurry happened again. I stepped closer and saw a scurry this time. It was The Boss, behind the mop, rummaging around in his cage. "Hey," I cooed. "What are you doing in here?"

He twitched his salt and pepper whiskers at me and that was all I needed to hear. I picked up his cage and turned around.

M and my dad were standing by the icebox. "Who put The Boss in there?"

My dad looked confused, but M looked away. Then we both looked at her.

"Dad," I pleaded. "It's freezing in there."

He stepped back. "Margie," he said carefully. But before he could say any more, she covered her mouth with her hand and ran out the door.

We both watched her go. I prayed she would run all the way out the front door and back to Brazil, but no such luck. Pretty soon she'd have to, though. Her work visa was only good for a year. Now, she just walked up the stairs, leaving a trail of Fruity Pebbles so she could find her way back for more glue after my dad left.

My dad sighed. "Sorry, Apron. I'll tell her she can't do that again."

I put the cage down. "He could have died," I told him. "Guinea pigs cannot survive below sixty-five degrees, Dad." Which may or may not have been true. My dad knew just about every fact out there, but hopefully not this one.

He looked at me, exhausted. "Just try to be a little more patient, okay?" He said this like she was our new maid, which, when I thought about it, made me wish she was. Then she could get fired.

"Dad," I said. "You're still married to Mom, right?"

He tipped his head at me. "Of course I am. Now get to school, Apron."

He walked out the door and I left The Boss on the kitchen table, twitching and munching, while I went back to the closet to get out the mop. The truth was, he looked plenty fine to me. But M hated him almost as much as she hated me. "Why do all you Americans keep rats for pets? It is disgusting."

I grabbed the mop. I had never trusted M around The Boss, and now that she dared get close enough to move his cage, who knew what she would do to him next. Maybe she'd even take him out and set him free.

The Boss stopped munching when he saw me. "Save yourself!" Jesus had warned everyone. But what he should have said was "Tell your owner to get a combination lock." Because in the real world someone had to save you.

3
Sona si latine loqueris.
Honk if you speak Latin.

Hello Maine! **was wrong as usual.** Today was going to be *humid, humid!*

When I finally made it to the bike racks at school, the back of my shirt was soaking wet and two seconds later the bell rang.

Before I got to my desk, I stopped at Rennie's. Today, her black pigtails were wrapped up in pink bows and her part was so straight it looked like a chalk line. "What, Apron?" she rolled her eyes at me.

"Hi," I smiled.

"Look. I need to talk to you at recess," she said, suddenly serious.

"Why?" The last time she said that, she told me there was a rumor going around that I had kissed Johnny Berman in the boy's room. I hadn't, but I couldn't say I wouldn't have. Maybe not in the boy's bathroom, but behind the lower school swing set, where everyone else did, I might have at least considered it. We never found out who started the rumor, but I kept hoping it was Johnny Berman himself.

Rennie's eyes flashed over to Jenny Pratt at the end of her row. "I can't tell you here."

"Why not?"

"*Because*, Apron," she said. But then she looked up at me. "Look, I think we need to start making new friends, okay?"

I felt like I had been punched in the stomach, but slowly, like I was watching it happen.

"I mean, we've been friends for so long it's just *boring*." She looked back over to Jenny Pratt. This time, Jenny turned her perfect face toward her and smiled. When she noticed me though, she scowled. Jenny was the most popular girl in our class and we hated her. The only way you could be friends with her was if she picked you to be.

I frowned at Rennie. "Jenny Pratt? But we hate her."

"I never said that," Rennie whispered, panicked.

"Yes you did. We both did."

"No. Apron. I never said that. You did."

I stared at her. I wasn't a liar and we both knew it.

Just then, Ms. Frane walked in and told everyone to sit. I gave Rennie one last look before I went to my desk, two rows in front of her.

When everyone was seated, Ms. Frane, who was kind of pretty but still wasn't married, probably because she always wore the same blue skirt and messy hair with two barrettes pulling it back for no reason, said, "Grammar books, please. Today we begin to study Latin roots."

Johnny Berman, who only sat next to me because Ms. Frane liked to keep things in alphabetical order, let out a groan. But I smiled. Even if you didn't know my dad was a Latin professor, you might think something was up from our bumper sticker: *Sona si latine loqueris!* "Honk if you speak Latin!" Hardly anyone ever honked.

I wasn't exactly good at it, but my dad was determined to teach me. For a while, things got too serious for me to practice. But now with M hanging around, I was back to studying it full time. She could hardly understand English, no way could she understand Latin.

"Page 132," Ms. Frane said. "Today we'll start with *homos.*"

Johnny Berman snickered into his hand. I felt my cheeks turn on. It *was* kind of an embarrassing word.

"Now. Can anyone tell me what the Latin root *homo* means?"

A few more boys chuckled and Johnny Berman whispered, "Paul Green," loud enough for only some of us, and Paul Green, to hear.

"Anne, do you know?"

A few seats down from Rennie, Annie Potts flipped her mousey brown hair over her shoulder and sat up higher. "Um. One?"

"One *fudge packer,*" Johnny Berman whispered, coughing to cover it up. But Ms. Frane must have heard this time. "Another interruption and you get a red card, Johnny," she warned, so he lost his smile. "Good guess, Anne. Not quite, though. Anyone else? Paul?"

"Man," Paul Green answered quietly, which made Johnny Berman cough again.

Ms. Frane said, "Yes," then added, "Perfect, Paul," because he was one of her pets. "Can anyone give an example of a *word* using this root?"

"Homicide?" Billy Moore called out.

"Good," Miss Frane nodded, writing it on the blackboard.

"Homosexual?" Lynn Aouerbach said, like she said the word out loud every day. Which maybe she did. She always wore black.

Johnny Berman let out a hoot this time and the room fell silent. Miss Frane turned to him with her lips pinched together. Everyone knew that if he got one more red card he was going to get suspended. "Yes. That *is* a proper use of the root. Lynn is correct." She didn't turn around to write it out, though. She just kept staring at Johnny. Deciding.

"Homo habilis," I called out quickly. Once in sixth grade, I'd seen him walking home in the rain, so I'd given him a ride on my bookrack. And ever since then he'd been nothing but nice to me.

Miss Frane shifted her stare over, impressed. "And can you tell us what this means, Apron?" She caught me studying my dictionary again last week. "You remind me of me when I was your age," she said, meaning to be nice but scaring me just the same.

"A species of primitive man that first used sticks and stones as tools." It said this a few pages later in our grammar book, but nobody else had probably read that far.

"Very good," Miss Frane said turning back to the board and writing *Homo habilis* on it. Johnny Berman exhaled and sat back. I smiled at him and he bugged his eyes out.

"All right, now. Please get out your writing notebooks and give me three full sentences using the Latin root for *homos*. And if you'll excuse me, I have someone waving at me from the hallway."

We looked over to the long skinny window inside the door, but all we could see was the back of a head. Principal Parker.

As soon as Ms. Frane was gone, everyone started talking. "I hope she's getting fired!" Johnny Berman said standing up. I watched Rennie stand too. But I got to her before she could go anywhere. "Rennie," I said, careful not to sound desperate. "We need to be Avon ladies this weekend."

"Ucch," she said. "See what I mean, Apron. *Boring.*" Then she shrugged and turned toward the end of her row. Toward Jenny Pratt. "We're teenagers now, Apron. Not babies."

I lowered my voice. "It's an emergency."

"What?" She turned back to me, which I hoped she would. Rennie loved emergencies.

"M's going to kill The Boss. I need a lock."

Rennie crossed her arms.

"She *is,* Rennie. She started hiding him in closets. You don't believe me?"

But then suddenly she looked like she did.

"Well, too bad," she said anyway. "It's the Meaningless Bowl. Seth Chambers's dad is bringing a real *Patriots* football." She said this loudly, but no one looked over, not even the boys.

I shifted in my sneakers. "It won't take very long. I just need one with a combination. They're cheaper."

Rennie pinched her forehead in. "They are?"

I nodded. She believed me when I told her things like that because my dad was a professor. Rennie's dad owned Perry's Plumbing so all he knew about were pipes.

"We can definitely still get to the game on time."

But Rennie shook her head and looked back around to Jenny Pratt, who had already stood up to go talk to Nan Wetherly, her last best friend. Rennie tried not to look hurt when she turned back to me. "No way. I have to make cookies. It's our turn. And this time I'm making little footballs. My mom says I need to make like a hundred." She flipped back one of her pigtails, which meant she was serious.

A few boys started clapping, egging Johnny Berman on to do something. Then we all watched him jump up on Ms. Frane's desk and start break dancing, which gets pretty boring pretty quickly without music. I turned back to Rennie.

"Fine. What if I help you bake them Friday afternoon?"

"So you're inviting yourself over now, too?"

"No, I'm not," I said begging my freckles to stop burning. We used to just swap weekends at each other's house. "Forget it. I'll do it myself."

She grabbed my arm. "Wait! You can't be Avon ladies *alone*. It's in the rules."

"No, it's not," I said pulling away.

But Rennie grabbed my wrist this time. "You can't sell stuff we found together."

I smirked. "Fine. I just found a new pair of sunglasses. With the tag still on." They were in the passenger side of our car, probably M's.

"Like movie star ones?"

I didn't even need to nod. Rennie huffed. "All right. You can sleep over. But only because Jenny is going away this weekend." It was sad for a second, the way she said it, like she wasn't entirely sure it was true.

But then she told me to bike over fast if we were going to get the cookies done by four-thirty, which I already knew. No one can be in their kitchen after four-thirty because that was when Mrs. Perry started making dinner. She went to cooking school with Julia Child, and there's a picture of her with bobbed-out hair in a yellow dress, holding a cake and smiling big in their dining room. Hardly anyone else knew that the cake was made out of wax and was so heavy that Mrs. Perry got tennis elbow from it. At six o'clock, usually something like a whole fish with a head on it comes out the door.

"She's coming!" Matt Curtis warned us. He was half the size of most of us girls, but might be foxy someday.

I got back to my desk and watched Johnny Berman rip it over to his seat. He was still panting when Miss Frane walked in. "Sorry, class," she said, like we were sorry about it too. "Never a dull moment. Now, who'd liked to read their sentence? Oh, and before I forget, each of you needs to pick up their reminder slip for year-end conferences next week. Your parents should have marked their calendars off when I met with them in the fall, but just in case."

I looked out the window. Outside, dark branches were criss-crossing everywhere and it would take until after lunchtime before the sun finally started shining down on them. But every once in a while a branch might move for no reason and then if you looked carefully you could see a bird in there, jerking its beak around, searching for something.

4
Consanguinitas
Blood relative

Stinky people buy stinky things. That was what Rennie talked about while she skipped ahead and I pulled our wagon through the bumpy woods between our houses. The Perrys lived off of Route 88 too, but closer to Portland, and their road was paved and smooth and had a name: Thornhurst Landing.

Pieces of Rennie's voice kept falling back on me about Mr. Solo and where he lived and how we could sell him some perfume to put on before he taught us eighth grade next year. It was a well-known fact, even for us seventh graders, that Mr. Solo smelled. But he biked the same way to school as I did and unless you've tried biking up that hill yourself, you don't know what you're going to smell like.

"Hey. Wait up," I yelled to Rennie when she reached our dirt road. We couldn't be Avon ladies on her street because she only had Mrs. Larry for a neighbor, who heads to Bermuda when the mosquitoes head to Maine.

"You better go first," Rennie ordered me, standing off to the side. So I yanked the wagon over roots that looked like they had come up for air a few million years ago and then changed their minds and gone back down again.

When I stepped out onto our road, sun was beaming down everywhere, frying the shadow off everything, and the air was so heavy you could scoop it up and drink it like soup. I ripped off my sweater. All you really wanted was for those degrees to make up their mind. It wasn't like spring was a big surprise every year.

"Water," Rennie gasped, fanning her tongue, looking down at my house.

"No way," I said. "M might be there."

"We have to get water from Mrs. Smeller then."

I nodded, even though the only thing Mrs. Weller ever gives you is orange Kool-Aid that tastes like syrup and makes you thirstier.

Everything looked the same as it had yesterday. The swing set in the Christiansons' yard had the same old rake leaning up against it, and the red pickup truck with ORD UCK on the back of it was in Mrs. Weller's driveway again. Lately, I'd been seeing it there. Mr. Orso lived across the street from Mrs. Weller. All you needed to know about him was that he barked and watered his lawn every second.

"Who is it?" Mrs. Weller asked in her scratchy voice when I knocked on her door. I waved at her eye in the peephole. If we were anyone else, she would have yelled, "*Go away!*" but after she saw it was us, she said, "Hold on," and started flipping back the locks.

Except what she *should* have said was, "Don't be afraid, little children, it's just me," because there was a rolled up bloody piece of toilet paper hanging out of her nose. Big blotches of bright red blood had dripped onto her orange nightgown and there were smaller ones on her ratty old slippers, which probably used to be orange too. Rennie looked at me like we should make a run for it, but I stayed cheery the way Avon ladies are supposed to.

"Avon ladies!" I said, as if all our customers had bloody torpedoes sticking out their noses. "Let's talk beauty."

Rennie groaned.

"How are you today, Mrs. Weller?" I asked, even though a blind person could tell she was bad.

"Damn nose again," Mrs. Weller said with that bloody torpedo bumping up and down on her lips.

"Oh," I said, *really* cheery this time, because the customer was always right.

We hadn't been Avon ladies since last year. Some people might think we were getting too old to be Avon ladies, but not her. "So what do you have, girls?" she asked, getting down to business.

Rennie looked surprised, but I didn't, because bloody nose or no bloody nose, Mrs. Weller was our best customer. She was always trying to look good, but the truth was she looked exactly like George Washington in a dress.

And this morning, she looked like an especially grumpy George Washington. "We have a lot of great supplies today," I said. But what she really needed was more Kleenex to shove up her nose.

Mrs. Weller gurgled something and walked past us to get to the wagon. The smell of pot roast and stale baby powder lingered behind. Rennie pinched her nose, but I tried to keep my face pleasant!

"*Milk* soap?" she croaked, holding up one of the tiny squares an inch away from the bloody torpedo. This was the bulk of our supply: little soaps and shampoos that Mr. Perry brought back from his trips. He was always giving them to Mrs. Perry, who just threw them into one of her drawers and kept using her fancy French stuff anyway.

"There's a special today. We'll give you three soaps for the price of two," I said, ignoring Rennie's open mouth.

Mrs. Weller dropped the soap back into the wagon and mumbled, "Smells like a frying pan."

A window slammed shut from somewhere behind me and when I turned around, I saw that it was mine.

I took off. It had to be M, snooping around in my room. And this time I was going to catch her.

I ran around to the front of our house, up the porch stairs, and opened the front door fast enough for it to slam against the wall. Then I took the stairs two at a time and turned into my room. And there it was: my shut window—sitting there like it wasn't even open a minute ago. Everything else was just sitting there too: one white sock hanging out of the drawer, exactly how I left it.

I walked over to my window and slid it open again. I could see Mrs. Weller down there, leaning into the wagon trying to smell something, and Rennie watching her with her top lip pinned up. Then I heard the toilet flush and M cough.

I walked into the hall, crossed my arms, and waited. *This* time I was going to tell her to stop snooping around in my room or I'd tell my dad.

Except everything changes when you hear someone throw up.

She threw up three times. Then I heard the toilet flush again and M start crying. Hard. Like maybe she had slammed her foot into the door. Suddenly, I just wanted to go back outside and talk beauty.

When I got to the wagon, Rennie's lip was still pulled up and Mrs. Weller was smelling a small bottle of blue conditioner with *Kennebunk Marriott* on it.

And then I knew what Rennie's face was all about. The torpedo had fallen half way out her nose.

Rennie put her finger down her throat and gagged, but Mrs. Weller was too busy to notice. She dropped the mini bottle back into the wagon and picked up another one. I shot Rennie a warning look. You can gag all you want unless you need a combination lock.

Across the road, Mr. Orso came out of his door and walked up to his car. He waved at us once, barking softly before getting into it. I waved back. He was our worst customer, if you could even call him that. He had never bought anything from us, ever.

"Damn nose," Mrs. Weller said. I turned around again. The torpedo had fallen out. A tiny speck of blood started dripping. "Wait here girls," she said tipping her head back and walking into her house like Frankenstein.

"Let's *go*," Rennie whispered.

I frowned at the bloody torpedo and the next thing I knew I was bending down to pick it up.

"*Ach*," Rennie yelled, slapping her hands over her eyes. "Sick!"

Even though she couldn't see that I was only touching the part without any blood on it, you couldn't blame her. Before M hijacked my life, I would never in a trillion years have picked it up.

"What are you going to do with it?" Rennie groaned through her fingers.

"I'll be right back," I said like I had a plan, which I guess going to find Mrs. Weller's trash can was.

I held the torpedo out as far away from me as I could and walked through the front door. Inside, it smelled like a million different things rolled into one, but mostly just plain old *oldness*. There were thickly brushed portraits of Mr. and Mrs. Weller hanging on the walls. Even though Mrs. Weller looked like George Washington *now*, she used to look pretty good once, like a younger version of him.

The only trash can that I knew about was in the kitchen under the sink, so I turned into it.

And stopped.

Jesus was eating some toast.

"Jesus!"

He looked up at me with his big blue eyes and said, "Sorry, did I scare you?"

I shook my head.

He was sitting at Mrs. Weller's kitchen table, and after he asked me that, he put his toast down and smiled. His nose looked a little bigger than it had on stage and his stringy blond hair stayed tucked back behind both ears, but anyone could tell it was him: Jesus Christ Superstar.

"Uh-oh," he said spotting the torpedo in my hand. "I keep telling her she should stay in bed when she gets one of those, but she doesn't listen. Trash is over there." He pointed toward the sink.

Up on stage you might not be able to see how blue his eyes were, but sitting there at Mrs. Weller's table, his eyes looked like perfect round blueberries. He was wearing jeans and a white T-shirt and sitting with his legs crossed like a girl.

I opened the sink door and threw away the torpedo. When I turned around again, he was chewing on the toast. Smacking it, really.

He smiled at me, then uncrossed his legs and sat up straighter.

You would think a Jesus's teeth would be perfect, but they weren't. They were kind of yellow and not exactly straight.

He pointed his crust at me. "You're April, right?"

"Ap*ron*," I corrected him.

"Oh yeah, sorry man. *Apron*." He held his arms up like he was under arrest and a few blond strips fell out from behind his ears. "The neighbor's kid. You have a brother or sister or something named Cricket, right?" He put his hands in his mouth and started picking something out of his teeth, way in the back.

I shook my head. "Wrong house."

He groaned, concentrating. "Got it," he said finally, pulling his hand out with something pinched in between his fingers. "Lettuce. Been driving me crazy."

I made a face. He stared at me. Then he stood and walked toward me. "I'm Mike," he said. "Mike Weller."

"Mike *Weller*?" I asked. He looked nothing like Mrs. Weller.

"Yip," Mike said holding out the hand he had just used for the lettuce, then thinking better of it and holding out the other one instead. "Millie's nephew."

We shook hands the opposite way, then I stepped back and saw that his jeans were dirty at the bottom and there was a hole right where the pocket should be.

"I gotta go," I said. "Nice to meet you." I walked out the door.

Rennie was sitting on the wagon braiding a piece of thick black hair straight down the middle of her face. She let it drop flat on her nose when she saw me. "Can we *please* go now?" she said. "I'm dying." She stuck her tongue out and fanned it.

"Yes."

Rennie jumped up so quickly the wagon almost tipped over. "Your house?"

"Fine."

A peep sound came out of her after that. The wagon was going to be hard to turn, but I didn't feel like helping, so I just kept walking.

"Hey, Apron?" someone said.

I turned around and there he was in the doorway.

Rennie's eyes went from me to the door, the one long braid still hanging down the middle of her face. "Look!" she said whipping her head back again so fast the braid made a thump. "It's Jesus!"

Part of a crooked smile happened on his mouth. "You guys saw the play?"

"The other night, didn't we, Apron?"

"Far out," he said. "I didn't know kids came to the show."

"It was great, wasn't it *great,* Apron?" Rennie gushed, with a big goofy smile.

"Did you guys come on a field trip or something?"

"A field trip at *night?*" Rennie asked him, like *he* was the one with the unicorn braid hanging down the middle of his face.

"Right," he said nodding to himself.

He was going to say something else when Mrs. Weller pushed by him with a new torpedo up her nose.

"Don't you girls go anywhere," she said shuffling up to the wagon.

"Whatcha got in there?" he asked Rennie.

"Beauty supplies," she said trying to tuck that braid back behind her ear. "Do you need some stage make-up?"

"Too bad we don't have any then," I said before he could answer.

"We have some *rouge*," Rennie said ignoring me. "And some movie star sunglasses."

"Back off!" Mrs. Weller waved her arms around like a seagull deflector. "I was here first!"

We all fell silent. But when she started opening up little bottles and sniffing them through her torpedo nose again, a smile snuck over Mike's mouth. He coughed a little and used his hand to cover it up, but Rennie had seen it too, so the same kind of smile started happening on her face. Mrs. Weller kept grumbling things like "uch, Pine Sol," before throwing another mini bottle back into the wagon.

"What do you think, Mike?" she asked straightening up this time with the oversized sunglasses on, the tag hanging down one cheek.

"Gorgeous," he said. "Audrey Hepburn all the way."

Even under those bug eyes you could tell Mrs. Weller was embarrassed about a boy telling her that. "How much?" she asked with the tag and the torpedo swinging toward me.

I couldn't look at Rennie. "$10.99."

We had never made that much money in one whole *day* of being Avon ladies.

Mrs. Weller looked back up at Mike, who whistled at her like she was a famous actress, not a George Washington look-alike with bug eyes. Then she turned and walked in through her front door again.

"Is she kidding?" Rennie asked.

"I don't think so," Mike said. "She's not really a kidder." He looked over at me when he said that, like he had been meaning to tell me that all along. I turned away. People who looked that much like Jesus shouldn't lie. Ever. And especially not to little old lady George Washingtons, even if it did mean our best sale.

"Are you a movie star, too?" Rennie asked with her eyelashes flapping all over the place.

For a second he had no idea what Rennie was talking about. But then he tapped his chest and said, "No, um. I own Scent Appeal, the flower store? But my partner, he owns the flower store with me, was the choreographer for the play, so . . ."—and with that, he flapped his arms down. Then he looked at me with his blueberry eyes and a sad ping happened in my heart. Maybe he couldn't help it that he looked exactly like Jesus.

Still, he could have dyed his hair at least.

Mrs. Weller walked back out with the sunglasses.

"Here, Apron," she said handing me eleven one-dollar bills soft as cotton. I reached into the wagon for our coffee can full of change and shook the coins until a penny popped up. "Thank you, Mrs. Weller," I said handing her the penny, which was so bright and shiny you would think I was the first person to use it.

"Bye now," she ordered us. Then she spun on her slippers and walked back into her house.

"Sha*bam*!" Rennie said. "That was scary."

Mike laughed. "That was *Millie*."

"Let's go," I said.

Rennie blew on her braid, picked up the wagon handle and said, "It was nice to meet you. You were really great." Then she walked past me toward my house. I waved once, then followed Rennie.

"Hey, Apron," Mike called after me. "Your dad's the professor. And the expert on Maine, all things about Maine. *The History of Maine*, right?"

"Yeah," I said. I thought of telling him the real title of the book, but ran to catch up with Rennie instead.

5
Audi, vide, tace.
Hear, see, be silent.

On the way to the Meaningless Bowl, it looked like rain. Rennie kept asking M over and over again about the chocolate in Brazil. Through the window, I watched those dark clouds sail in. There were only three seasons in Maine: July, August, and winter.

It had started raining lightly by the time we got to the soccer field. Most of us kept our hoods up, so no one did much talking while the moms unloaded the cars and the dads got ready to tackle each other in their sweat pants and tunics, either blue or green, which I had remembered to get at school after all. My dad was the blue captain. Mr. Perry and my dad used to be on the same team, but this year Mr. Perry was a green.

Rennie had run straight over to her mom and Eeebs when we pulled into the Falmouth Middle School parking lot. M followed her and hugged Mrs. Perry like they were long-lost friends. Then the two of them stood next to each other until Mrs. Perry walked away and went to go talk to another mother instead. I stayed two mothers away from M and watched Rennie walk over to Seth Chambers's mother and start talking to her.

Seth Chambers and some other eighth grade boys were biking around the field, but Eeebs kept standing there, holding a green tunic in his hand, waiting for someone to get hurt so he could go in. Mrs. Perry was never going to let him play touch football, though, and everyone knew it except him. "They're like animals out there," Mrs. Perry complained last year, closing her eyes and shaking her tight curl. "I'm just not going to let Ebert play until he's at least fifteen."

"Good idea," another mother had said.

Eeebs never put his tunic down, though, which was blue last year too.

Finally the rain stopped and the birds started singing. Some people, like M and Mrs. Perry, unfolded their blankets and lay them on the wet grass, and Rennie and I passed around the football cookies. I knew almost everyone, but I kept my big hood up so I didn't have to talk much. Right before halftime, it started raining hard enough again for one of the dads on the green team to make a big T with his muddy hands, and for my dad and the others to make a huddle.

After that, my dad came over and told all of us that it was a tie and that we could go home. My dad went over to M and helped her pick up our blanket and put it in the bag. I heard him say, "I'll meet you in the car. Where's Apron?" even though I was standing right there. M didn't answer him, though, or maybe I just didn't hear her with that rain beating down on my hood. Everyone started walking fast to their cars, except me, who took my time. Rennie didn't even say good-bye.

Before I reached the parking lot, I heard some loud voices behind me. When I turned around, I saw two men, one blue and one green, standing across from each other in the middle of the field. They were moving their hands around fast. Then the blue man punched the green one in the stomach. When the green man crumpled over, his hood slid off and I saw that it was Mr. Perry. The blue man turned around and started walking off the field.

And when he got up to me, still standing there watching, he said, "Let's go, Apron."

6
Pistrix! Pistrix!
Shark! Shark!

I thought my dad would save it. It looked like he might, his hand extended out like that. But he didn't.

"Sorry," I whispered.

He shook his head and leaned down for my tray.

I should have seen it then—all the other things about to come crashing down. But instead I watched *Juan Busboy*—it said so on his tag—walk up to me with a mop. "It's okay," he nodded. "I take care of it, no problem."

My dad slapped his hands on his pants and stood. "I'll get you another one. We're not paying twice."

Since the Meaningless Bowl, my dad had been in his office grading papers. He didn't tell me what happened with Mr. Perry, and I didn't ask. Rennie and I made enough money for a combination lock, but now I needed to get to the store to buy it. When I told my dad I needed a new lock for my bike, he looked at me crooked and said he just bought me one. "I know," I answered. "But tornado season is coming up. My bike could get blown away." He told me Maine hadn't had a tornado since 1972, the year I was born. But then he told me he'd try to get me there by the end of the week.

Which meant seven more days of M trying to kill The Boss.

I stepped back and watched how quickly *Juan Busboy* wiped up the spaghetti with just a few twists of his mop. After he dropped an orange danger cone with *Maine Med Cafe* onto the wet spot, he winked at me and left. I sighed. At least M wasn't there yet.

Carlos Manager must have told *Barbara Cashier* not to charge him again because she brushed my dad away without tapping on her register. I could see meatballs all over the place when he handed me my tray and said, "Try to watch it this time," before walking his red head over to the water fountain. I hadn't had a sip of water since last week when we studied amoebas in Science. After watching those hairy little cells banging into each other under the microscope, I decided I was never drinking water again.

I went to go save our seats inside the handicapped section, which was the last place I wanted to sit, but it's quieter in there. Grandma Bramhall says my dad has been agoraphobic since he was a boy, but when he hears that he just shakes his head. "Your grandmother's starting to lose some of her marbles, Apron." Which might be true. Lately she'd been forgetting things. And the little people were back, too. They were there when she went down to get some juice in the middle of the night, sitting at her kitchen table, or standing there doing nothing at all. The little people had started coming last year, but then stopped all of a sudden during Christmas. "It might be a busy time of year for them," Grandma Bramhall said, her head shaking back and forth. "Who knows?" But my dad just rubbed his hands. "Dennis," she said, still shaking, "You can put me away if you want, but I swear on your father's grave, those little people are nice as pie."

Grandma Bramhall's head never stops shaking. Ever. If you didn't know about her, you might think she was saying no every second or trying to get a mosquito off her head, but she wasn't. It was just her neck plugged in wrong. "The head's nothing to worry about," my dad promised. "It's been shaking like that since before you were born. This little people thing could be the beginning of the end, though."

Now, my dad sat across from me and cracked open his paper.

President Reagan Promises to Keep AIDS out of America was the headline. There was a picture of President Reagan under his promise too, looking as handsome as ever. Grandma Bramhall kept a picture of him in her bedroom, right next to Grandpa Hub. "He was in the movies, you know," she'd wink and shake.

"What *is* AIDS?" I asked. I knew it killed you, but only gay people.

A corner crinkled down and he studied me for a moment. "A very bad disease."

I nodded at the front page. "But only for um, *some* men right?" I wished President Reagan was talking about nurses' *aides* though, then M would be long gone.

"No. Not only for *some* men, Apron. There's an entire continent of people dying from it. Men *and* women. *Kids*. What do they teach you in that school?"

"Everything," I shrugged, leaning down to get my Latin dictionary.

"Doesn't sound like it. Maybe I should come in and talk to Miss Frame."

"*Frane*," I corrected him.

"Frane," he repeated to himself. Then he flicked his paper back up.

I put the book on my lap and looked at those meatballs. None of them were getting any closer to these lips, so I started squeezing my peanut butter muffin into a ball. Across the room, a girl was reading. She didn't look anymore handicapped than I did. There were no crutches anywhere and her long blond hair came down past one shoulder. *University of So Maine* it said on her sweatshirt.

I waited to see if she noticed my dad, maybe she'd taken Latin with him or knew about, "Maine Matters," the column he wrote about Maine. We were going to be rich beyond belief and buy a new house as soon as he published the book, *Maine Matters.* She didn't even look up, though.

A nurse walked into the handicapped section, but it wasn't M so my stomach sat down again.

At the beginning, I liked M. She used to come into my mom's room and say, "Can I get you somethings, Mrs. Bramhall?" And my mom would smile like nothing hurt and say, "How's the search going?" Then M would sigh, "Not so good yet," and my mom would say, "You'll find Mr. Right someday." But M would shrug and say, "He's having to come in eight more months," which was when she had to go back to Brazil. It used to be funny. But that was before she decided to make Mr. Right my dad.

A loud siren made me jump. The emergency room was right next to us—all those people bleeding or dying while just one wall away we were eating meatballs. When the siren blared again, M walked through the door.

She put her hand on my dad's shoulder. He smiled and said, "Hey there," and stood to kiss her.

"Hi, Aprons."

"Hi." I thumbed through the dictionary until I found it: *Blandae mendacia linguae*; the lies of a smooth tongue.

My dad pulled out a chair for her and they both sat. "So what did they say?" I sucked in my smile and tapped my foot and waited for the good news: hardly anyone gets asked to stay another year as a nurse's aide, she had told me that herself, all wrong in English, and now her year was up next month.

Instead of answering out loud, M put her hand up to my dad's ear and whispered something, which even if you're from *Brazil* is the rudest thing you can do.

My dad's face turned weird. He stared over my head and M looked down at my muffin ball. Sneering. Like Jenny Pratt.

Before he said anything, my dad glanced at me and that's when I saw it —a flash, a tiny tick of sad crossing his face.

He turned to M with a half smile. "Welp," he said. "Whadda ya know."

She blinked at him. I'd never seen her look so nervous.

"What *do* you know," he whispered to himself.

Bad news pulled down on me like a shade. I looked at my dad's newspaper and saw a picture of a skinny African girl wearing a pot on her head and a baby on her back. Nobody ever smiled in newspaper pictures.

"Apron," my dad turned to me clearing his throat. "Margie's *gravitas*."

"What?"

He nodded toward my dictionary. "*Gravitas*," he said. "Look it up."

M lay her head on his shoulder and squeezed his arm.

I flipped through the pages and moved my finger down slowly. I wanted it to mean sorry. Sorry that she had ruined everything for so long; sorry she hated American girls; and sorry, but she wouldn't even write to us. *Gravitas.*

But it didn't. Pregnant. That's what it meant.

I looked at my dad. He waited for me to say something, but I couldn't get my throat working. So he blinked his eyes off mine and started sliding his newspaper back and forth with one finger making it look like that African girl was trying to walk off the page. When his finger stopped, you could see that girl was still there, though. Stuck like me.

7
Mea culpa.
Oops.

The church smelled like leftover tears. Sadness was tucked into corners and hidden under beams and pasted so thick on the walls that it was hard to breathe.

My dad and M were getting married during dodge ball. I know, because we were still waiting for M to walk down the aisle when the bells rang eleven times, exactly when we had gym class. My dad and M had to get married on a Friday because the church was booked up solid from now all the way through summer, and Grandma Bramhall said they were just lucky that Reverend Hunter would marry them in the first place. Grandma Bramhall didn't like M any more than I did, you could tell by the way she called her "the girl."

We were supposed to be done by noon because a real wedding was in the church tomorrow and they needed to start setting up for it. My neck kept itching and my butt was digging into the pew. On the other side of the aisle, Nurse Silvia was sitting with a lady I didn't know, but who was probably a nurse because they stuck together like glue. Nurse Silvia worked in the kid's department, but she was from Brazil too, and even though she was the one who brought M to America in the first place, I kind of liked her. She was short but pretty and she always had brown lip gloss on. She waved to me when she sat down, so I waved back.

Finally, after about a year of me turning my bracelet right side up and then upside down again, someone started walking down the aisle because both Reverend Hunter and my dad shifted their eyes back there. It turned out to be Grandma Bramhall though, wearing a brown skirt with pineapples on it and a yellow button-up shirt. She waved a flat hand up to my dad, or Reverend Hunter, you couldn't tell, and then sat down next to me.

"This is craziness," she said giving me a butter-scotch drop. I unwrapped it quietly. After I put the ball of melting happiness in my mouth, Grandma Bramhall took my hand inside her boney one and said, "Forgive them, Lord, for they know not what they do," with her eyes closed. But with her head shaking like that, it looked like she was secretly asking the Lord *not* to forgive them. Sometimes I heard people whispering about her behind her back, but I couldn't imagine Grandma Bramhall's head staying still like everyone else's. You might think she can't read a book, but people can adapt to anything. Just look at how monkeys turned into humans.

"Where is she?" Grandma Bramhall asked loudly, not whispering like everyone else. Even with pink lip-stick on she had my dad's exact same face minus the freckles.

I pushed the butterscotch into my cheek and said, "I don't know."

My dad waved to someone else back there, which turned out to be Mr. Haffenreffer and his wife, who was wearing the same bright pink dress with yellow flowers and green stems on it that Mrs. Perry wore sometimes, plus a matching headband. They sat down behind us and Mr. Haffenreffer leaned his face in between us and said, "Nice to see you, Mrs. Bramhall." His breath smelled like old coffee.

Grandma Bramhall nodded and said, "Nice to see you, too," without turning around. Then she lifted her chin up toward my dad and cleared a frog out of her throat.

"Hey, kiddo," Mr. Haffenreffer said, getting way too close to my ear and rubbing the top of my head like a boy. "Exciting, huh?"

It was lucky for him I *wasn't* a boy, because if I were, I would have slugged his pasty white face and shattered his big round glasses. But all a redhead girl sitting next to her grandmother could do was shrug and move away. I looked up to make sure my dad wasn't watching, but he was having his millionth conversation with Reverend Hunter.

Before any more of that breath hit my face, the music started playing from somewhere loud and high. Mr. Haffenreffer sat back and Grandma Bramhall and I both turned around, but my eyes crashed right into Mrs. Haffenreffer's, whose mouth was so tight it looked like you needed a key to open it. She gave me a little nod, but you could tell she didn't want to be here any more than we did. Which made me kind of like her.

Someone we didn't know was walking down the aisle. I looked at my dad to see what he was going to do about that: the wrong bride walking up to him. But he just stared at her, bouncing up and down on his toes like he does when he's nervous.

I looked back at the bride, getting closer. Turns out it *was* M. Her hair was pulled up into a bun and she had a white veil hanging down over her face. Her dress was so big and frilly you would never know there was a little whatever growing in there. She was carrying dark red roses tied up with a yellow ribbon, and even though both of her nurse uniforms were white, I had no idea that M could look this good. But when she got up to Grandma Bramhall and me, she looked over and there was her same old mean face with rouge on top. Then the back of her dress floated up next to my dad, who took her hand and the two of them turned to face Reverend Hunter together.

"Dearly beloved," Reverend Hunter started, "We are gathered here today to join this man and this woman in holy matrimony." It was the same thing people said on TV. I would have given a million dollars to be able to change the channel on this, though.

I looked at Grandma Bramhall's watch. Everyone in my class was running around, dodging rubber balls or throwing them. Even if you hit someone so hard they cried, you didn't get in trouble, not even Johnny Berman, because *that's* dodge ball. But I was stuck inside this soggy church, wishing someone would smash a ball into me and get me out for life.

I looked past my dad and M, and up to the rug on the wall with the picture of Jesus hanging on the cross. Pieces of blood were dripping out of his hands and down his feet. He had been hanging like that since my mom's funeral. Since forever. Just hanging there. Not saving anyone. Not even himself.

Reverend Hunter kept blabbing on in one long sentence. My cheeks burned and I looked down at my mom's hospital bracelet. I hadn't taken it off since she died. But now, I slid my finger underneath it and started pulling.

Reverend Hunter stopped talking so Grandma Bramhall and everyone else could say, "We will." But I clamped my teeth down as hard as I could and kept pulling, like I was trying to unplug something big enough to turn off the whole world. The edge of the bracelet was starting to dig into my skin. I looked up at Jesus again. He could have saved Nutter at least.

A snap happened. My arms flew apart so fast I hit Grandma Bramhall right in her chest.

"Uh!" she groaned, loud enough for everyone to hear, including Reverend Hunter, who stopped talking.

"Sorry. I'm sorry, Grandma Bramhall. Are you okay?" My jaw was hard to get moving again, but my hand went right to her heart and started rubbing out the dent I just made. Grandma Bramhall kept looking straight ahead and blinking, and then her head started slowing down.

I rubbed her chest harder. "Grandma Bramhall, are you okay?"

Mr. Haffenreffer and his breath poked in between us again, but this time I didn't shrug away. He squished his eyebrows together and looked at me and said, "What happened, Apron? Why did you hit your grandmother?"

"I didn't mean to. I'm sorry. Are you okay?" But Grandma Bramhall stayed staring straight ahead. Then she started gasping.

"Apron, what did you do?" my dad said, walking down the steps back to us. M looked at me with such meanness on her face that for once anyone could have seen it, if they were looking. But no one was, because everyone was looking at us. Even Reverend Hunter put down his bible and started walking toward Grandma Bramhall, whose head kept getting slower and slower.

Mrs. Haffenreffer came around and knelt by Grandma Bramhall. "Are you having trouble breathing, Mrs. Bramhall?" Grandma Bramhall tried to croak something out. Nurse Silvia and the other lady, who was definitely a nurse by how she kept saying "Okay, everyone, give her some room," were standing there now, too.

"Move, Apron," Nurse Silvia ordered me through her shiny lip gloss.

I slid away and looked up at that Jesus and prayed for him to help Grandma Bramhall. *Please*, I said, putting my hands together. *Do something.* But of course he didn't. He just hung there and when I looked back over to her, Grandma Bramhall's head was almost at a standstill.

They started to lay Grandma Bramhall down across the pew, so I slid all the way over to the other side and ran up the aisle, slapping my palms against the entrance door.

Outside, the sun burned straight into my eyes. I ducked my head and ran down the stairs, past the statue of Mary holding her baby with the chip in his foot.

And got struck by lightning.

It cracked my forehead and split me down the middle. Everything went dark. I fell to the ground.

And then there was Jesus, down from the rug, shaking his long blond hair over me.

8

Semper ubi sub ubi ubique.
Always wear underwear everywhere.

Two blurry faces were leaning over me. One of them was Jesus and the other one was bald. Both of them knew my name.

"Apron," they kept saying. "Can you hear us?"

Somebody else was hammering a nail into my head. I closed my eyes. "Stop it."

"What?" Jesus asked. And then I saw the crooked teeth.

I covered my face with my hands and groaned. I had been hiding from these teeth since Saturday. Every time I saw that ORD UCK in Mrs. Weller's driveway, I biked by it so fast I had to pull over and catch my breath.

"Looks like she's got a hard-boiled one, Mikey," the bald man said. "I'll get my Big Gulp." I heard him walk away.

Mike touched my shoulder. "Man, I'm sorry, Apron. You just ran smack into me."

My teeth throbbed. I looked through my fingers and saw Mary and her baby smiling down at me. And then I remembered Grandma Bramhall's head.

"I have to get out of here," I said, sitting up.

"What *are* you doing here?" Mike asked, easing me down again.

A car door slammed and the bald man yelled, "She comin' around, Mikey?"

"Think so," he answered.

"I'm fine," I said sitting up again. I tried to stand, but my head split further apart so I let Mike take my arm and help me.

"Good thing you're a kid," the bald one said in front of me now, studying my forehead. "That'll be gone by tomorrow." I studied him back. He was bald but young, like Mike, only skinnier and shorter and he had a big black birthmark on his neck.

Mike took the Big Gulp from him and handed it to me. "Put this on your head, Apron. You sure you can stand?"

I nodded and put the melting drink on my forehead. Down at my feet there were white flowers and pieces of broken glass inside a puddle. In the parking lot, there was a white van with its back door open and *Scent Appeal 321 Center St. Portland* written across it.

"We're doomed," the bald man said, squatting down, shaking water and glass out of the flowers.

"Stop it, Chad. I'll get it." Mike let go of my arm and yanked him up by the wrist. Chad turned and walked back down toward the van.

"You sure you're okay?" Mike asked me.

I told him yes, but his eyebrows still didn't believe me. He knelt down over the pile and started shaking out the flowers himself.

"Wait a minute. Did I do that?"

Mike smiled. "It's okay."

But I knew that it wasn't. Casablancas were expensive, and hard to get in Maine, and now they were all bent or broken.

"But they're Casablancas," I said.

Mike looked up at me, surprised. "It was my fault. I didn't see you until it was too late."

He must have seen my underwear. People who bang their heads into huge vases and fall down in their mini long-sleeved Lilly Pulitzer dresses have to show their underwear at some point along the way. I smoothed my dress down and watched Chad pull another bunch of Casablancas from the van.

The Big Gulp was starting to feel good on my head.

"Apron, why are you here?" Mike asked.

"My grandmother." I pointed to the church door. "She's in there."

"Your grandmother?" Mike stood up fast. "Does Millie know?"

"It just happened. Her head's probably stopped by now."

Mike's forehead squeezed together. Mrs. Weller and Grandma Bramhall had been friends since before Maine got electricity. In the distance, I heard a siren getting closer. "What are you talking about?" Mike asked, his blueberry eyes drilled straight into mine. "Does she need help?"

"Coming through," Chad panted behind us, struggling with another huge vase. Mike whipped his head around, his blond hair shimmering like the sun on top of Grandma Bramhall's pool. "Whoa, Chad. Let me get that."

Chad handed him the vase, then wiped his sweaty forehead with his sleeve and headed back down toward the van again without saying thank you. The sirens kept getting closer.

"Apron, does your grandmother need *help*?" Mike asked again, but not waiting for an answer this time and walking by me with the flowers. Below in the parking lot, an ambulance pulled in and stopped right behind the *Scent Appeal* van. Chad had his hands on his ears when he ran out from behind the door and jumped up onto the path. Mike stopped and all three of us watched two men in dark blue clothes, one old and one medium-old, leap out of the ambulance, run to the back and pull out a gurney. The older one asked Chad something, but he shrugged and looked up at us.

"The victim inside?" the same man asked when he got up to us, not even stopping for the answer, those wheels crunching over broken glass.

"Yes," I said. Then they were gone.

"What is going on?" Chad yelled up to us, throwing his hands in the air.

"Apron's grandmother," Mike yelled back, starting up the path again. I put the Big Gulp down by the baby Jesus's chipped toe and followed him.

9

Fiat lux.
Let there be light.

The church was darker than I remembered it. Mike looked around for a place to put the vase down, but there wasn't one. M was sitting on the top step of the altar, her elbows on her knees and her face in her hands. Mr. and Mrs. Haffenreffer were sitting to the side of her. My dad, Nurse Silvia, Reverend Hunter, and the other nurse were spread out behind the paramedics, who were picking Grandma Bramhall up gently. I could see Grandma Bramhall's eyes were open and one of the men was talking to her. Mike moved a few steps ahead and placed the vase down carefully on one of the pews. Chad stepped in behind us, breathing heavy.

"Is she all right?" Mike asked.

"I don't know," I said.

"Isn't that your dad?"

I nodded.

"He's getting married?"

"Uh-huh," I said. But really, I didn't want to talk about it, so I stepped away from them.

Grandma Bramhall was in the gurney now, sitting up with a mask over her mouth. The older paramedic was talking to my dad, using his hand to tap on his own chest like a monkey. It made my dad look worried instead of mad. Then the other paramedic started rolling Grandma Bramhall toward us. Before she reached me, I saw her head shaking. It might have been a little slower than normal, but it was her same old shake all right.

"Grandma Bramhall?" I leaned into her as she went by. "I'm so sorry."

She said something, except I couldn't hear what under the mask.

After she was out the door, the other paramedic and my dad walked past us. My dad looked over at me with his face stone cold. "Stay with Reverend Hunter, Apron. Until I get back."

Mr. and Mrs. Haffenreffer walked by us next. Mrs. Haffenreffer's arm was tucked inside Mr. Haffenreffer's elbow and her eyes were pinched up as much as her mouth now. Mr. Haffenreffer nodded at me, but in a thank-God-you're-not-*my*-kid kind of way.

"Who's the bride?" Chad asked way too loudly.

"M," I answered. I was glad about Grandma Bramhall's shake, but now I was stuck with Reverend Hunter.

"*Who?*"

"She's from Brazil."

Chad just said, "Oh."

Down at the altar, Nurse Silvia and the other nurse were pulling M up by the elbows. The veil was flipped over her head so you could see her red, crying face. Reverend Hunter said something as he walked by her and headed into his office. After that, all three nurses headed up the aisle toward us.

M hissed at me. If she were a lion, I would have been dinner. Nurse Silvia didn't look at me, but there wasn't a speck of brown shine on her lips anymore.

"Whoa," Chad said trying to shake M's mood off his arm. "If looks could kill."

I swallowed. They didn't know the half of it.

Outside, the siren turned on again. At the altar, M's red roses were lying on the top step.

"Did your grandmother have a heart attack?" Mike asked.

"Maybe."

"Do you want us to drive you to the hospital to find out?" he asked. Chad's face scrunched up next to him.

"That's okay. Her head's still shaking. And my dad told me to stay here."

"You sure?"

I nodded.

"But don't you, like, go to school?" Chad asked.

"Not when your dad's getting married," I mumbled. Mike flashed Chad a look.

"Well, any*who*," Chad said clapping his hands and heading back up the aisle. "We have work to do, Mikey."

Mike smelled like soap and Mr. Solo mixed together. "Don't lift anything heavy," he warned Chad.

"Okay, *Mom*," Chad sang back to him.

"That's *Mother* to you," he called back.

I looked around the Church of Sadness, wondering where the least amount of tears could be stuck. Mike was watching me. "Did you bring anything to do? Homework or anything?"

I shook my head.

He started to say something but then took my arm instead and hooked it under his. Pressed together like that, the thing in my belly button pinged on again. "Tell you what. Let's go find the Reverend," he said, walking me down the aisle.

When we got to the end, Mike let go of my arm and picked up the roses.

"For you," he said. "I now pronounce you . . . a kid."

He handed them to me and I stared into the dark red swirls, which were perfect except for the fact that they were M's. I looked back up at Mike, and then I was looking at two Jesuses: one standing in front of me, bowing slightly, and the other, on the rug hanging above him.

"Wait here," Mike said. Then he walked over to Reverend Hunter's door, knocked, and stepped in.

After he said something, he waved me over and I put down the roses.

Reverend Hunter had changed into black pants and a white shirt, and one of his arms was in the middle of sliding into a black sleeve.

"That's a terrible story, son. I'm sorry for you both," he said. "Did they get into your shop?"

"No," Mike shook his head. "The shop's okay. But we're running a little behind."

Reverend Hunter handed Mike a keychain. "Take all the time you need," he said.

Mike nodded. "Thanks for the second chance, Reverend. I'll make sure to lock it this time. Thanks. Thank you."

Reverend Hunter dipped his chin and finished getting into his coat. "Very good," he said gathering some papers together. When Mike turned to me, he winked.

"And one more thing, Reverend. I know Apron's dad told her to stay with you until he got back—"

Reverend Hunter's eyebrows lifted. "Oh dear," he said, just noticing me. "I'm due at a meeting in twenty minutes. I guess you can come if you like, Apron. Or I could drop you off at school?"

I looked down. If I showed up at school like this, in the Lilly Pulitzer dress Mrs. Perry gave me for Christmas, Rennie and Jenny Pratt would know I had been lying when I told them I was having my teeth pulled.

Mike was watching me. "Well actually, we were wondering," he said with his hands on his hips. "If Apron might be able to stay. We could use the help. It's a big wedding, the Farmington wedding. And her dad's expecting her to be here anyway. Right, Apron?"

I tried not to smile, but one side of my mouth snuck up there anyway.

"Apron? Did your father ask you to wait here?" Reverend Hunter leaned onto his desk and waited for my answer. I nodded. So he started buttoning his coat. "Fine then."

"Great," Mike smiled. "That's great."

Reverend Hunter started to leave but when he got up to me, he stopped.

"I'm praying for your grandmother, Apron," he said, before stepping through the doorway.

Mike smiled at me and was about to shut the door behind us, when we both noticed Chad, struggling with another vase halfway down the aisle. Mike groaned and dropped the key in my hand, "Hold this, would you?" he asked. "He's like a toddler." He ran up behind Reverend Hunter, who nodded at Chad while Mike grabbed the vase out of his hands.

I looked down at the brass keychain; a small Jesus on a cross. I couldn't get away from this guy.

10

Nemo saltat sobrius nisi forte insanit.
Nobody dances sober unless he's insane.

"Apron," Chad scowled. **"How'd you get a name like that?"**

"My mom," I told him.

"What's your brother's name, Oven?"

Mike nodded his head toward me. "This is the girl I told you about. The one who saw the show last week. Apron, this is Chad. My friend. He's the choreographer."

Chad curtsied. We were all at the top of the aisle now.

"Looks like we've got ourselves another set of hands, Chaddie." Mike cheered like we were at the Meaningless Bowl instead of in the saddest church on earth.

Chad crinkled his sweaty forehead together. Then he flipped his hand down like he was showing me his engagement ring. "Whatever floats your boat," he said, heading down to the altar. Except every few steps, he held his arms out like he was waltzing with someone, spinning them around in graceful swirls.

"Follow me, Apron," Mike said. So I did. All the way outside.

At the statue of Mary, Mike stopped. "You're saving me, Apron. Chad isn't feeling too well and we have to rig up this whole place up by three o'clock. And I have to rest the cords for tonight." He smiled his blueberry eyes at me, tapped on his throat and turned back down the path again.

I picked the Big Gulp up off the statue and carried it down to the trash can. Mike opened the back of the van and inside were bunches of flowers wrapped in newspapers. Dozens and dozens of them, smelling like happiness. "Wow."

"You can say that again. It's a big wedding. You ready?"

I stuck both arms out and Mike dropped a dripping bunch into them.

"Fleabanes."

"Hey, how did you know that?" he asked with his head inside the van.

"I just do," I said.

After three deliveries of Casablancas, white peonies, and bluebells to Chad at the altar, I stopped to watch him start arranging bouquets. A few times he changed his mind and started over again. And every time I brought him another bunch, the church smelled a little lighter. Then one time, the flowers Mike placed in my arms turned out to be a boom box instead.

"Just remind him to keep it down," Mike warned. "Tell him to remember what happened the last time." I nodded, but didn't say anything at all when Chad plugged the box in and Madonna came out.

At first Chad kept the music low, but every time I walked back in with another load, it seemed to get louder. I kept sneaking looks at him tiptoeing in between piles of flowers, then spinning fast and shaking quick. His blue jeans were so baggy you could see the top of his underwear, and his T-shirt had circles of sweat under each arm. But he moved so smoothly it was contagious. My body kept trying to copy him, one hip going this way and one shoulder going the other, while he danced to "Lucky Star." Mike smiled when he walked in and saw Chad. But then he said, "All right, Material Girl, tone it down a bit," looking a little worried instead. He had me fill up a lemonade pitcher with water in the girl's bathroom and bring it to Chad. "Make him drink it, Apron," Mike said. I tried, but Chad just pointed to a spot on the floor where I should leave it. He probably knew about the amoebas, too.

Once all the flowers and vases were inside the church, Mike went to park the van.

I hoped that Chad would be too busy dancing to notice me watching him. He was the best dancer I had ever seen, even better than the people on *Dance Fever*. But when I sat down in the first pew, he looked up at me and snapped off the music.

"So Apron, how old *are* you?" he asked out of breath, sitting down on the top step right where M had been bawling her eyes out.

"Thirteen," I answered, waiting to see if that was good or bad.

Chad raised his eyebrows. "Thirteen, huh? I was thirteen once."

"Yup," I said, politely. I was used to Rennie saying dumb things like this, but not a man.

Chad looked at me funny. "What do you think? I was never a *kid*?"

I pulled my shoulders up to my ears. But truthfully, it was kind of hard to imagine.

"Fine, I'll prove it," Chad said. "When is the best time to see a dentist?"

"I don't know."

"Tooth-hurty!" he said slapping his hands on his knees. "Get it? Tooth—*hurty?*"

"Pretty good," I nodded. I thought about telling him the only people I knew who told jokes were preschoolers and old people. But when he closed his eyes I could see he was really sweating.

"Whew," he said wiping his forehead and lying back on the floor with his arms spread out.

It *was* getting kind of hot. I wished I had kept Chad's Big Gulp now. I made it through two weeks without water. My dad told me I was being ludicrous. "What are you going to do when your science teacher shows you the bugs on your eyelashes, rip your eyes out?"

"*There are bugs on my eyelashes?*" I yelled at him, my stomach suddenly clawing to get out.

"Sorry, kiddo," he said calmly, getting back to his newspaper. "I didn't write the rules."

Now, I looked at Chad's pitcher. I had to admit, I had been getting some pretty bad headaches.

"Can I have a sip of that?"

Chad threw a hand up in the air then let it flop back down on his stomach. So I picked it up, squeezed my eyes shut, and had it almost to my mouth when Mike yelled, "No!" so loudly that a wave of amoebas shot out and splashed onto my face. "Don't drink that, Apron. Come *on,* Chad."

Chad sat up on his elbows and blinked at me. "Oh yeah, better not."

"Chad has a bug," Mike said walking down the aisle in loud clomps and taking the pitcher from me.

Mike gave Chad a hard look, but Chad started swiveling his hips again. "Yup. It's a bug that I got! So let's dance 'til we drop! Huh, Mikey?" Then he stood.

"Uh-oh," Mike said. But it was too late. Chad had already turned up the music so loud I kept waiting for the Jesus on the rug to fall off. Mike tipped his head back in a smile, then raised his arms and swung his hips, dancing all the way up the aisle again. Even me in my freckles and Lilly Pulitzer dress couldn't stop moving something. I thought Mike was leaving, but then he locked the door and turned around with a huge smile. "Lord, let the Reverend remember his robes this time!" he prayed to the ceiling.

And then no one talked and we all got to work. If Mike asked me for lilies, let's say, he would point his hip out at that pile, and I would twirl around once and hand it to him. And if Chad wanted the asters he might break-dance after I gave it to him. When the vases were full, Mike and I moved on to decorating the pews while Chad rested on the altar.

We started on the back rows, thumbtacking big thick pink bows at the ends of each one. Most of the time, Chad just sat and watched us, sipping a little of the water, but once in a while he might scoot around on his butt, dancing like he didn't have legs.

And even though I had freckles and red hair and almost killed Grandma Bramhall, I danced like I didn't. I danced like I didn't know that Rennie was having Jenny Pratt over for the night, and I danced like my dad wasn't going to ground me for hitting Grandma Bramhall. And mostly, I danced like it was all a mistake—M wasn't pregnant and she'd be gone by the Fourth of July.

When we got down to the pew where Mr. and Mrs. Haffenreffer had been sitting, Mike leaned over and picked something up: a long curly piece of white plastic.

I grabbed for my empty wrist so fast I forgot about the thumbtack in my other hand. Mike was already reading *Holly Bramh #08092* out loud when that thumbtack pierced my skin and I yelled. Mike grabbed my hand, straightened my elbow, and plucked it out. Then he pressed down on top of the bloody spot and screamed, "Chad, turn that crap off!"

My mom's broken bracelet was still in his other hand when he lifted his finger to take a look, thinking that was where it hurt.

11
Serva me, servabo te.
Save me, and I will save you.

Mike and Chad gave me a ride home in the Scent Appeal van.

"Thanks," I said when we piled into the front. My wrist was still throbbing a little, but I had a Band-Aid on it now. Chad found it in the glove compartment. My dad hadn't come back like he said he would, and Mike and Chad had to get going.

"No problemo," Mike nodded gunning it out of the church driveway. With the back of the van empty now, it smelled like happiness lost. "Your house is kind of on our way anyway."

They had to get back to Scent Appeal to make the wedding party bouquets.

"You should see the bouquet of bluebonnets and lilies of the valley that Chad is making for the bride," Mike smiled, driving down Route 88 while Chad flipped through the radio, never stopping on any one song long enough to start caring about it.

"Yup," Chad nodded, knocking his shoulder into Mike's. "When we get married, I'm making that one for me."

I looked at Chad. Chad looked at me. But Mike looked straight ahead.

"What?" Chad shrugged. "We flipped a coin. I'm the bride." Then he turned to Mike and said, "Right, Mikey? And I get to wear *heels*."

My blood felt like it had been mixed in with baking soda. And Mike must have known because he tightened his jaw. "Cut it out, Chad," he said seriously. "I don't know what's gotten into you today. You've got diarrhea of the mouth or something."

Which meant it was true: Mike and Chad were gay. I had worried about it a few times when we were decorating, but when you're inside a church you don't want to think about that kind of stuff.

But now, I couldn't stop looking at them, first Mike, then Chad, and then back to Mike. I had never met a real live gay person before. Even though everyone said Paul Green was one, we all knew he couldn't be one *yet*. You can't be gay until you're at least old enough to drive.

Finally Mike turned to me. "Chad's kidding, Apron. We're not getting married."

I made myself nod and look away.

"A girl can dream, though," Chad sighed. "I have a dream," he said in a deeper voice, wagging his finger, imitating Martin Luther King Jr. exactly. But Mike elbowed him kind of meanly this time, so Chad leaned forward and started switching the channels around again until he found *Wake Me Up Before You Go-Go*, turning it up high enough for the glove compartment to rattle.

The air was different now, though, and all three of us knew it. I hoped Chad couldn't tell when I moved a little farther away from him.

"Thanks," I said after Mike pulled into our driveway.

"Is anyone home?"

They both looked at me, Chad's knee touching Mike's while I sat with my hands in my lap, rolling up my straight line of a bracelet.

I shook my head. "But it's okay," I said looking into the empty garage ahead of us, which didn't mean that M wasn't there. Nurse Silvia could have given her a ride back, her white wedding dress piled up underneath her like a booster seat. You never knew where M might show up.

"Thanks for the ride," I pulled the thick metal handle up and stepped out. My high heels sunk into the dirt.

"Can thirteen-year-olds be home alone?" Chad asked Mike, sliding over and looking down at me like I was an experiment.

"I don't know," I heard Mike say. He left a note for Reverend Hunter saying he had taken me home. "Probably. Apron, is it okay?"

"I'm fine," I said shutting the door harder than I meant to.

Fog was rolling in as I climbed the porch stairs. Mike honked twice. I looked back and waved and watched the van head out. Then the fog blew over my ears and followed me inside.

"Hello?" I called into the hallway. I was so thirsty my brain was starting to buckle. I heard the long blow of a foghorn outside, but inside, no one was yakking or crying as far as I could tell. My heels clicked across the kitchen floor. This morning seemed like a long time ago now, when I sat at my lobster watching my dad and M get ready for their wedding. M's dress was already in the car, and she wore high heels and big hair when she came downstairs. She looked different these days. Not young and tan like she did when she was my mom's nurse, but older, like her skin was starting to get stale. And if you didn't know about that little whatever in there, you would think she ate half a soccer ball for lunch.

The kitchen clock said four o'clock, twenty minutes after school got out.

After I drank half the lemonade, I leaned against the counter. My cereal box was still on the table and dishes were piled in the sink. M wasn't neat and she wasn't nice and now she wasn't even married. I picked up the cereal, climbed onto the counter, and hid it behind a box of instant mashed potatoes.

Upstairs, my room still smelled like sleep. But there was something new in it too. Which must have been me. Because even though I ruined M's wedding and almost killed Grandma Bramhall, the truth was I hadn't laughed or danced like I had with Mike and Chad since way before my mom died. I slipped my broken bracelet into my sock drawer and decided to go check on the closet while M was gone. I hardly ever got to go in there anymore.

My dad's room was starting to smell a lot more like M and her oatmeal now. Pants and socks were everywhere and the bed wasn't made. Both dressers were covered with M's tipped over bottles of beauty supplies and there was an open soda can on one of them. I plugged my nose and walked around to the closet.

There were only three dresses left inside. One was white with daisies on it, one was pink, and one was the velvet one Grandma Bramhall had spilled champagne on a few New Year's Eves ago. So far, my dad had kept his promise not to let M put her stuff inside. This was the last place on earth that still smelled like my mom.

I stepped into the dark quickly and shut the door behind me. When I pulled on the light switch hanging from the ceiling, I knocked off an empty hangar. And when I leaned over to pick it up I heard a thud.

Reverend Hunter's key.

It was my fault. I should have remembered to give it back to Mike, except he hadn't remembered to ask for it. But Mike had promised Reverend Hunter he wouldn't forget to lock the doors.

I picked it up and closed the door behind me. Then I went back to my room, found money for the bus, and ran down the stairs. I grabbed my backpack before I hurried out the door.

It was even foggier outside now. The Scent Appeal van had said Center Street on it and that was near Bramhall Street. You would think those old Bramhalls would have wanted to put something else besides a hospital on their street.

Just as I was about to run up the dirt road, I heard tires. Mr. Orso was backing out of his driveway in his little white car. *Pinto*, it said on the back, like the bean.

I hurried up to his car and waved my arms. When he stopped, I walked to his window. "Sorry to bother you, Mr. Orso. Hi. Um, my grandmother's in the emergency room. My dad just called. He was wondering, if you could maybe—if it's not too far out of your way—drive me there?" My skin prickled from the lie, but I didn't know what time the buses came anymore; it had been more than six months since I'd taken the last one.

Mr. Orso looked at me like he couldn't remember where he had seen me before. "I'm Apron," I said, waiting. He nodded, then brushed off the passenger seat.

I got in and pulled my backpack onto my lap. His car smelled so clean my nose stung. "Thanks, Mr. Orso." Sitting this close to him, I could see how much he looked like an elf. Gray hair was growing out of his ears and he had hardly any neck at all.

"Roger that," he said. I looked straight ahead while he changed gears and started up the dirt road, barking softly, almost like a hiccup, clearing his throat in between.

It was Tourette's syndrome, what he had.

Mr. Orso slowed down at the top.

"Maine Med?" he asked staring straight ahead.

"Yes," I nodded, so he gunned it left, across the road.

I didn't know what else to say after that, sitting this close to him, trying not to notice him trying not to bark. No one should have to bark like that. God might be busy running the world, but he could still take the time to zap the bark out of a guy who probably never even hurt a fly.

And then we were there, turning onto Bramhall Street and pulling into the emergency entrance.

Mr. Orso put his bean in park without looking over. "Sure hope Doris is all right."

I blinked at him. "You know her?"

"Ah-yuh," he said, looking down at his radio. "Went to school together."

Grandma Bramhall had never said anything about going to school with Mr. Orso.

"She was quite a looker back then, Dory," he said. "Still is." Then he barked, so we both stared down at his radio, hot shame leaking out of my heart. I wondered if he had barked like that in school, too. And if that was why Grandma Bramhall never talked about him.

"Thanks, Mr. Orso," I said. "I'll tell her you brought me."

I grabbed my backpack, opened the door, and stepped out. Somewhere along the line, the fog had cleared and now it was hot, hot.

I waved. But Mr. Orso didn't wave back. He just drove off in his bean.

12
Damnant quod non intellegunt.
They condemn what they do not understand.

Standing in the Maine Med parking lot, I thought about how my life had turned into one giant trip to the hospital.

I wanted to go in and make sure Grandma Bramhall's head was up to speed again, but it was too risky. You never knew where M might show up.

So I walked out of the parking lot. By the time I got to Center Street, my mouth felt like I had been sipping on glue.

I crossed the street and turned left. This was the crummier part of Portland, where we went to *Portland Bagels* sometimes. After you've tasted those once, though, your mouth spends the rest of its life wanting more. I glanced up at the big digital clock on top of the *Bank of Maine* and then the sidewalk slammed into me.

It hit my knees first, then my hands, and after that, my face. My bottom lip felt like a safety pin was being pushed through it. I heard someone scream, which turned out to be me. And then I saw a ladder—the one I hadn't seen before, but should have.

Bad things happen in threes, Grandma Bramhall said, and today it was Grandma Bramhall's chest, my cracked forehead, and now my split lip, which had a flap of skin the size of Maine barely hanging on in there. Two perfectly white sneakers rushed up to me.

"Hey. Are you okay?"

I looked up and saw Chad.

I blinked to make sure, but it was definitely him, in the same clothes he had on before: blue jeans that were too big for him and a light blue T-shirt with *Tears for Fears* on it. He looked better now, though. Not so sweaty.

"Apron?" He leaned down. "Is that you?"

I nodded.

"Do you wear glasses?"

I shook my head.

"So you're just uncoordinated?"

I moaned.

"I like that in a girl," he said. "But you're bleeding. You better come in." He took my backpack and helped me up. Then he spun me toward a window with *Scent Appeal* painted across it like growing ivy. Except you could barely read it because of what was spray-painted over it: *homo* and *faggot* and *fudge packer*, written in bright red paint.

"What happened?" I asked, trying to get my fat lip out of the way.

"A friendly visit from our fan club," Chad said walking through the door. My heart stung for him. If I had a window on a sidewalk, I bet Jenny Pratt would have spray-painted nasty things about me on it too. I wanted to tell him that, but instead I mumbled, "Sorry," and followed him in.

Chad shut the door behind us and locked it. And suddenly it smelled like someone forgot to turn on the gravity. The air was so fresh and light you could practically float on it. Flowers were everywhere, all of them bursting with color. Tin buckets of tuberoses and lilies were lined up on the floor, and smaller flowers like tulips and daisies were sticking out of buckets set on top of old bleached-out lobster traps.

Chad dropped my backpack on the couch against the wall and said, "Hey, Toby, we got any ice?" then disappeared around the corner.

Someone said, "Why?" and wheeled out from behind the long counter. I jumped back.

"Sorry, little lady," the man in a wheelchair said. "Didn't mean to scare you."

He had dark black skin and was wearing all white. His chest and arms were normal looking, but his legs were too skinny and his ankles were too close together. Sadness hit me harder than the sidewalk. "I'm Toby," he said with a wave.

"I'm Apron," I said, my swollen lip getting in the way. "Are you a nurse?"

His laugh was so deep it sounded like we were sitting at the bottom of Grandma Bramhall's pool.

"Only to Chaddie boy," he said. "But that's a good lookin' lip you got there." He didn't sound like he was from Maine, but from somewhere fancier, like Boston.

Chad came back holding a paper towel and some ice in a bag. "Hey, Toby, did she tell you she loves my jokes? Watch, I'll prove it. What did the digital clock say to his mother?" he asked, wrapping the paper towel around the bag of ice before handing it to me.

"Look ma, no hands," I answered, taking the ice and tapping that coldness lightly against my lip. "Thanks."

Toby laughed at that, the oldest joke on Earth. "Fantastic."

"Isn't it though?" Chad smirked. "She's fab. She's also *here*," he said putting his hands on his hips and turning to me. "Why?"

"I was trying to—"

"Oh, find the hospital," Chad answered for me. "Is your grammie okay?"

"I don't know," I said, pulling the key out of my pocket. "But I forgot to give this back to you."

He widened his eyes and took the key. "Oh, man. Not again."

"I'm so sorry," I slurped through my hunk of lip. On his wrist, there was another black splotch like the one on his cheek.

"Well. Screw 'em if they can't take a joke," he smirked at Toby, who chuckled again. "Hey, how did you know where to find us?"

"Your van." I turned toward the window, which from this side looked even worse. The paint was puke-brown and you could see how thick it was, barely letting any light in.

"Where's *Papa* Apron?" Chad asked suspiciously. "Is he waiting for you out there?"

"I got a ride from my neighbor." I sucked on my lip. It was getting bigger by the minute. "I'll probably take the bus home."

Chad looked mad. "I knew Mike should have made you stay there and wait for the Reverend. I told him not to mess with dads and kids."

"I'm *thirteen*," I said, putting the ice on my lip and preparing for the burn.

But before I felt anything, there was a *shot!*

Chad grabbed my shoulder and pulled me down with him. "Get back!" he yelled to Toby, who reversed himself around the counter. Chad and I stayed pinned down with our hands covering our heads until nothing else happened and we heard car tires peeling out.

Chad looked up. "Holy crap." The window was shattered. Broken red glass covered the floor.

"You two okay?" Toby asked, wheeling around the corner.

Chad nodded. "Apron?"

I nodded too. But my heart had been knocked out of its socket. I tried to take in a breath, but I couldn't fit it in. Toby looked okay, but Chad's eyes were darting around like a flashlight.

"Was that a *gun*?" I asked, getting to my knees.

"A rock, looks like," Toby answered, leaning over his tire to grab it. He held it up, a rock the size of his fist, with something written on it: *Get out fags.* Chad stood, but Toby ordered him to get down again. "There might be another one."

Chad ignored him though and walked to the door with glass crunching beneath his perfect white sneakers. Then he swung it open and yelled things I would be grounded for life for if I ever said.

After a few more swears, he shut the door. "They're gone. Those pieces of scum."

"I'll call the cops," Toby said, rolling over crunching glass and around the corner again. I stood, but blood was pounding so hard in my lip I could barely close my mouth. The ice was on the floor.

Chad looked at me. "Man, I'm sorry about that, Apron. You sure you're all right?"

I nodded, even though my shaking had turned into shivering. I suddenly wished Johnny Berman were here.

A door next to the couch opened to a set of stairs and Mike standing at the bottom of them. His wet hair was pulled back into a ponytail and he was wearing jeans and a blue jean button-down shirt, way more open at the top than my dad ever wore. "What just happened?" he asked, his eyes wide. "Is everyone okay?"

Chad nodded. "Our fans came back." His voice was shaking now too.

Mike's mouth tightened and his eyes landed on me. "Apron?"

"Oh. And we found a little stray," Chad said. The truth was, Chad wasn't much bigger than me.

Mike crunched toward me, crinkling his blueberry eyes into a worry. He smelled like an Ivory Soap commercial. "Did they get your lip?"

I shook my head. "I tripped, outside. Before."

Mike looked confused but moved on to Chad. "Are you bleeding anywhere?"

"Nothing," Chad answered, holding up his hands to prove it.

"Where's Toby?"

"Right here," he said wheeling out from around the corner. "Cops are comin'."

Mike sighed. "What else can happen today?" None of us answered. But it was a good question.

Chad leaned down to pick up a shard of glass.

"What are you *crazy*?" Mike yelled, slapping his arm fast enough for the glass to drop and shatter all over again. "You two get upstairs," he snapped, pointing to us. "Toby and I will take care of it. Last thing we need is for either of you to start bleeding again."

A knock on the door startled us all. Through the windowpanes, two policemen were waiting. Chad started toward them, but Mike caught his elbow. "No."

"I was the one who saw it," Chad pleaded.

"Take Apron and go upstairs," Mike ordered him. "Now."

Chad stepped back and sighed, letting Mike open the door. "We meet again, officers," Mike said, trying to be funny but sounding sad instead.

"Come on, Apron," Chad said, and we started up the steep stairs. Toby must have wheeled over and shut the door behind us because then it was darker, and Chad was climbing the stairs so slowly in front of me I could count ten throbs in my lip before each one of his steps. At the top landing, he leaned over. "Well, I won't miss those," he said out of breath.

"You're moving?"

"Biggest move of all, my teenage runaway," he panted. Then he turned and stepped in through a doorway. I ran up the rest of the stairs and followed him into an apartment.

13
Melita, domi adsum!
Honey, I'm home!

"Welcome to our humble home," Chad said.
There was a small kitchen to the right, and a couch and TV in front of me. It smelled like asparagus had been cooked recently. Pictures of Mike and Chad were everywhere, some big and some small, but in all of them they were hugging each other way closer than normal men. I was glad no one from school could see me. Suddenly I wondered if maybe Mrs. Perry had thrown the rock; she and Eeebs, screeching off in their Cadillac.

Chad walked over to the kitchen and put together another bag of ice, then handed it to me with a paper towel.

"Thanks," I said, lifting it up to my lip, feeling the burn right away this time.

He walked passed me to a closed window and craned his neck to look down through it. After a minute he gave up and walked over to the brown leather couch. "Sit," he said. I did, in a brown leather chair, while Chad kicked his shoes off and lay back. "Bet you wish you'd just kept the key."

"Do you know who it was? Who did that?"

"Just some kind soul who wanted to tell us how much they love us," Chad sighed, like I was born yesterday. Like I didn't know what the rock said.

"Oh. *Okay*," I was mad now. "And I'm sure it had nothing to do with you and Mike being—"

Chad picked his head up, daring me. I couldn't say it though so he did, "Gay?"

Blood flew up my cheeks. "Sorry," I said, pressing the ice on my lip, embarrassed for being so rude.

"Sorry for us, or sorry for you?"

"Them," I said in a deeper voice than I knew I had.

Chad stared at me, but I stared at him harder, ignoring the ice burning through my lip. After a moment, his face softened and he nodded. "Okay," he said, dropping his head back again.

I sighed quietly, trying not to let him hear it. "But did you do anything to them? Before? Like, were they fighting back or anything?"

Chad chuckled. "You don't have to do anything for some people to hate you, Apron," he answered, staring up at the ceiling. "You're just not old enough to know that yet."

"Guess what. You don't have to be *old* for some people to hate you, either," I said.

"Touché," Chad pointed at me. But I knew the kind of hate he was talking about was deeper than anything I had ever felt. Even from M. Last year a boy named Edward Carter moved to Falmouth and had two dads. One of them picked Edward up from school every day, like a mom, and the other one went to work like a dad. They even wore rings like normal people. Some parents had tried to get Edward kicked out of school. They blocked Principal Parker's car with signs that said, "No queers! Not in here!" And one of them was Mrs. Perry. But Principal Parker sent out a note saying that Edward was staying. He didn't, though; he left at Christmas.

Chad jumped when Mike walked in. "You guys didn't see *anyone*?" he asked.

"Nope."

I shook my head.

"That's what I told the police," Mike sighed. "All right. Next problem," he walked over to me. I was that problem. He put both hands on my freckles and angled my face so he could see my lip. "Ow," he said. "Do you think you need to go to the emergency room?" I shook my head, which was hard to do in his hands. Then he crossed his arms and stared at me. "Do you wear glasses?"

"Asked her," Chad said.

"Uh-uh."

Mike stepped away. "So what are you doing here?"

I told him about Reverend Hunter's key. Chad pulled it out of his pocket and threw it onto the coffee table.

"But you didn't have to bring it all the way *here,* you know," Mike said.

"I didn't want you guys to get in trouble again. You said it was your last chance."

Mike and Chad shot each other a look.

"Well, thanks, Apron."

I nodded.

Then there was a pause. A long pause. I stood up.

"So I'll see you later," I said, turning for the stairs.

"Wait, how are you getting home?" Mike asked.

"Bus," I said, as if I took the bus home at night all the time. As if my dad wouldn't ground me for doing *that* too.

"Does your dad know you're here, Apron?" Mike asked Chad, not me. Chad made a face and Mike lifted an eyebrow.

I shook my head. "But it's okay."

Mike flapped his arms down. "I have to be at the theater in *ten* minutes," he told Chad, as if Chad had just asked him to drive me home.

"I told you we should have waited for the Reverend," Chad said, adding a cough. "I told you we'd get in trouble."

I shouldn't have come. "It's fine—"

"It's just that, it's final performance tonight," Mike sighed, flustered, walking to the closet and taking out a jean jacket. "Can your dad come get you, do you think?"

Suddenly I wanted to get out of there as much as they wanted me to. "I'll call him," I said starting for the stairs again. "From the bus stop."

But Mike stopped me. "No. You're not doing that." He looked at Chad who shook his head in agreement. Then he wiped off the phone before handing it to me.

No one was home.

"No answering machine?" Mike asked, looking nervous.

I shook my head. I had overheard M telling my dad that she needed one now, though, so that her friends from Brazil could leave messages all wrong in English. My dad said he'd think about it, which meant yes.

"Well, you're just going to have to keep trying him, then. Chad's right, we're kind of responsible for you."

I was about to tell him I'd go wait for my dad in the hospital, but Chad sat up. "Oh let her stay," he said. "I need a little girl time anyway. Go away, Mikey."

It was nice, the way Chad smiled at me.

"Hold on, Chad," Mike said, annoyed. Then to me he said quietly, "You sure you don't mind staying here with Chad? He's going to need to rest, and there's really not much to do."

"No, I don't mind," I said.

Chad smirked at Mike.

"Okay," Mike nodded. Then he walked over to Chad who lifted his hand. Mike took it and the two stayed like that, in a frozen handshake. "And you stay put," he ordered him quietly. He let go of Chad's hand and turned toward the stairs.

"Say hi to that whore Mary," Chad called after him. "Tell her everything's all right, yes, everything's fine."

Mike waved back and then he was gone.

14
Bis pueri senes.
Old men are twice children.

"What kind of animal should you never play cards with?"

"I don't know," Chad answered.

We were still in their living room, having gone downstairs once to find the window covered up with garbage bags and masking tape in a thick X. Toby had made me give him our number so he could keep trying my dad, too. And later, he yelled up, "Got him, he'll be here around eight." Then said, *"Adios amigos"* and left. Chad and I had already made macaroni and cheese, except Chad hardly ate any and I was so hungry I had three bowls of it. That was when Chad said he better start making the bouquets for the wedding tomorrow, so we brought up the flowers, ribbons, and scissors, and got to work.

"A cheetah," I said.

"Good one," Chad nodded. Already I had told him at least ten jokes. I didn't even know I still knew them. But there they were, hiding somewhere inside my brain.

Chad only had two faces; happy or bothered. If he wasn't smiling, his face was frowning, like that was where it was normally set. Once in a while he went to the bathroom and stayed there for a long time, sometimes flushing the toilet twice. So I snooped around while he was in there. A few pictures of Marilyn Monroe were on the walls, but the rest of them were all of Mike and Chad with their arms wrapped around each other, on a lobster boat, or in a restaurant. I wanted to ask if people had stared at them when they posed like that. But I didn't. Usually not talking around someone made me nervous, but with Chad it was just normal.

"What do kids in seventh grade do now?" he asked one time, after another trip to the bathroom. "Are you on to heavy drug use yet?"

I was finding out that Chad said stuff like this once in a while, too, usually after coming out of the bathroom. But they were just things he said, not things I was supposed to answer.

"Seventh grade was the first time I fell in love," Chad said, laying back down on the couch and smiling. "Chris Baladucci, spitting image of David Cassidy." He asked me if I had a boyfriend. I said no, but told him about Johnny Berman anyway.

"What does he look like?" So I told him blond hair, blue eyes, nice smile, and then realized I could have been talking about Mike.

"Sounds dreamy. Has he tried to kiss you yet?"

"No," I said. But my cheeks got hot anyway.

"Bet he will. What about word problems? Do they still do that? Bobby has seven bras and Jeffrey has four, so how many do they have all together, kind of thing?"

I told him we learned that in first grade. He asked what we were learning in social studies and if we had sex ed yet. "No," I said. "Next year."

"Well, it's boring. I used to cut that one." He picked his head up and grinned at me.

I wanted to ask if that was why he was gay. Maybe if he'd gone to the class he would have turned out normal. But instead I told him that we got suspended if we cut classes more than three times.

Right after eight o'clock, when we were watching *Cheers*, something knocked on the front door. Chad looked over at me before starting down the stairs. I followed closely behind. "Who is it?" he asked at the bottom. But we both knew who it was. You could see my dad's red head through the window. I lifted my hand up to hide my lip.

"I'm looking for my daughter," my dad said, his voice muffled through the door.

Chad flipped back the lock and waved him in. He wasn't wearing his wedding clothes anymore, just his same old khakis and green button-down. He nodded at Chad, glanced around at the flowers, and then shot me a look. Bad news was coming and my stomach knew it.

He turned to Chad. "Dennis Bramhall," he introduced himself, extending his hand. "Thanks for keeping Apron."

"Chad," Chad said shaking it. He looked like a ninth grader next to my dad.

They both turned to me.

"Let's go, Apron," my dad said. When I dropped my hand down, his face folded. "What happened to your lip? Did someone hurt you?" He stepped toward me. "I saw the window?"

"No, Dad. I tripped outside. On a ladder."

My dad didn't look like he believed me. He turned back to Chad, who sunk his hands into his pockets. "We didn't think she needed to go to the hospital, otherwise—"

My dad sighed hard enough to growl. "Let's go, Apron."

I picked up my backpack still on the couch and walked toward the door. "Thanks, Chad," I said quietly. But it came out wrong, like it was Chad's fault that my dad found me.

"It's been real," Chad said sadly. "See you, Apron."

"Thanks again," my dad said. "And here." He was trying to hand Chad some money, but Chad put up both hands. "No, no," he said. "I should be the one paying you. She's like a dictionary of jokes. And she makes a mean bouquet," he smiled.

My dad nodded, no smile, and flashed a quick look around the room. I was so used to the flowers I couldn't even smell them anymore. All I could smell now was my dad's sharp look. "Okay then," he said, disappearing out the door. "Come on, Apron."

Chad looked worried, but I shrugged like I was used to getting in trouble, then I waved and followed my dad.

Outside, we walked to our car without talking.

"How's Grandma Bramhall?" I asked in a small voice when we were both inside.

My dad wrapped his hands around the steering wheel.

"Fine, Apron," he said. "You knocked the wind out of her, but they let her go as soon as she got to Maine Med. Margie and I brought her home in time for that trunk show she wanted to get to. But you have a lot of explaining to do. You shouldn't have left with those boys, Apron." He looked at me. "You have no idea who they are. Look at their window for Christ's sake. They aren't the type to be hanging around with."

"They're really nice," I said. "I helped them decorate the church for a real wedding tomorrow." I realized my mistake and waited for him to get mad, but instead he shook his head.

"Well, you were supposed to stay there."

"I was there for two hours, dad. Reverend Hunter had to go somewhere so Mike and Chad took me home. And then I forgot to give them back Reverend Hunter's key so I came here and they wouldn't let me take the bus home by myself. I tried calling you. Where were you?"

He paused. "Getting married," he said, starting the engine and backing out of the parking spot.

An elevator dropped in my stomach. "What?"

He put the car in gear again and told me they went to the courthouse right after dropping Grandma Bramhall off at Mrs. Finn's trunk show. M was still in her wedding dress because she said she wouldn't take it off until they got married. And my dad said she meant business because he had never seen her cry like that.

Mr. and Mrs. Haffenreffer were their eyewitnesses and my dad tried to call Reverend Hunter's office, but got the answering machine telling him what time Sunday Service was and to go with God, so he decided maybe Reverend Hunter had taken me out for an ice cream. And the courthouse only had a 5:35 appointment left, so sorry, Apron, but it seemed the best choice at the time.

My dad told me all this without looking at me once. I didn't look at him, either.

"Apron?" he said finally, turning to me at a red light. "It was a rough day for Margie."

I looked at my empty wrist. If I hadn't broken my bracelet, almost killed Grandma Bramhall, smashed my head into a vase, and split my lip open, today would have been a rough day for me, too. *"Nemo sine vitio,"* I mumbled. No one is without fault.

"Nemo sine vitio est," he corrected me. "And Margie wasn't the one to knock the wind out of Grandma Bramhall."

I looked out my window.

"Why did you hit Mr. Perry?" We hadn't talked about it once since it happened.

My dad didn't answer for a moment. "He cheated," he said finally.

"How?" I crossed my arms.

"Illegal tackle."

I looked over at him. "Why?"

My dad shook his head. "That's just what some people do."

I looked back out at the road. A green car switched into our lane too fast, and my dad honked. "Idiot," he said. And I agreed.

Later, I didn't get into as much trouble as you might think. But only because a) Grandma Bramhall's head was all the way back up to speed again and b) I went into the kitchen after we got back from Scent Appeal and looked M straight in the eye and said, "Sorry," while my dad stood in the doorway watching.

Behind M's eyes, you could see that she didn't mean it when she smiled, or when she said, "It's okay,

Aprons. Come to gives me a hug," opening her arms like a pterodactyl. I had to hug her if I knew what was good for me, so I held my breath and waited for it to be over. You could feel that round bump of little whatever in there.

"My new daughter," she said trapping me and rubbing my back so my dad could get a good look. Then she stood back and took my shoulders in her hands and laser-beamed me with her brown eyes. "Now we are one big happies of family."

My dad stepped up. "All right, Apron. Up to bed," he said, taking M's arm off of me and wrapping it around his own waist. It was like watching a commercial for life insurance, the two of them standing together, smiling, and only I could see the black tornado spinning toward my dad.

"I have to feed The Boss first," I said. Except then I noticed his cage wasn't where I left it. My throat jammed. I glared at M. "What did you do to him?"

She faked a stunned look and my dad's forehead pinched together. "Don't talk to Margie like that, young lady. The Boss is in the pantry, on the counter."

And that's when I realized she could have poisoned him. Just a little mouse poison and he'd be dead in an hour. A lock wasn't going to save him anyway.

I narrowed my eyes at M's lying face. There was no way I was going to make it through a whole summer with her. One of us had to go.

15

A.M.

Before midday

A moaning sound was coming from somewhere inside the house. I rolled over and looked at my clock. It wasn't even seven yet and it was Saturday, when my dad went to get the paper at Town Landing. I shut my eyes but then I heard that moan again.

I sat up.

There it was again.

Except this time it was in a small animal kind of way, like a cat had gotten its paws stuck somewhere.

The Boss's cage.

M.

I jumped out of bed and practically fell down those stairs. Then I ran through the kitchen and into the pantry, and sighed. The Boss was twitching away in his cage. But behind me the moan happened again. This time, I followed it through the living room and onto the back porch. And when it happened again, I didn't wonder who it was anymore. It was no cat. It was M.

She was lying on the couch facing away from the door, curled up on her side, making that moaning sound and crying hard in between. My blood turned into a slushy and my feet felt like they were stuck on flypaper.

I had never heard anyone make that sound before, not even the bear at the Portland Zoo. She moaned again. I thought about calling 911, except my dad might end up getting mad at me, and after last night I didn't want to risk it. I squinted to make sure she was still breathing, which she was. She was wearing a white T-shirt and tan shorts and her hair was sprayed out around the couch cushion.

I was about to say her name, until another groan came out of her. And then she did something that made me stop breathing. She slapped her bump. Not in a nice, tapping way like you did on a fish tank. She slapped her belly hard with the palm of her hand. "Uh! Uh! Uh!" she groaned each time, and then did that moan, and then just cried.

Before I could move, she rolled onto her back and turned her head toward me, slinging her arm over her eyes. I unglued my feet and made a run for the door as quietly as I could. Behind me, I heard her moan again.

Upstairs, I ran into the bathroom and shut the door. That little bump of whatever was just sitting there, growing a leg or an ear like it was supposed to, and then all of a sudden getting slapped for it. Something deep in me burned when I thought about this. Even though it was M's little whatever, it still didn't deserve to get hit.

I looked in the mirror at my blotchy freckles and red eyes and fat lip. *Apron*, I told that person, *you have to stop her.*

I opened the door but waited when I heard footsteps. My dad.

I ran downstairs as fast as I could to tell him what I just saw, but when I stepped into the kitchen and opened my mouth and said, "Dad!" M looked over at me. She was holding a tea bag in mid-air, dripping it into my mom's *Tap Your Life Away!* mug.

"Your father's not back yet," she said. Her face was puffy but her hair was tucked back, neat now.

I looked down at that bump.

"Getting bigger, no?" she said trying to sound like a real mom.

A tidal wave of sadness hit me.

She turned away, stirring her tea, and I knew that if my dad walked in right now and I told him how I saw M banging on her bump like she was making home-made pizza dough, he would never believe me.

"I pray to Gods it doesn't have red hair," M mumbled, still stirring her tea. She didn't look at me when she said it, which is how I knew she meant it.

I turned and walked out the door.

Then I walked upstairs and climbed back into bed, remembering in a dream how loud the rock was when it shot through Mike's window.

16

Accipe hoc!
Take this!

When I woke up again it was nine o'clock and everything was quiet. No moaning anywhere. And downstairs, the kitchen was empty. No M and no *Hello Maine!* I got my cereal, dropped a few pieces of it on the floor, and sat at my lobster.

I had come up with a plan. My dad might not be able to see the M that I could, but there was no way he could miss what a slob she was. My dad was a neat freak and it wouldn't take long for him to realize he'd just married a mess. And messes can be divorced.

"Morning, Apron," he said walking in. He was dressed in his usual jeans, yellow button-down shirt, and red hair, but something was new about him and when he sat down at his lobster, I could see what it was: a gold ring on his left finger.

"Where did you get that?" I pointed to it.

My dad looked down and scrunched up his nose. "Yeah," he said. "Margie's idea. I told her I didn't know how long it was going to last, though. It's already driving me crazy." He spun it around with his thumb.

A piece of cereal swelled up like a log in my throat. I had to look away. My dad never wore one for my mother. I waited for him to mention it—that he was sorry he had to marry M. That he'd *just* promised me he was going to stay married to my mom forever.

Except he hadn't. I swallowed. He hadn't said that at all.

"So is it me or Perry today?"

I turned back to him quickly. "Did she call?"

"Not yet," he said flicking open his newspaper and disappearing behind it.

Hope drained out my feet. Rennie wasn't going to call, but my dad didn't know that. And this is what he always asked every Saturday morning: who was dropping off whom, at whose house, for a sleepover?

"We're not friends anymore, Dad," I said, stirring pink milk.

My dad lowered the paper and looked at me. "What? *Why?*" I wondered if this was the way he talked to his students. *Why*, he might ask, *do you think Maine matters?* He was a Latin professor, but they made him teach a class about Maine too, which is why he wrote the book.

"Forget it," I said standing up.

"Sit down," my dad said. He had said that a million times before, but this one surprised me. I sat right away.

"What happened with Rennie?"

"She's best friends with Jenny Pratt now and they hate me."

My dad folded the paper, clasped his fingers together, and looked at me. "Well, that's just not right, is it? What did you ever do to her?"

I shrugged. "You don't have to do anything for some people to hate you, Dad," I said. "Look at Chad and Mike. People throw things through their window just because they're gay."

My dad considered me. "*Homosexual,* Apron. That's the proper word. *Gay* is slang. Along with a host of other words, some of which were written on their window."

I nodded. I started to tell him that I had been there when the rock smashed it, but caught myself. "Dad," I said quietly. "Why do people hate them anyway? They're not hurting anyone."

My dad sat back and crossed his arms. "*Men vereor they quis they operor non agnosco.* The age-old reason, Apron. Men fear what they do not understand."

"Do you hate them?" I'd heard him joking with Mr. Haffenreffer before, about how they'd had to share a bed in a motel once so they lifted up the dresser and put it down between them.

"No. I don't hate them."

"Mrs. Perry does. She hates them. And Eeebs, he does too. But I don't think Mr. Perry does."

My dad's face tightened up. "Listen, kiddo, I'm sorry about Rennie. I don't think I can fix that one for you. Maybe it's time we all move on."

It was the same thing Rennie had said. Time to be friends with someone else.

"But what if you don't want to?" I asked.

"Sometimes it's not up to you, is it?"

He squeezed my hand and disappeared behind the news again.

I went to the sink and washed my bowl. Then I got out the saltines and crushed a few onto the counter. They were M's favorite crackers.

I left through the back door.

Outside, it wasn't raining exactly, just sort of spritzing on my face every second. I walked around the house and into the garage for my pogo stick. Then I bounced up to Mrs. Weller's driveway to see if Mike's truck was there. It wasn't. Her orange love bug was though.

I knocked on her door and prayed she didn't have blood on her anywhere.

All clear, but her George Washington face was as cranky as ever.

"Yes?"

"Hi, Mrs. Weller."

"Are you selling today?" she looked behind me for the wagon.

"No. I just came over to see if Mike was coming by anytime soon."

She sneered at me. "Mike's in the hospital."

I shook my head because I thought she said Mike was in the hospital. "He *works* near the hospital," I told Mrs. Weller carefully.

"I didn't say that," she snapped. "I said he's *in* the hospital. You need one of these." She pointed to her hearing aid.

"What happened? Is he okay?"

Mrs. Weller smacked her lips together. "You kids," she said. "You all watch too much damn television and now you can't HEAR right," she yelled. "What I said was, Mike's not sick. His little queer friend, Chad, is."

17

Fors fortis
Fat chance

I kept the TV on low in case Mike's truck drove into Mrs. Weller's driveway. Mrs. Weller knew nothing else about Chad, not even which hospital he was in. "I'm not sure they let queers into Maine Med," she said before shutting the door so close to my face my eyelashes blew back. "He might be at Mercy."

Finally, I let my fingers do the walking and called Scent Appeal. After three rings, Chad's voice said, "Hello. You've reached Scent Appeal. Floral arrangements for every occasion."

I left a message, then heard a car bumping down the road.

Just like I thought, my dad bought M an answering machine and a million things for that little whatever. I helped them get everything out of the car and up the stairs. At dinner, they yakked on and on about cribs and strollers while I pushed my Hungry Jack instant mashed potatoes around and thought up more jokes to tell Chad. *What bird sings the saddest song?*

"Apron. The Boss has to go."

"What?" I dropped my fork. "No way."

"Margie feels, no, *we* feel that if some of the feces gets near Margie, she could get sick, Apron. Really sick."

I glared at M. She stood and picked up my dad's plate.

"But she doesn't even have to go near him. She doesn't even have to *see* him. He can live in my room from now on. *Dad*," I told him quietly, "Mom gave him to me."

He looked at me with drooping eyes and whispered, "She's afraid of him, Apron."

"Then *she* can leave," I whispered back, with a growl in it.

My dad almost got mad, but then he leaned forward and put his hand on top of mine. "We've already decided."

A bluebird. A bluebird sings the saddest song.

I pulled my hand away. "Where's he supposed to go?"

My dad sat back. "I don't know, Apron. Anywhere but here."

Which was exactly where I was going.

I stood and headed for the door, but stopped when I heard a pan crash. "Oopsies," M said, squatting down to pick it up.

My dad stood to help, but I walked out.

Later, when my dad was in his office and M was upstairs glued to more reruns of *The Love Boat*, I went back into the kitchen. Soaking pans and crumbly counter tops were everywhere. Still, I took some paper towels, wet them into little blobs and dropped them all around the stove. Then I picked up the phone.

It took years for Grandma Bramhall to answer.

"Hi, dearie," she said, but carefully.

"Are you okay, Grandma Bramhall? I'm so sorry."

I could hear a lawn mower in the background, which meant she was sitting in her screened-in back porch, surrounded by the plastic green frogs she had lined up in certain directions for good luck. "Yes, dearie, I'm fine."

But you could tell she was waiting for me to tell her why I hit her.

"My hand just flung out like that. I was trying to take my bracelet off and it just snapped."

"Really, dearie, I'm fine. The hospital was very relaxing and I needed a little tune-up anyway. And those paramedics were just divine." I heard the lawnmower move farther away so she must have walked into the kitchen.

"They got married anyway."

"They did?"

"Yup." I told her how M wouldn't take off her dress until they did.

"That little tart," she said, throwing something that sounded like ice into a glass. "I should have known when she wouldn't take that damn dress off in the emergency room, not even a heart attack would slow her down."

"You had a heart attack?"

"Well, no."

She asked me what I was doing tomorrow: did I want to go to church with her and then out on Mr. John's lobster boat for a picnic?

"Grandma Bramhall?" I asked, twirling myself all the way up into the phone cord.

"Was that yes or no, Apron?" You could hear the lawnmower behind her again. Our phones were all stuck to walls, but she could go anywhere with hers, even to her pool if she wanted to. "I couldn't hear you."

I untwirled an inch. "Do you think I can come live with you?"

For a second, the only noise was the lawnmower.

Then I heard Grandma Bramhall's shoes clicking up the stairs.

"Oh, dearie, wouldn't that just be the monkey's uncle?" I heard a squeak and water running. "Now listen, did I tell you about the cruise that Mr. John is taking me on?"

I didn't say anything.

"Apron? I'm starting a nice hot bath. You sure you won't come tomorrow?"

I spun myself out of the phone cord.

"I'll pick you up at nine forty-five?"

I said no, thank you, I had a lot of homework.

"All right. But we still have a Handy's brunch date, with or without the bride and groom. Preferably without. Next Saturday, then?"

I didn't say yes or no, just something in between.

But Grandma Bramhall wasn't even listening. "I'll tell you all about the cruise," she said.

After we hung up, I stared at the phone and swallowed the piece of my heart that was lodged in my throat now. She was my last chance.

18

Et tu, Brute?
You too, Brutus?

**Nobody talked about The Boss, who was still in
the pantry, and all my dad and M did the next day was
walk around the guest room deciding where the little
whatever's crib should go and what color they should
paint its room.** While they were up there, I took a used
tea bag out of the garbage, put it in an empty mug and
left it on the living room table. M was the only one who
drank tea around here.

Upstairs, I stayed on my bed, studying different
stages of a cell's life and wishing I were one of them.
Cells could never be lonely, all they had to do was di-
vide themselves up. We had lab on Monday and Johnny Berman and I were already assigned to be partners. I
had decided I was going to wear my pink short-sleeved
button-down with Rennie's lace undershirt that she left
at my house once. A few times last week, I'd caught
Johnny staring at me when Ms. Frane wasn't looking,
the drill in my belly button happened every time.

Later, I rode my bike to the Foreside Market.

My forehead was dripping sweat by the time I got
there. It smelled awful at the deli, like *Mr. Clean* mixed
in with things that used to have eyes. But even if you
didn't live in Falmouth Foreside, you would probably
come all the way here to get your Italian sandwiches,

which are the best in Maine. A few people were waiting for their order so I squished by them, and heard my
name. When I turned around, Mrs. Perry was watching
me.

"Hi, Apron," she smiled, her tight curl tucked perfectly under each ear. I was almost as tall as she was
now.

"Hi, Mrs. Perry."

"Getting lunch?"

"Not really." Except standing there smelling the
green peppers and vinegar, you couldn't help but want
an Italian of your own.

"Well, we heard the good news," she leaned into
me and whispered.

"You did?"

"A teensie weensie bit of good news?"

I kept my face blank.

"Marguerite's having a baby?"

I hadn't told Rennie anything about M and her little
whatever.

"Apron?" Mrs. Perry dropped her smile. "Oh gosh.
You did know that, right?"

I nodded. She said, "Phew," and, "For a minute
there." Then she gave me a weak hug and her big curl
smooshed into my cheek and you could smell cigarettes
in her hair. "Good for your dad," she said. "Life goes
on then, doesn't it?"

When she was done hugging me, I stepped back so
she couldn't do it again. "How did you find out?"

Mrs. Perry threw an arm up and said, "Well, let's
see. Rennie's grandmother told me, and, well, you
know how those ladies can talk."

"Does Rennie know?"

"Of course, Apron," she said. "She's already suggested some names to Margie. Good old-fashion American names."

"But Rennie never called me," I said shaking my head. She never called.

"Margie called us, honey. To tell us herself. And besides, Rennie said you've been too busy with schoolwork to come over. Sure I can't get you something for lunch? We're off to the boat show today, did Rennie tell you?"

My hair melted. Rennie was a traitor, all right. Just like Judas. Next, she'd probably tell M where I would be on Thursday.

19

Amantes sunt amentes.
Lovers are lunatics.

"Love," Ms. Frane said, throwing her hands up and looking out the window. "Is in the air."

What we were talking about was our last English assignment of the year: free verse poetry. "You can write about any kind that you want, but the topic is: Love. What does it mean to you?"

Someone burped.

"Now. There are many kinds of love," Ms. Frane said in a big smile. With the sun hitting the blackboard behind her, it looked like it had been bleached by mistake.

Anne Potts dropped her pencil.

Monday mornings we were like caged monkeys, Ms. Frane said, scratching our ears and picking our teeth. "Love for your family, your friends, games, sports, or even *romantic* love."

The boys groaned at that, and Sherman Howl said, "This stinks," loud enough for Ms. Frane to hear. Rennie and Jenny Pratt looked at each other with their hands over their mouths. You could tell they were whispering about Seth Chambers, how much they loved him and he loved them, when, really, he didn't know they were alive.

Ms. Frane wrote, *Love: What Does It Mean To You?* on the board and started writing out examples of free verse poetry.

Johnny Berman was absent; I'd worn the lace undershirt for nothing.

Sherman Howl and Mark Lippett stood and put their hands over each other's mouth and pretended to kiss. Ms. Frane didn't even turn around when she said, "Sherman and Mark, sit back in your seats by the time I count to three."

They made it.

"If love means kissing another boy to you, that's fine."

Everyone said, "Yuck," but I didn't, even though it was pretty weird when you thought about it lip by lip. I tried not to imagine Mike and Chad kissing, but it was impossible not to, so I thought about Mike kissing me instead.

"Just remember," Ms. Frane said leaning onto her desk. "I'll be showing them to your parents at conferences next week." The boys straightened up in their seats after that. But I slumped down. I still hadn't given the reminder slip to my dad. It was for Thursday at 10:15, which he wasn't going to be able to make anyway. Love didn't mean missing work.

Jenny Pratt got called to read the example.

Love means helping someone when they get hurt.
Love means sharing your umbrella in the rain,
Or taking your grandmother's hand,
Or having a picnic on the beach.
Love means boat rides and seashells,
And hugs from your friends.

Ms. Frane nodded. "Very nice, Jenny. Okay, everyone, remember to elaborate. It counts toward your final grades. Six lines. Due next Monday."

Jenny Pratt sat back in her seat again and Rennie batted her eyelashes at her, like love meant waving to the person who read the example out loud.

At recess, I lay on the grass making an obstacle course for the ants. They were too fast to do much with, but every once in a while, one of them fell into the snake pit that I made out of twigs and branches. Maybe love meant falling into my trap.

Four matching pink shoelaces stopped next to me. I looked up. They were standing with their arms crossed, Rennie's shoulder only up to Jenny Pratt's elbow, both of them smirking at me playing with my sticks.

A full moon of trouble rose in my stomach.

"Oh, look at the cute toddler," Jenny Pratt giggled. Her long nose was pointing straight down at me and her lips were crunched up together, like she just tasted something that didn't have sugar on it yet. "Are you, like, playing with *bugs*?"

"Shut up," I said, pushing myself onto my knees and standing as fast as I could. Rennie and I had made up the game together. But now she just sneered at me.

"We heard about your dad getting married," Jenny Pratt said. "You must *love* your new mom. *Everyone* knows about their *love* child, too. Guess your dad just couldn't keep it in his pants."

Someone slapped me, but Jenny Pratt's arms were still on her hips and Rennie's were still crossed in front of her. I looked at Rennie, who forced a chuckle. I wanted to punch Jenny in the face, but she was right.

And M's baby was coming in September, right after we started eighth grade. Which meant she'd been pregnant for a lot longer than anyone knew.

"Well," Jenny continued, "at least he's got a shot at getting a girl this time."

Even Rennie looked confused. "What are you talking about?" I asked. "I don't have a brother."

Jenny lifted her hand to her mouth in mock surprise. "Oh my God. I'm so sorry. All this time, I thought you were a boy," she glanced down at my chest, and then smoothed down her own; two mounds under her shirt. "Hey," she said slapping Rennie's shoulder. "Maybe we should ask Apron to come bra shopping with us sometime, what do you think, Ren? She might like the one we just picked out for you."

And then I saw it; Rennie was wearing a bra. I had never seen such big mounds on her chest before, which had to be mostly padding. We'd even touched tongues on it: that we would buy our first bras together. The moon of bad news exploded inside my flat chest and landed in between Rennie and me, burning the space between us forever. I looked at her for the last time as my best friend. Something in her face knew it, too.

"Hey, Jenny?" I turned to her. "Why don't you ask Rennie about how she calls Seth Chambers and pretends to be you?"

Rennie dropped her arms, her face looking sorry now, all right. But I tightened my mouth and flicked my eyebrows. Even though she had only done it once, way before we stopped being friends, turns out once was one time too many.

"What?" Jenny Pratt said whipping her head back and forth between Rennie and me, stopping on Rennie. "Did you really do that?"

I turned and walked away, loving it.

20
Pactum factum
A done deal

At the end of school, I pedaled across the field where my dad hit Mr. Perry and turned left down the big hill, hoping I wouldn't run into Mr. Solo. He was always warning me that if he saw me empty-headed one more time he was going to call my parents. It had been plenty more times, but you could always tell when it was Mr. Solo biking by because of the dentist mirror taped onto his helmet for a rearview mirror.

At the bottom, I started pedaling hard, my backpack heavy again, especially with the conference reminder slip that was light as a feather unless you counted the rocks it put in your stomach if you were me.

When I reached our mailbox, I slipped my feet off the pedals and opened it. The mail was in a perfect pile with an L.L. Bean catalogue folded around it. Until a car zoomed past me so fast my hair blew into my eyes and most of the mail flew out of my hands. One of the letters had sailed onto the yellow line in the middle of the road, so I put my kickstand down and ran in to get it.

There was a picture of a seal on it. After another look, I could see it was a picture of seal*s*. *Save the Seals,* it said in big black letters. *Do Something.* On the back it had some news about seals and a picture of a red log in the middle of a snowfield. But when you looked closer, you could see that that log was a seal. And the rock to the side of it was a baby seal, its two black eyes staring at his dead mother.

You Can Help, it said. But I just shoved it in my pocket and rode home.

I called Scent Appeal right after I stepped into the kitchen. I had called so many times in the last two days, I could dial it with my eyes closed. And still, no one answered.

In my room, I said hi to The Boss. He and his cage were hiding in my closet now. So far, my dad hadn't mentioned him again. I did my homework and tried to decide if love meant letting your guinea pig live in your sock drawer for the rest of its life. But there was the poop to consider, so I wasn't sure. I picked up *The Long Winter*. Laura had a hard life all right—like her sister going blind and her dad always off hunting and her whole family almost getting scalped—but she had a better shot of writing a poem about love than I did.

Later, my dad's car crunched down the dirt road and the same old bangings started happening in the kitchen. Until a huge high M scream happened.

I jumped off my bed and flew down the stairs, ready to see blood or broken bones. But when I got there, M was jumping up and down next to my dad and both of them were reading a letter. M's face was pink and smiling, but my dad's was just kind of frozen, like he fell out of the freezer and couldn't remember where he was.

When M saw me, she squealed. She was in her nursing clothes, looking kind of plumped up everywhere now, not just in her bump anymore.

"Aprons," she said. "Your father's famous!" She grabbed his arm and jumped up and down with it until my dad pulled it back. Then she stopped jumping and started some chipmunk clapping instead.

I looked at my dad to see what was going on. "Well, Apron," he nodded. "I'm getting published." Then he shook his head. "*Exsisto curiosus quis vos opto, is may adveho verus.* Look it up," he told me, walking out the door.

M and I looked at each other, our eyebrows pulled up into a question mark. But then, in the next second, we both got busy. M started banging more pots and I walked over to the table and picked up the letter. Casco Bay Publishing was pleased to inform my dad that they were interested in acquiring his book, *Maine Matters*.

I knocked two times softly.

He was sitting behind his desk, grading papers like usual. But he stopped when I walked in and placed his letter on top of a pile.

"Be careful what you wish for, right?" I asked. It was just a guess. *The secret to deciphering Latin,* it said on the back of the dictionary, *is that much of it can be inferred.*

"Very good," he nodded down to his work. "Just give me one second here."

I watched him, trying to find that same happy freckle-faced boy that was in the picture by Grandma Bramhall's bed. But I couldn't find him anywhere.

"Okay," he said ready for what I had to say.

Which was: "Aren't you happy?" I nodded toward the letter.

He looked off to the side. "I just wish it had happened a lot earlier." He cleared his throat.

"Are we going to move now?" I held my breath. "Or anything?"

He shook his head. "No. Nothing is going to change, all right?" He meant it to be reassuring, but staying the same was the worst thing that could happen now.

21

Sit vis nobiscum.
May the force be with you.

"Hello?" Mike answered

"Hello?" I answered back, like it was a wrong number. I had been calling since Monday. And now it was 8:31 on Thursday night.

"This is Scent Appeal, can I help you?"

"Mike?"

"That's me."

"It's Apron," I said, but carefully, in case he didn't remember me anymore.

"Apron!" he said. "How are you?"

After three days of watching Jenny Pratt and Rennie whisper about me, one visit to the nurse's office to get checked for lice, and three different kinds of M's meatloaf for dinner, this was the first time anyone one had asked me that. I told him I was fine.

"Listen," he said. "I wanted to ask you something, if it's okay with your dad, of course. Chad was in the hospital. He's okay now, but we have another big wedding on Saturday and he's a little, a little tired. So I was wondering, because—you know, you were so great with all the flowers and the decorating."

"I can help." I jumped down from the counter. "I'd love to."

"Really?" Mike asked sounding surprised. "You have school tomorrow, right?"

I said right, but then realized too late, that I should have said no.

"Okay, what time can I pick you up?"

"Three-thirty."

"I'll see you then. Make sure it's okay with your dad, though. Unless you think I should ask him myself?"

"No," I said. "He's working, I'll ask him."

"Thanks, Apron," Mike paused. "You're saving me."

Mike hung up after that, but I stayed there with the phone still tucked into my neck thinking that he had taken those words right out of my mouth.

I walked out of the kitchen and knocked on my dad's door. Every single night this week he had left me alone with M before dinner was finished to get back to work. He wasn't just grading papers anymore, he told M when she put on her pouty face. He was grading *finals*.

"Dad?" I opened the door.

There were so many piles on his desk that all you could see was the top of his red head.

"I'm really busy here, Apron. I have six different finals to grade."

"Sorry. Um. Can I go help Mike after school tomorrow?" I whispered.

Two of the stacks parted and in between them my dad's face appeared. "Mike?"

I nodded.

"Just a second," he said, annoyed now, lifting one hand up in a stop sign and scribbling down a few more notes.

I stood quietly turning the doorknob back and forth.

The first night after Chad went into the hospital, my dad came into the kitchen and asked who I was calling. I told him Scent Appeal, and that Chad had gone into the hospital.

"For what," he asked. I said I didn't know but that Chad seemed to sweat and get tired a lot. He frowned and went back to work, but he didn't tell me to stop calling them.

And last night while we were getting the garbage, my dad told me that he had actually met Mike before. He hadn't met Chad, but he did remember meeting Mrs. Weller's nephew in her garden one day. I tried to picture it: my dad, my mom, and Mike, all hanging around Mrs. Weller's yard together, talking about flowers and drinking orange Tang.

"It wasn't like that, Apron," my dad said, dumping the bathroom trash into the garbage bag I was holding out for him. If you paid money, the trash truck came all the way down your dirt road, but if you didn't, you had to go to the dump every Wednesday night like we did. We usually took Mrs. Weller's garbage too, and you could tell which bags were hers by how bad they smelled.

"I'm sure your mother saw Mike more than I did. She saw a lot of people more than I did." My dad put the trash can back down again and leaned over to collect the small bits of toilet paper on the floor next to the sink—which I had scattered around that morning. I had pulled off some red hair from my brush and dropped that around too, until I woke up and smelled the coffee on that one.

"So how come she never told me about him?" I asked.

"She kept good secrets," he said, walking out the door. I stopped to look in the mirror at my freckled self. Mike and my mom were friends. Mike and my mom were *friends.*

"Anyway," my dad said from the hallway. "What's with the sudden friendship? You should be making friends with people your own age. Did these guys even go to college?"

I told him I didn't know. In the living room, the couch cushions were sticking up in all the wrong places and a vase filled with droopy dead peonies was on the table. I felt bad about it, but after I picked them the night before, I hid them in the corner of the pantry. Then later, when they were perfectly sagged, I slid them into the vase and put them on the table.

My dad scooped up some pages of M's magazine while I held out the garbage bag and picked up a dusty picture of me sitting in a yellow car that I couldn't remember.

I put the frame back and followed my dad upstairs. His shoes crunched a little, just like I hoped. I made sure there was no sand on the floor going into my room, only into the little whatever's room. Finally, in the hall bathroom, he sighed. "Apron," he said, picking up a trash can overflowing with toilet paper and old toothpaste tubes and a few of M's empty creams. "This place—" but then he sighed again and shook his head. I coughed not to smile. M was in his bedroom watching *Wheel of Fortune*, you could tell by the dinging and clapping. She said she needed to watch it so she could learn English better, but even *loud holiday in July* for a clue was too hard for her. We didn't say good-bye when my dad and I drove to the dump. We used to get ice cream afterward, but these days my dad needed to get home to start grading more finals and I needed to get back to calling Scent Appeal over and over again, which I did until bedtime.

Tonight, though, I just needed permission to help Mike after school tomorrow.

Finally my dad put down his pen and said, "There," rubbing his eyes and staring at me in between the Himalayas of papers. Ms. Frane had just taught us about Mt. Everest, and Sherman Howl said his uncle made it to the third step but then went snow-blind and had to turn back. None of us believed him.

"I don't know," my dad said. "Why doesn't Mike go and get some real help?"

"It's just this once. Remember I told you Chad was in the hospital?" He didn't answer. He took a stack of papers from one pile and stacked it on top of another. "Mike said he would pick me up and bring me home. So can I?"

My dad started flipping through the papers. "And when is this happening?" he sighed, like it was already on the calendar.

"Tomorrow. After school."

"You've got to be kidding," he said shaking his head and flipping through more papers. "There's no name on here."

Which may or may not have meant yes, so I said thanks and left.

22
Licentia vatum
Poetic license

The next day after school, I biked by Mrs. Perry's white Cadillac in the pick-up line. She waved to me, but I saw two heads in the back, Rennie's and Jennie Pratt's, so I didn't wave back.

This morning I had made it almost halfway up the big hill before getting off my bike to walk. Mr. Solo noticed how much farther up I was getting these days. He said, "Looking good," when he passed me, nothing about my head, so I gave him the thumbs-up inside his dentist mirror.

Nobody was home. It was M's last day of work and some nurses were taking her out for dinner afterward. When my dad told me this at my lobster this morning, I thought he might say, *And that's why you can't go help Mike later.* But he didn't. So I waited for Mike in my room, reading more of *The Long Winter* and letting The Boss wander around my room until I heard tires crunching.

I rolled off the bed, dropped The Boss back in his cage in the closet, and grabbed my backpack. I was standing in Mrs. Weller's driveway by my next blink.

"Hey, Apron," Mike said, climbing out of the Scent Appeal van. He still looked like Jesus, but a paler, more tired one now. His white T-shirt smelled clean when he hugged me, though, and he was wearing his same old jeans.

"What happened to the ORD UCK?"

"Had to sell it," he said. "Listen, thanks for helping me out. I'm sure you had some fun kid things to do today."

I looked up at him. "I don't do fun kid things," I said. But it came out as I don't do *fun* kid things, which was worse.

A chipmunk whizzed by like a rocket and disappeared up a tree.

"You never told me you knew my mom."

Mike nodded. "I met her right before . . ." He looked down, flashing his eyes right and left, remembering. "Before Halloween. She was helping Millie with a broken cupboard. She was nice, Apron. And beautiful."

A shooting star went off in my stomach.

"I saw her a few times after that in her garden," Mike looked over at my house. "But you were always at school, or someone's house, maybe?"

"Rennie's," I said. "We used to be best friends. Now we're not."

He nodded absently. "Listen. I better go check on Millie for a sec."

I said okay and walked across her yard and sat down against a tree. An ant crawled over my ankle, but I just let it.

After a whole city of ants had used my ankle as a bridge, Mrs. Weller came out on her doorstep wearing her orange sweat suit with white sneakers and an orange bandana wrapped around her head like George Washington playing Little Orange Riding Hood.

"Hi, Mrs. Weller," I waved, brushing the ants off me and standing.

"Did you hear about your grandmother's cruise?" she clucked.

I nodded, but I wasn't sure if she could see me this far away, so I said, "Yes."

"Your grandfather would roll over in his grave if he knew about that. But then again," she said nodding over to my house. "Apple doesn't fall far from the tree."

Mike walked back out wearing orange gardening gloves and holding some clippers. "I'll be just a minute, Apron," he said, crossing the lawn to Mrs. Weller's rose garden. Mrs. Weller walked back inside, so I went over to watch Mike snip off branches of perfectly good orange roses and let them fall to the ground.

"Why are you doing that?"

"Pruning?" he asked, another branch biting the dust.

It smelled like the best perfume in the mall right there. Another chipmunk zoomed by, but stopped in the middle of nowhere to look around when it heard the snap of the clippers. It took off again when Mike said, "It takes a lot of energy for a plant to keep the old buds alive, when it could be used to help the new buds grow."

Mike kept clipping while he spoke, moving in and around the bushes, flipping his hair back off his shoulders once in a while. "Out with the old, in with the new kind of thing," he said after another bush had been knocked off. Last year, Mr. Burke told us in Science Lab that if you hooked trees up to tiny microphones and then chopped them down, you could hear them scream. "Our ears can't hear it, though," he said pulling on his black moustache. "Their screams are that high-pitched." Everyone thought he was making it up. Except me. Because unless you were a tree, how would you know?

I picked up an orange rose. "*Collige virgo Rosas,*" I said quietly.

"Did you just say something in another language or am I hearing things?" Mike smiled.

"Latin. *Pick, girl, the Roses.* It means stop and smell the roses."

"I like that," Mike said.

"My mom did, too," I told him. It was the only sentence she liked in Latin.

↗   ↗   ↗

When we got to Scent Appeal, Mike opened the back door of the van and filled my arms with flowers. "I'll get the rest," he said. "If Chad's awake, go sit with him. He's been waiting to tell you something."

The window was still covered with garbage bags and tape, and inside it didn't smell as good as it used to. Some of the flowers were sagged over or dried up.

Upstairs there was a long lump under a white blanket on the couch. It was so hot in the living room you didn't even need your skin on. But Chad's blanket covered his whole body all the way up to his chin.

"Hi, Chad," I whispered.

His eyes popped open and he pulled himself up. "Apron." He groaned a little, like he was getting a Band-Aid ripped off. "Come here."

I put the flowers on the floor and walked over to him, feeling guilty for ever being mad at my freckles. At least they were normal ugly. Chad's face had two new black spots on it that were so big and uneven it was hard to stop looking at them. One was next to his ear and one was on his chin. His face looked like the skull that Mr. Solo kept in his classroom, but with a little skin on it.

I tried to smile.

"Listen," Chad said, letting his blanket fall off. He was wearing a dark blue sweater. "What goes ninety-nine clunk, ninety-nine clunk, ninety-nine clunk?" He grinned at me. You could tell he had no idea how much worse he looked in just a few days. That's what a hospital could do to you.

"I don't know," I said, wishing I hadn't come up here without Mike. "A pirate with a lot of friends?"

"Close! A centipede with a wooden leg! Hah!" He pointed at me and laughed, and really did look a little better.

I tried to laugh back. "Good one. Where did you get that?"

"Hey, man, I have my sources."

He waved me over to sit on the floor next to him. The coffee table was gone. The TV was too.

"Where's your TV?"

"Sold it," Chad shrugged. "Drug money. You know."

I said oh.

"So what's been going on around the school yard?" Chad asked, snapping his fingers. "What's the word. What's the haps. Everyone talking smack about *Back to the Future?* Think they're going to go out and get themselves one of those fancy time-warp cars?"

"You're a freak, Chad," Mike said walking in with more flowers. "*You're* the one who wants that kid's car."

"Ooh," Chad said wiggling his eyebrows. "Me, Michael J. Fox, suddenly back in homeroom class, *dissecting* things."

Mike tried not to laugh, but you could see the corners of his mouth begging him to let them go. Chad blew him a kiss and Mike finally gave in, both sides of his smile, and most of his eyes, turning up.

"Okay," Mike said putting the flowers on the floor. "We're going to do these up here today so Chad doesn't have to move." He headed back down the stairs again.

"I must really be close to the end then, huh?" Chad winked at me.

I didn't answer. Chad lay back down on the couch and closed his eyes. I tried to unwrap the newspaper as quietly as I could. I knew the names of all the flowers, but I made up new names for them anyway as I rolled them out of their newspapers. Names that matched their smells like: "No More Jenny Pratt" and "Sea Glass Cave." All of them, especially "Gone Back to Brazil Forever," made the room start smelling better. After his last delivery, Mike walked into their kitchen and got himself a glass of water. Chad still hadn't moved yet, but Mike wasn't looking too worried about it. Mike put his glass down and started telling me how many of each flower went into the arrangements.

"And *Lisianthus*," Mike said walking over and pointing to the last pile. "Wait, what did we say, Chaddie? Five or six of each?"

Chad lifted his head like he had been awake the whole time and looked over at us. "Three," he said. "Makes a statement," then flopped his head back onto the pillow.

"It's all a big blur to me now, what we learned in school. Like, I think we learned verbs in fourth grade, is that right?" Chad mumbled while Mike and I started grabbing from this pile and taking from that, saying, "Oops, sorry," once in a while when we bumped wrists. Being this close to Mike made the cramp in my heart loosen up a bit, like little shingles were falling off of it.

I told Chad no, that happened in first grade, even though you really learn your verbs from *Schoolhouse Rock!* before that. Chad and Mike said, "Oh yeah!" at the same time, and then Chad started singing "Conjunction junction what's your function?" And Mike and I started singing it, too. You could hear what a good voice Mike had when he started harmonizing. They had both forgotten the *noun* song, but when I said, "A noun is a person, place, or thing," they caught on again.

"Cool. We're all nouns. Wait a minute, have you had to write a *thesis* yet?" Chad asked.

Mike chuckled. "Where'd you go to seventh grade, Harvard? Didn't know that was your alma mater."

I looked at him. "That's Latin, you know. It translates as 'nurturing mother.'"

Chad whistled. "Kid's a scholar."

I shrugged. "My dad teaches it."

"So it's not dead after all," Mike said.

"It teaches you the English language. That helps with spelling and stuff."

"You're scary," Chad said.

"You're speaking it all the time. You just don't know it," I argued.

"I'd know it," Chad chuckled.

"Okay, fine," I said. "So you and me and Mike, we're all—?"

"Present?" Chad guessed.

I shook my head. "No. We're all homo—?"

Chad and Mike looked at me, surprised.

"Sapiens," I finished quickly, my cheeks heating up. "Men. I mean *man*." I looked down at the flowers. No wonder Rennie and Jenny Pratt hated me.

Chad propped himself up on his elbows and said, "Or just plain homos, in Mike's and my case."

"Chad," Mike warned him.

"Oh come *on*, that was funny," Chad said while I untangled some stems.

My cheeks were still rug burned, so I leaned into a bunch of babies' breath and pretended to smell them, hoping they wouldn't remember that babies' breath doesn't even *have* a smell.

"Anyway, tell us some more things we used to do in seventh grade, Apron."

"Geometry and social studies," I said happy to change the subject. "And we have to write a free verse poem. By Monday."

"A free verse poem," Chad said dreamily. "Now *those* I remember. Don't I, Mikey?"

Mike shrugged. "Probably not," he said counting out some irises. "What's your poem about?"

"Love," I groaned, like it was the worst news in the world. "What it means to you."

"Love!" Chad clapped. "So what *does* love mean to you, Apron?"

I told him I thought it was a dumb question.

No one said anything for a second, but I could tell they were eyeballing each other. Then Chad said, "Yeah. My mom's dead, too."

"She is?" I stopped untangling stems to look at him.

"Will you knock it *off*, Chad," Mike warned him meanly this time.

"What?" he said throwing his hands up. "She *is*, to me. Haven't spoken to the woman in twelve years. That's pretty dead."

"Nice," Mike mumbled, shaking his head.

I focused on figuring out the tallest daisy, then snipping it.

"Tell you what, Apron," Chad said. "I'll write the poem for you." He lifted himself up on his elbows again. "I'm a hopeless romantic-type, right Mikey?"

"You can't do that, Chad. Apron could get in trouble. Teachers have a way of knowing stuff like that. You're not *actually* a seventh grader, remember?"

Chad pouted. "Well, then, can I *help* write it? Please? I'll take you to Dairy Queen?" He blinked at me, then Mike. "Fine. *Mike* will take us to Dairy Queen."

Mike gave a quick nod.

"Great!" Chad smiled, even though I still hadn't agreed to anything. He stood and shuffled over to the kitchen for a pen and some paper, then shuffled back to the couch. "What Love Means to Me," Chad said, writing. "By Apron Bramhall, the loveliest noun I know. Get over here, noun."

So I did. And while Mike drove off to deliver the flowers, Chad and I wrote my free verse poem together.

And later, when Chad slid the poem into my backpack he said, "You're gonna get an A. You wait."

23

Draco dormiens nunquam titillandu.
A sleeping dragon is never to be tickled.

If you thought M looked bad before, you had to see her now. She had black circles under her eyes the size of a football player's and her mouth hung so low she probably couldn't lift it up into a smile if she tried. Even though she didn't look as bad as Chad did, she looked like she could check into the hospital for a nap at least. And if *she* looked this bad, you could only imagine what that little whatever in there looked like. Which is why, when I saw her carrying a load of laundry up the stairs, I heard myself say, "I'll do it."

She looked up at me like she was too tired to play games.

So I stepped down and took the pile out of her hands just to prove it.

"What do you want?" she scowled.

"Nothing," I said. "It's just that you seem kind of tired this morning."

Turns out I did want something, though.

In the bathroom, I pulled the green curtain back. The other side was the laundry room, and the hamper against the wall already had a few arms and legs hanging out of it. I dropped M's pile, dumped the hamper out on top of it, and started sorting. When I was done, I plucked my dad's bright red shirt, which always bleeds, out of the darks and dropped it in with the whites, which had his favorite summer pants and white button-down shirt. Sadly, I was going to have to sacrifice my white *Portland Pottery* T-shirt to make things look real.

I was putting in the load when I noticed M through the space between the curtain studying herself in the mirror. She pulled both cheeks back with her palms and opened her mouth as wide as she could. Then she dropped her eyes to her bump and turned sideways, smoothing my dad's plaid shirt over it. She tried to suck in her stomach, but it wasn't going anywhere. That little whatever was going to have to come out one way or the other now. M let the bump go and put her hands over her face and started crying; silent and quick with shaking shoulders.

Even though she wasn't hitting her bump this time, that same tidal wave of sadness crashed into me. When Mrs. Christianson was pregnant, she rubbed her stomach so nicely you practically wanted to climb in there yourself. But M just hated it, you could tell.

Maybe I needed to cut back on the messes I was making. At least for a few days. My dad had started clenching his jaw again, what he always did when he had a low-grade problem, and M had started stepping away from him. I pulled my dad's red shirt out of the load and threw it back down with the darks. Then I opened the curtain. But when M saw my face, her eyes hardened. "This laundry should be your job anyway, Aprons. You American girls are all so spoiled," she hissed, walking out.

So I picked up the red shirt again, dropped it back in with the white load, and started the laundry machine.

By the time I got downstairs, M was standing in front of the stove cooking runny eggs. "Morning, Apron," my dad said sitting at his lobster. Last night after Mike dropped me off, he had yelled out from his office, "Is that you, Margie?" I had made it home before M, who was still out with her nurse friends. I poked my head in through his doorway. "Oh. Apron. How'd the flowers go?" he asked. So I told him. And he told me to make sure the front door was unlocked and to go on up to bed, it was late.

Now, I got down my cereal, but something was too thick around here and it turned out to be their moods. M put some eggs in front of my dad and asked me if I wanted any. My dad was watching so I looked her straight in the eye and smiled when I said, "No, thank you." She looked away and sat down. My dad took a few bites of the glop, but M stared at hers, not eating a thing.

"Better eat," my dad said nodding to her plate.

M shook her head and said, "I cannot."

"Serves you right then," my dad said, pushing his eggs away and cracking open his paper. "It wasn't a bachelorette party."

M cleared her plate and left. I poured some cereal into my bowl and read the *Do You Knows* on the back of the box. Just like the good old bad days.

24
Satine caloris tibi est?
Hot enough for you?

Grandma Bramhall's brown car jiggled down our dirt road right on time.

"Hi, dearie," she said screeching her car into the driveway and waving her hand out the window. "Don't you look pretty."

You have to wear a dress to Handy's so I was wearing the yellow one she gave me for Easter. Already it was so humid out that winter was starting to sound good again.

I waved back and ran into the garage to put my pogo stick away. When I came out, my dad was standing at the top of the stairs.

"Hi, Mom," he said, one hand in his pocket and the other one lifted, palm out, in a wave. He looked tired, and tired of it, the way he always did now.

"Hi," Grandma Bramhall said, poking her head out the window. "How's the girl?"

"A little under the weather," he shrugged. My lips made a U-turn. I kept my smile low when I walked to the passenger side of her brown square car.

"Well, dearie, if you're going to make your own bed," Grandma Bramhall sighed, throwing her hands off the steering wheel.

I knew the rest: if you're going to make your own bed, *you better be willing to lie in it, too.* Grandma Bramhall said it a lot. But what it really meant was: who's sorry now?

My dad started down the stairs, both hands in his khaki pants. "When do you think you'll bring Apron home?"

"Oh, well, that depends," Grandma Bramhall said, turning her head to shake it at me, sliding into the passenger seat. "On whether we decide to have dessert or not, doesn't it, Apron? Did I tell you we are making *three* stops on the cruise, two in the Caribbean?"

I bugged my eyes out for her and rolled down my window. My dad said, "Sounds a lot more fun than fly-fishing." Last summer she went to fly-fishing school and left notes all over the kitchen that said, *Dear little people, I've gone fishing. Make yourselves at home.*

Grandma Bramhall jerked the car into reverse before my dad could lean into the window. "Call me if she gets to be too much for you, Mom. I'll come pick her up," he said.

"Oh for God's sake, Dennis. She's more of an adult than you are."

My dad tipped his head towards the stairs. "Yes. But it'd be a great way for me to get out of this shindig."

"A man at a baby shower. Honestly," Grandma Bramhall grumbled, turning around to see where she was backing out. Her head shook even cranked to the side like that, just a little slower, like it was up against something.

We couldn't hear what my dad said next because of the dirt crunching under the tires. But when I looked up again, he was climbing the stairs, his hands still in his pockets.

After that, we were on our way. I punched around on her radio until I heard, "We Are the World" with Cyndi Lauper and her friends.

"Oh, I love this one," Grandma Bramhall said, putting the petal to the metal and gunning it out onto Route 88, cutting off a *#1 Maine Movers* truck behind us. The driver let out a huge long beep, but Grandma Bramhall just threw her hands off the steering wheel and said, "Turn this up, dearie, will you?"

The driveway into Handy's Boat Yard was so full of potholes that if you closed your eyes, you might think you were on a ride at Funtown Splashtown instead. Half-way down, there was a parking lot full of boats with every kind of sailboat and speedboat you could think of just waiting to be fixed or painted. There were long boats that could fit my entire class in them, and tiny boats that could only fit two people. But all of them had names like *Sunrise Surprise* or *Sailendipity*. I thought about what I'd name mine; nothing with an M in it.

Grandma Bramhall got going so fast down the driveway it looked like she was trying to launch *us* off the docks. Then at the last second she turned into the parking lot, tires screeching. Seagulls cawed all over the sky and the air smelled like God just burped after eating fish for lunch. White poop was drizzled on everything, including Grandma Bramhall's brown hood already.

"Damn birds," she said, shutting her door. Then we started up the walkway with old wooden piles roped together. I held the door for her, which had a knob like a helm.

"Thank you, dearie," she smiled at me.

In the restaurant, the air conditioner was practically below zero and the fish smell from the outside turned into a fish smell sprayed with Pledge on the inside. Grandma Bramhall told a lady who looked too old to have bangs our names. Then we followed her into the dining room with dark wood everywhere and old people eating piles of fried clams.

Out the window, you could see the launching slope, where a medium-sized sailboat named *The Portland Polly* with a green hull was halfway into the water, waiting to go.

"I don't think so," Grandma Bramhall said when the bang lady stopped at a tiny table in the middle of the dining room. "I asked for a window. So my granddaughter can watch the boats."

The bang lady pinched her face into too many wrinkles, just like I thought, and seated us at a new one.

"Isn't this lovely," Grandma Bramhall sighed bringing some ice water to her shaking lips. Even though her head moved a thousand miles an hour, she knew exactly how to sip without spilling a drop.

"Thanks for bringing me here, Grandma Bramhall," I said putting my napkin on my lap and slipping my flip-flops off my feet, against the law but who was going to see.

"Nonsense," she said opening her menu. "Anything you want. The world is your oyster." She laughed at that. Then she leaned into her bag and pulled out three brochures, each of them with a big white ship on the front. "Did I show you these, Apron? Look where Mr. John is taking me," she said holding them up like a fan.

I plucked out the middle one and unfolded it. There were pictures of happy people eating in fancy dining rooms or dancing under big chandeliers. And pictures of tan ladies sitting around the pool with one knee up reading, and pictures of people with their arms wrapped around each other smiling big while the sun set behind them. Not a person with a freckle anywhere. When I was done, I smiled up at Grandma Bramhall, who was looking down at another brochure now, studying it really, bending it this way and that, trying to find something. It wasn't people with freckles though, because Grandma Bramhall didn't have any. Just like me, my dad caught them from his dad.

I put the brochure back down and opened the huge book of a menu with so many adjectives Ms. Frane would have had a field day. *Succulent*, *ripe*, and *perfectly roasted* were all over the place. Plain tuna salad is my favorite, but at Handy's the tuna is so *fresh* and *chunky* you can't even eat it. Which is why I usually got the fried clams, except now it reminded me of the seals I needed to save. Yesterday, I took the pamphlet out of my drawer and checked off the *Yes, please send me flyers to distribute* box. You didn't even need a stamp to mail it, that's how desperate they were for help.

A waitress with tall hair and bright lipstick came over and said, "Mornin' to yuh, ladies."

Grandma Bramhall put on her glasses and held the menu about a mile away from her and said, "Yes, I'll have a bloody mary and my granddaughter will have a—?" then waited for me to fill in the blank. I said,

"Shirley Temple, please," and then Grandma Bramhall said, "And I'll have the crab roll and my granddaughter will have the—?" I said, "Grilled cheese, please," making a heart on my sweating water glass before I took a sip. I was back to drinking water full time again, even though I could practically feel those hairy amoebas sliding down my throat, eyes closed and laughing like they were on a water slide. But I was finished eating meat. Hamburgers had parents, and I wasn't about to eat anyone's mother.

After the waitress took our menus, Grandma Bramhall put her napkin in her lap and said, "Excited for school to get out, dearie?"

"Yeah," I said. But I wasn't. I'd be spending most of my time trying to avoid M.

I picked up my fork and tried to balance it on one finger.

"Grandma Bramhall?" I asked quietly. "What does love mean to you?"

Something about that was funny to her, so she laughed. "Well, let's see then, a three-stop cruise in the Caribbean?" My fork dropped, clanking against the water glass.

A few times while we were eating, Grandma Bramhall caught someone's wrinkly arm walking by and asked, "Do you know my pretty granddaughter, Apron?" Then I would stand up to shake their cold hand and watch Grandma Bramhall smile big and say, "Oh, did I tell you about my cruise?" Two ladies said, "Yes, Dory you did," and kept walking, but one old lady with a needlepoint lobster on her pocketbook shook her head and said, "No, for gracious sakes, Dory, do tell." So Grandma Bramhall told her to pull up a chair.

I looked outside so I didn't have to see those happy people dancing under chandeliers again. *The Portland Polly* was in the water now, puttering past the docks. Way out in the harbor, boats were bouncing up and down against the waves like pigeons pecking at birdseed. A small blue sailboat named *2 Have Fun* was tied onto the dock and someone in red Nantucket pants and a dark blue polo shirt, wearing a white baseball hat, was spraying the bow down with a hose. I watched those seagulls dare each other to land on deck but then chicken out when the man aimed the hose at them.

"Did your grandmother tell you about the beluga whale?" the woman with the lobster pocketbook asked me. She was as old as Grandma Bramhall, but dressed fancier, with big gold earrings that matched her necklace and a red coat with gold buttons.

I shook my head and looked at Grandma Bramhall, in her same blue dress with white squiggles on it, a matching belt tight around her waist, always thick and soft. But Grandma Bramhall kept staring at one of the brochures while she said, "I don't know anything about a whale, Betty."

"Oh, you do too," the pocketbook lady said, slapping the air in front of her. "That poor whale has been stuck in the harbor for days. Lost its way."

"Well, I haven't *been* here for days, Betty," Grandma Bramhall said, picking her head up.

"I can't remember there ever being a whale around here, can you?" the pocketbook lady asked.

Grandma Bramhall shook her shaking head at me. "No," she said, her voice lifting a little. "Actually, I can't either. Go down and have a look, dearie."

I turned to the window and sighed. I didn't want to go take a look, but Grandma Bramhall and the pocketbook lady had already swapped brochures once and were about to do it again, back to talking about upper decks and pineapples. So I stood. We weren't allowed to be home until after two o'clock anyway, when M's nurse friends would be gone. I had heard my dad on the phone last night promising to get them all back to the hospital by then, the beginning of their shifts.

I smiled at the bang lady on the way out, but she didn't smile back.

25

Tempes omnia revelat.
Time reveals all things.

It felt like I stepped into a dryer by mistake. But the closer I got to the docks, the cooler the wind got, blowing across my forehead and whipping up my red hair.

I crossed the pebbled path and headed straight down the ramp, steep now at low tide. Everything creaked on the way down, so I held onto the railing. When I got to the bottom, the man in Nantucket pants was on his knees tightening a knot in the cleat. I walked over to the edge of the dock and looked into the deep green water. No signs of a whale anywhere.

"Apron?" someone said.

When I turned to look, I saw it was Mr. Perry. He wiped his hands on his Nantucket pants and stood.

"Hi, Mr. Perry," I said turning back down to the water. I hadn't seen him since the Meaningless Bowl.

"Well, hi, is your dad here with you?" he said checking out the ramp behind me.

"No. Grandma Bramhall is taking me to brunch."

"Oh," Mr. Perry said, worry falling off his face. Then he looked down at my dress. "Well, you're a picture of loveliness."

"Thank you," I smiled, my freckles burning. In the water there was still nothing but slapping waves.

"Are you looking for the whale?" he asked, stepping closer to take a look for himself. "It's a baby beluga, all white."

I nodded. Mr. Perry was even more handsome with a hat on.

"Haven't seen it myself. Though supposedly it's been hanging around for a few days, must have strayed from its pack."

That got me worried. "Are they going to kill it?"

"No," he said quietly. "No one's going to hurt it. All we can do is hope that it finds its way back home soon enough, while it still stands a chance."

I nodded and then we stood on the edge of the dock together like that, waiting. Small bits of wind were blowing here and there, but the sun was still beating down, hot.

"Mr. Perry?" I asked softly. "Can I ask you something?"

He cleared his throat. Then with his voice much lower he said, "What is it, Apron?"

"Did Rennie have Jenny Pratt for a sleepover last night?"

He didn't answer me for a second. "Jenny Pratt?" he said with his voice up to normal again. "As a matter of fact yes, she did, Apron."

My stomach dented. Just off the docks, a man in a Boston Whaler screamed, "Yo' Perry, you done?" But Mr. Perry didn't answer. He waved him off with a flick of his wrist and said, still looking at me, "Uh-oh. Did Rennie make plans with you first?"

I watched that man turn his boat around and zoom off. And just when the wake from the Boston Whaler slammed into the side of the dock, I shrugged.

"Gosh, I'm sorry about that. You two remind me of sisters, though, and sometimes even sisters fight." Mr. Perry said, smiling in a big goofy way.

I hung the ends of my flip-flops over the water and watched the waves banging against the docks. It had a life of its own now, the water, splashing back onto itself so hard that even the seagulls stayed away.

"Hey, I know," Mr. Perry clapped, perking himself up and pointing to the boat tied next to him. "Do you want to take her back to the mooring with me?"

I turned around and looked up at the restaurant, then back to Mr. Perry who dropped his hose again, waiting for an answer. "You'd be my first passenger?" he said. "Just launched her this morning. Not even Rennie's been on her yet."

So I nodded and climbed aboard the *2 Have Fun*, thinking of exactly how I was going to tell Rennie and Jenny Pratt that I had been on the boat before they had.

On deck things were really rocking. I held onto the side of the boat while Mr. Perry got in and pulled up the bumpers. Everything smelled new, like shoe polish, and the floor was the sandy color I should have had for hair.

Mr. Perry said, "Not yet," when I asked him if he needed any help, so I leaned against the side of the boat and watched him wrap and store and turn things on. My dad gets too sunburned to sail, but Mr. Perry was brown as a bear.

"Okay, Apron," he said, undoing the cleats and throwing the ropes into the boat. "We're going to motor out to the mooring."

I leaned over the side and dipped my hand in the water, watching five long fingernails grow. After they dripped off, one by one, I did it again and again. Until the motor slowed and Mr. Perry said, "Take the helm, would you?"

I looked around to see who he was talking to, but no one else was there and he was already walking up to the bow. Which meant for a moment, we were just floating; unmoored. We could have drifted anywhere—all the way up to Canada or straight into the rocks. Only time would tell.

I stepped over and took the helm. "Which way?" I yelled to Mr. Perry sprawled out on his stomach and leaning down over the side.

"*No* way," he said to all the lobsters and clams zipping along down there. "Just hold her steady right where she is."

So I did. And even though I was still nervous, I could do it. I looked around at the names of some of the other boats. *No Billow Bertha* was black and long, and *The Lazy Daisy* was as yellow as my dress.

"There. She's on," Mr. Perry said, standing up and clapping his hands on his Nantucket pants. He walked back toward me with two dark handprints above his knees. "Time to call the launch. You're going to love this."

He told me to let go of the wheel, the boat wasn't going anywhere now. "On the right side is a foghorn, can you go down and get it?" He pointed to the stairs leading into the cabin.

Below, there were two red cushioned benches, plus a sink with wine glasses hanging upside down over it, swaying back and forth with the waves. There were life jackets and radios and compasses, all tucked neatly into a shelf under the two round windows on either side.

"Wow," I said.

"Great, isn't it?" Mr. Perry yelled from the deck, winding up something else. Then, when I turned around again, I saw the foghorn hanging on a hook and my mom.

I froze.

It was a picture that I had seen before, when my mom volunteered for the sponge toss at the Falmouth Fair. Her hair was in a ponytail and her wet cheeks reflected like mirrors. She was laughing at the camera, at the person taking the picture, and right then I remembered Mr. Perry hitting her flat in the face with a sponge while Rennie and I watched from the side, grabbing each other's shoulder to see if she was going to be mad about it, then watching her come around from the painted backboard with holes for heads, and smiling at Mr. Perry. That was when he took the picture.

I tried to act normal when I went back up on deck and handed Mr. Perry the foghorn. But I couldn't look at him. He told me no, Apron, you try blowing it. But not how loud it was going to be, and when I squeezed that bubble, my ears felt like someone was trying to pull them inside out.

Mr. Perry said, "Good job, kiddo," after I handed it back to him.

I said, "Thanks," but not: why don't you have a picture of *Mrs. Perry* taped on to the wall down there instead?

Mr. Perry hung the foghorn on his belt loop, whistled something, then started tying and folding, while right in front of me three seagulls dive-bombed the water. You couldn't see what it was, but something was stirring under there and all three of them knew it.

The launch motored up to us and the launch boy took my arm when I stepped into his boat. Mr. Perry went downstairs to close up and when he came back, his face looked like it had been painted white. That foghorn wasn't hanging on his belt anymore, either.

He didn't look at me when he said, "Wait a minute" to the launch boy, he just kept walking up to the bow with a green plastic snake in his hands.

The launch boy said, "Don't worry, it's not real. Old lobsterman trick, supposed to scare off the seagulls."

But I wasn't tricked at all.

After Mr. Perry climbed on board with us, he stayed in the stern, one foot up on the side of the boat, looking back the whole time. I kept my eyes peeled straight ahead. The wind was blowing so hard it could practically erase your mind, unless you were me, who had too much to think about now. Like Mr. Perry and my mom, and my dad and M. You're only supposed to love one person, *that's* what love was supposed to mean, but no one was getting it right around here.

As soon as the bumpers hit the docks I jumped off.

Mr. Perry stepped off behind me and caught my arm before I could go anywhere.

"Wait, Apron," he said. "I've been meaning to give this to you."

He slid the picture into my hand and just then something big splashed next to us. Mr. Perry and I saw it at the same time: a long shiny white back.

"Will you look at that," he whispered, leaning over the edge of the dock.

I stepped up. Shimmers of light exploded on top of the water faster than I could blink them out. He turned to me, but I kept my eyes down. I thought the beluga would be huge, but it was the same size as the dolphins I was going to save.

Mr. Perry started to say something but the whale surfaced again, blowing water out of its spout before disappearing again deep into the green.

He shook his head. "It never should have strayed."

I held the picture out for him to take back.

"If you're going to make your own bed," I said quietly, then spun away and started up the ramp.

26

In loco parentis
In the place of a parent

It was three o'clock by the time Grandma Bramhall bounced us back down our dirt road. But even hearing "Glory Days" twice on the radio didn't take the splinter out of my stomach.

Grandma Bramhall told me to go on in and take some Maalox right away, that I was probably coming down with something, but I told her I was fine, just not hungry for dessert.

"Grandma Bramhall?" I asked, looking over at her. "Can you come to my parent-teacher conference on Thursday?"

"Thursday?" she repeated, her shake cranking up. "I wish you had asked me sooner. I have Bertha's twenty-year widow party. Sorry, dearie."

I folded up that last bit of hope and put it away on the top shelf of my life. Grandma Bramhall smiled, then she jutted her cheek out for me to kiss it, so I did. "Bye," she said after I shut the door. I waved and climbed the porch stairs.

Inside, I made sure to shut the screen door quietly.

Halfway up the stairs, I heard my dad and M in the bedroom.

"*Because* Margie," my dad said. "I told you why."

"Uch. It's a *closet*," she said, slamming a door.

I stopped when I heard that.

A screech of hangers pushed together. "What are you doings, Dennis?"

"Take mine," he said. "I'll move everything into the guest room." My dad walked out with a pile of clothes hanging over his arm and stopped when he saw me. "Hi," he said, looking down at the clothes and then back up to me. "How was lunch?"

"Good."

"Good," he said. Then he turned into the guest room.

I started climbing again and when I got to the top, he walked back out carrying an arm full of M's clothes. "No one's taking your mother's closet, Apron. Don't worry."

Later, during dinner, right when I was putting more salt on my peas and M was eating her seven hundredth baked potato, and my dad's face was pressed up against the TV watching the Celtics, the phone rang.

"Who the hell would be calling during the play-offs?" my dad asked. M and I shrugged, but not at each other, and my dad said, "You get it, Apron." So I put the salt down and stood. It could have been a lot of people, even Grandma Bramhall calling to tell me she could come to the parent-teacher conference after all.

But it was Mike.

"Hey, Apron," he said. I stretched the phone cord all the way out of the kitchen. "How's it going?"

"Okay," I said.

"Thanks for your help yesterday. I don't know what I would have done without you. That wedding was *serious*."

"You're welcome," I said, even though, really, Mike could have done all of it without me. I had spent most of the night sitting with Chad. "Is Chad better?"

"Well," Mike said. "You know."

I nodded.

"Hey, listen, what can we do to pay you back?"

"Nothing."

"Oh come on. Can't we do anything for you? That's twice you've saved us."

In the background, Chad yelled, "We can kick that Jennie Pratt's butt for you. Maybe put a few worms in her locker?"

"Who's Jenny Pratt?" Mike asked both of us. Behind me in the kitchen, my dad yelled, "Way to go, Chief!" and banged the counter a few times.

"Actually," I smiled. "There is one thing I need."

"Ooh, there's one thing!" Mike said to Chad. Then there was some shuffling.

"Hi, exquisite human being," Chad said, sharing the phone now.

"Hi, Chad. Well, I know this is weird," I squirmed. "But my dad is too busy with everything else these days, and M hates me, and my grandmother has a new boyfriend, and I don't know anyone else old enough to ask. But the thing is," I hesitated. "I need a parent."

Behind me in the kitchen, the crowd was going crazy and my dad was screaming, "Come on Bird Man, send them back to L.A.!" But on Mike's end it went quiet.

"Hello?" I said. "Mike?"

"Listen, Apron," Mike said seriously. "We'd love to. You're great—"

"Greater than great," Chad said.

"But we can't," Mike answered.

I nodded to the wall. My heart was standing on its last leg around here.

"No one is going to let *us* be parents, Apron. And even if they did, well, Chad's *really* sick. We couldn't be responsible for anyone else right now."

I shook my head. "Wait, I don't mean a *real* parent. I just need one for my parent-teacher conference on Thursday. To go over my grades and stuff."

Neither of them said anything for a second. Then they both laughed.

"I'm the mom," Chad shrieked. "I'll be the mom. Can I wear a dress? Please please please? Oh! Can I wear heels? I have an outfit that will be just perfect, now that I am a size 0. It's to die for Apron, just fab."

"Hold it, Chad," Mike said. "She just needs *one* parent." Chad went silent. "And seriously, Apron, there has to be someone else you could ask. I'm not sure either of us would be able to fool your teacher."

"No. There's no one else. But it's okay. I'll figure something out."

Mike paused. "Your dad really can't be there?"

"It's his finals week."

"And you don't think he'd have a problem with me showing up, instead?"

"No. He hardly ever comes to my school."

There was another silence, then I heard Chad whisper, "Please? I'll be good. I won't even talk," and Mike say, "Chad, this is serious. Okay? Come on."

Finally Mike said, "Well, I could be your Uncle? Is that close enough?"

"Yes!" I said, because even though we did reports on our families at the beginning of the year there was no way Ms. Frane would remember that Uncle Hippie died in a motorcycle accident when I was two. "You can be my uncle who's dead."

Mike didn't say anything but Chad said, "Then I'll be the aunt who's dead! That's perfect for me." Mike said, "Hold on, Apron," and covered the receiver. When Mike's voice came back on, it was decided. "Okay, Apron. I'd be glad to be your uncle."

Chad groaned in the background, like Nutter used to when he had his rubber hamburger taken away. "Chad!" Mike scolded him, mad for real now. "Go back to your bed. Right now. Go. Go. All the way. Keep going. All right. Bye. Bye-bye."

Mike let out a heavy sigh. "Just tell me when and where, Apron."

"Mike," I said. "Is Chad going to get better?"

In the kitchen my dad yelled, "*Foul!* Blatant foul ball, Ref! Open your beady eyes."

"No," Mike said finally, evenly. "He's not. He's not going to get any better."

"Then can Chad be my aunt?"

Mike sighed. "You sure? What about your friends? He won't make just any old aunt, you know."

"I don't have any friends," I told him.

He didn't say anything for a moment. Then he said, "Well. He does look good in heels."

I laughed and so did he, but we both stopped at the same time because my dad started screaming in the background. "Air ball!" Then the TV turned up so loud the floor rattled. "*Unbelievable. They did it. The Celtics are the 1985 World Champions!*"

"What's going on back there?" Mike asked.

"I think the Celtics just won the play-offs. I'll call you tomorrow, okay?"

"Good-bye, my gorgeous niece," he said.

And after we hung up, his words buzzed like an overtime air ball straight into me, too.

Later that night, I slipped my free verse poem out of my backpack and stared at it for a long time, deciding. Then I took a pencil and wrote: *by Apron Bramhall and Chad Weller*.

27

Exsisto curiosus of quis vos opto.
Be careful of what you wish for.
(Johnny Berman)

On Tuesday morning, with only two more days of seventh grade left, I made it all the way up the hill without getting off my bike once. No one was there to see it except me. Not even Mr. Solo, who probably biked to school early because of parent-teacher conferences.

At the top, I raised both hands over my head like Bruce Jenner did when he won all those gold medals at the Olympics. And gliding down the other side, with my legs pounding and leftover sweat dripping into my underwear, I knew exactly how he felt: tired.

Rennie's parents were still talking to Ms. Frane when the bell rang, so the rest of us had to wait in the hall. Most of the boys started chasing each other and slamming into lockers, while most of us girls, and Paul Green, leaned up against the wall, one knee bent back, reading or pretending to. But Rennie and Jenny Pratt kept sneaking looks over at me and whispering. "Nice socks," Jenny Pratt said, pointing at them. I looked down without wanting to and saw what she could: too much of my white socks showing. Somewhere along the way, I was getting taller and now my jeans were too short.

Rennie and Jenny Pratt turned into each other to giggle some more, but I flipped through the pages in my Latin dictionary until I found it. "*Asinus asinum fricat*," I said loud enough for them to hear, shaking my head sadly. Paul Green and Annie Potts looked at me. "Conceited people flatter each other about qualities they do not possess." I had found this quote the other night and doggie-eared it. I knew it would come in handy sooner or later. Paul and Annie looked afraid for me, but Jenny Pratt scrunched her face into grandmother wrinkles and said, "You are such a loser." Rennie nodded along but kept her mouth shut tight and her Bambi eyes blinking.

Finally, Mr. and Mrs. Perry walked out waving thank you to Ms. Frane with big smiles everywhere. Mrs. Perry said hi to Jenny Pratt, but Mr. Perry looked over at me. I lifted my dictionary up in front of my face and stayed like that until Ms. Frane said, "Come on in, class."

Just before I walked in, though, someone tugged on my arm. Johnny Berman. "Hey, Apron," he said, looking kind of pale, but in a cute way. "Meet me by the swings after school?"

The doorbell rang in my heart. I wished I'd brushed my teeth this morning. "Sure," I said in a really high voice, like a squeak. Which might have sounded too eager, so I added, "I guess."

He nodded and walked into the room. I followed closely behind so everyone could see we were together. When we sat down in our seats, he didn't look over at me. But my stomach was going to be stuck on tingle all day. Johnny Berman wanted to meet *me* at the swings. I glanced back at Rennie, pulling books out of her backpack. A few weeks ago I would have passed her a note with a billion exclamation points next to his name. But now I just turned around again and stared at the blackboard. *Conferences today*, it said in the corner.

Last night when I gave Mike the directions to my classroom on the phone, he said, "Hey, wait a minute, you'll have to start a little further back than the main entrance." Turns out he wasn't from Maine. He was from St. Pete, Florida.

And yesterday, when Ms. Frane walked around collecting our free verse poems, she leaned down and said, "Apron, is your dad coming tomorrow?" I nodded and said, "Yes," which was all part of the plan. Chad said everything would go smoothly as long as I played my part. He told me to "act perplexed when Uncle Mike and Aunt Chadalina arrive to fill in at the *n*th hour for your dad, who is stuck consoling a suicidal filly over a failing grade." In the background Mike said, "Where did you *come* from Chad? Just have Apron tell the teacher he's sick."

So when the bell rang for first recess at 10:10, I followed Chad's plan. Johnny Berman took off right away, but I hung around the classroom until everyone else was gone, and then bugged my eyes out when Mike and Chad walked in, arm in arm.

But the truth was, my jaw really did drop. They didn't look like anybody's parents that I knew. Right away, I wished I had just told Ms. Frane the truth: that my dad was too busy to come in and talk about me.

But Mike had already asked Toby to open Scent Appeal for him, and Chad had gone to a lot of trouble just to get off the couch, so it was too late for me to back out now. I turned to Ms. Frane, trying to act as *perplexed* as I could. I had practiced in the mirror last night, staring at myself for so long that my forehead cramped. All I had to do was think about M and my face just naturally pinched together.

Mike was wearing glasses and his hair was brushed back into a wet ponytail. He had on white pants and a blue tie and was holding a briefcase in one arm and Chad in the other. Only if you didn't know it was Chad, you would never have believed it was him—or any other *him*. He was wearing a tight black dress and high heels, and a wig with bangs like Rennie's hair only shinier. He wore bright blue eye shadow and bubblegum-pink lipstick. A thick white scarf hid the black spot around his neck, but the one on his cheek was still visible.

"You must be Ms. Frane," Mike said, putting his briefcase down. Chad looked over at me for a second, then blew me a kiss without even cracking a smile.

"Yes," Ms. Frane said, turning around from the blackboard, only half of it erased. We'd been going over the summer reading list. *To Kill a Mockingbird* was still there. "Can I help you?"

Next to Chad, Ms. Frane looked just plain, *plain*. Her brown hair hung down her face like a flag with no wind in it, and her unpainted eyes looked like a sketch compared to the watercolor of Chad.

"Indeed," Mike said, sticking out his hand. "I am Mike Weller, Apron's uncle, and this is my wife—"

"Chad," Chad said curtsying a little.

"Chadalina," Mike said. You could see why Mike got the lead in *Jesus Christ Superstar*. He could have said Chad was a chipmunk and people would have believed him. Ms. Frane looked at them a little crooked, but put down the eraser, rubbed her palms together, and shook both their hands.

"Unfortunately, Dennis won't be able to come this morning. He's having a small emergency at his school, so he called to see if we could come meet you instead. He feels terrible about it," Mike apologized.

"I don't see it as a problem," Ms. Frane smiled. "Apron, is this all right with you?"

All three of them turned to look at me. I felt bad for lying. Ms. Frane had even come to my mom's funeral.

"Um. Okay," I shrugged. "Thanks, Uncle Mike and Aunt Chadalina." Then I stood and walked straight out the door without saying another word. Mike winked at me, but I kept my face perfectly perplexed.

Outside, Johnny Berman was playing soccer with his friends like he always did. Annie Potts walked over to me and said, "Who are those people? Are they movie stars?"

I said, "Who?" just to make it seem like having a famous family was old news.

"*Those* people, that came in to talk to Ms. Frane. Those movie star people."

"Oh *them*. My aunt and uncle. Yeah, they're famous. They live in Hollywood, but they wanted to come to Maine and see what a regular school looks like. So my dad let them take his place for the conference."

"Wow," Annie Potts said.

Sherman Howl walked up to me next. "Hey, your aunt's weird-looking." I flicked another ant off my knee. "Well, she's famous." Which ended up being a good enough reason. I waited for Rennie and Jenny Pratt to chime in, but they didn't. In fact, they weren't even at recess. Annie Potts said they had been picked to help with the graduation decorating committee, and it hit me then: if Rennie had seen Mike, she would have remembered exactly who he was. I sighed so hard I almost fell over. Annie Potts said, "Are you sick?" But I smiled and said, "No, just perplexed."

After school, I got my bike and walked it down to the lower school swings. My stomach had already started to curdle and I didn't want to risk sweating anywhere, especially on my lips. I wished I could have asked Chad what to do; I bet he'd kissed plenty of boys in seventh grade.

The swing sets were empty. I leaned my bike up against a tree and slipped off my backpack. Then I waited. Johnny Berman played lacrosse in the spring, and suddenly I worried about whether or not he meant for me to meet him after practice. I sat on a swing. Lacrosse practice went for at least an hour, and I wasn't about to wait that long. I stood up to go, but sat back down again. If I left, he might not ever ask to meet me again. And the fact was: my middle school life depended on it. If word got around that I had kissed Johnny Berman, no one, not even Jenny Pratt, would really mean it the next time they called me a loser. Ugly or weird, but not a loser. Johnny Berman didn't kiss losers.

After a few hundred swings, though, I decided to leave. Just as I stood, Johnny Berman, in his lacrosse uniform, came running over.

"Hey," he smiled, whipping his sweaty hair out of his eyes.

"Hi," I said. I never really believed that thing about someone's knees getting weak, until now. Mine were shaking like Grandma Bramhall's neck. I had to concentrate to keep them from collapsing. Johnny Berman was a little shorter than me, but standing there alone with him he seemed like a giant.

"I gotta get back to practice," he said. *Smile. Whip.*

"Okay."

"But listen," he pulled a tightly folded piece of paper out of his shoulder pad. "I was wondering. Would you give this to Jenny Pratt for me?"

"What?" My knees hardened into cement.

He handed the note to me, so I had to take it. It fit into my palm.

"Thanks, Apron. I knew you were cool."

"But, I'm not, really friends with her," I stuttered.

He looked at me surprised. "I see you together all the time. Look, if you don't want to, I can ask someone else."

I wanted to say that was a great idea, ask Rennie. But I didn't want to risk a cry. I should have guessed it would turn out this way. Johnny Berman wasn't anywhere near the hottest guy in school, but even he was too good for me. "I'll give it to her."

He slapped me on the arm. "Thanks. All right, see you later." And with that he jogged off, hiking his lacrosse stick over his shoulder.

28
Nemo surdior est quam is qui non audiet.
No man is more deaf than he who will not hear.

"What did you say?" I asked Mike on the phone later, after I biked back from school so fast that my lungs still didn't know I was home yet.

Turns out I had looked sad instead of perplexed. Mike said Ms. Frane was worried that I was upset about my dad not showing up and asked a lot of questions about how I was doing at home.

"I told her you were doing as well as can be expected, with everything that's going on. A new mother and new sibling on the way."

"You told her about the little whatever?" I asked, opening a jar of peanut butter, not sure if I should be mad about it. Although once Mrs. Perry knew something you might as well put it on a bumper sticker.

"I wasn't supposed to? You should have told me that."

Mike said that aside from Ms. Frane worrying about me, they had a great time. "In fact, she asked for our card."

"You *told* her about *Scent Appeal?*" I stopped the peanut butter jar mid-rotation and pulled my finger out, a plop of it hanging there.

"Yeah," Mike admitted. "We never even got to the Hollywood part. She mentioned the shop right away, said she thought she'd seen us before."

"So you mean she's seen Chad, as a boy?"

Mike didn't say anything for a second. Then he said, "She did seem awfully familiar." And even though my throat was still clogged up with all the things I wanted to call Johnny Berman, we got laughing so hard that my head cramped. I thanked him again for going to the conference and he said, "No, Apron, thank you." He hadn't seen Chad having that much fun in a long time. After we hung up, I took Johnny Berman's note and threw it in the trash. I might have given it to any other girl, but not Jenny Pratt.

On my way upstairs I heard a laugh coming from the back porch. My dad's laugh. He was lying down on the couch with his head in M's lap.

"There," M said. "He moves."

When my dad saw me, he sat up. "Hey, Apron. How was school?"

I would have told him the truth: that it was its usual horrible self with a sprinkle of Chad and Mike on top. But M was there, waiting for me to complain about something so she could complain about *me*.

"Fine."

"You want to feel your little brother? Margie's sure it's a boy," he looked over at her with a smile. Then he looked back at me. "Come on."

The truth was I *did* want to. So even though it was inside M, I decided I could close my eyes and hold my breath and pretend it was Mrs. Christianson's stomach that I was feeling. My dad moved over for me and I placed my hand on top of M's mound. Nothing moved except M's breath. I picked my hand up to leave, but M caught it and moved it over to her other side. And then I felt it—a squirmy kind of roll. "Weird!" I said, smiling up at M. And M smiled back, making everything doubly weird.

Next to me my dad said, "It's a real live person, all right. That's going to be needing a whole lot of real live taking care of pretty soon. Which is why his real live mother needs to do some real live settling down before he gets here."

It was funny, all the *real lives* he used, and I waited for M to chuckle about it, too. But instead, her grin fell off. She plucked off my hand and stood. "I forgots the meatloaf," she said. Then she turned and waddled by us without another word.

I looked at my dad to see what had happened, but he looked just as surprised as me. He sighed and folded his fingers together.

"Hey, Apron, I have to talk to you about something."

It wasn't going to be good whatever it was. I could smell the dusty couch cushions filled with so many Maine winters it could choke you.

My dad kept his fingers folded in his lap. "I can't come to graduation," he said, looking up at me like I was going to be upset about it. "I mean, if I hadn't found out about it *yesterday*, maybe I could have done something about it. But I have a three-hour final exam to give in the morning to a hundred and twenty-eight students."

"Only eighth graders graduate, Dad," I said, perplexed.

"I know," he said, tapping his fingers together. "But. Listen, I'm just sorry I can't be there, that's all."

Suddenly, I wanted to tell him about Mr. Perry. Except looking at him like that, with his legs crossed and his fingers mixed up in his lap, you could tell he was already filled to the brim with trouble. He didn't need any more.

"It doesn't matter," I said, looking out through the screen and watching some birds peck at the grass. Already mosquitoes buzzed at you every chance they got, and this was only the beginning. By August you would only have to walk across the grass once for your ankles to look like they had the chicken pox. One of the birds stopped pecking to chirp, then jerked its head around fast, trying to figure who had just made that sound. Before, I might have asked my dad why they did that, couldn't they tell it was only themselves making that chirp? And he might have said, "No, Apron, they have peas for brains." But these days, we just sat there, saying nothing about the same thing.

"Dad," I said, finally.

"Yuh?"

"Do you think M likes it here?"

He jerked his head over to me faster than one of those birds.

"Of course I do, Apron," he said, bad mood back on his face. "Listen. You're going to have to face it. This is our new life. *Dixi*. Look it up."

He stood and walked by me, leaving a cloud of madness behind. And when the screen door slammed shut, every single one of those birds got scared off, too.

29

De fummoin flammam
Out of the frying pan and into the fire

Seventh graders don't graduate, but we still have to dress up and watch the eighth graders. I had no choice but to wear my Avon lady dress. I kept telling my dad I needed to get a new dress, the Lilly Pulitzer one wasn't even an *option* for school, but he just kept on grading his papers so I gave up.

When I finally got to the bike racks, I could see that only four other people had biked to school besides me, and two of those bikes had been sitting there since March. I pulled off my sneakers and slid into my high heels, which were too small for me now. I decided not to tell my dad we were getting dismissed at noon today in case he made me go shopping with M for diapers, so I just said, "Bye" like any other morning. We hadn't said much to each other since he scared off the birds in the backyard and I learned what *Dixi* meant: "I have spoken—say no more on the matter."

Graduation was supposed to be outside except for the chance of rain so Principal Parker moved it into the gym. There wasn't a cloud in the sky, though. Ms. Frane wore a pink sundress, but didn't really look any different other than that. The two barrettes in her frizzy brown hair still weren't pulling anything out of the way. After both homeroom classes squished into our room, she put us in one long line according to the alphabet, which meant I was in between Joe Blink and Jimmy Cannon. Both of them were pretty normal, except Jimmy Cannon's eyes were crossed and he wore glasses. Johnny Berman was on the other side of Joe Blink. "Hey, Apron," he whispered to me as soon as Ms. Frane walked away. "Did she say anything?"

Jenny Pratt was in the back of the line, a head taller than every single boy around her. And Rennie's dress was so puffed out it looked like she was going to need two chairs to sit. When they first saw me this morning, Rennie pointed at my Avon lady dress and whispered. I turned my back to them. You don't have to do anything for some people to hate you, but it would have been nice to have a better dress.

"Yeah," I told Johnny. "She said she'll be there."

Hi Jenny, There is a guy that's totally into you. Meet me by the swings on the last day of school so I can tell you who.

Johnny Berman

That's what his note said.
"Cool. Thanks."
"Cool," I smiled.
"Come on, kids," Ms. Frane said. So we started walking in tight steps down the hall and the stairs, and past the cafeteria, which smelled like bleach now instead of meatloaf. When we finally snaked into the gym, the sun was shining so brightly through the windows some people in the bleachers had their sunglasses on. Every year a lot of people think Principal Parker's

time has come and gone, but after every summer it always comes back again.

Our class walked over to the seventh grade section where somebody had lined up chairs. The eighth graders had another section with fancy white ribbon wrapped around their chairs and flowers at the ends of each row that would have looked a lot better if Mike and Chad had put them there.

Ms. Frane told us to move it, so we picked up the pace and sat down. From my seat I could see every single Perry in the history of the world sitting in the top bleachers. For a second, I thought I saw something, so I blinked hard and shook my head and then opened my eyes again and saw the same thing: M. She was sitting in between Mrs. Perry and Rennie's aunt, waving her arms around like a crazy person, but not at me, at someone behind me. *Rennie.*

My blood boiled hotter than the square of sun coming through the window and frying the *F*s at the end of our row. I started fanning myself with the song sheet, but sweat kept pouring down my back and behind my knees. I turned my head like everyone else and clapped for the eighth graders walking in, but kept my eye on M, who leaned over and laughed at something one of those short Perrys said. I tried to sneak a look at Rennie, but I couldn't see her behind the *LMNO*s.

Music started playing and Principal Parker got up and said what a great school Falmouth Middle School was except for the library that got caved in by the big tree after lightning struck, so now there were only about three books left in it. Everyone laughed. Then we stood and sang the school song. I could see M singing all wrong in English, even though she was reading the song sheet. On the second verse she said something to Mrs. Perry, who put her hand on that bump and smiled. Finally, Principal Parker started calling up the eighth graders so the rest of us sat there clapping one solid clap.

Huge squares of sun were blazing down and frying almost half the alphabet now. I looked down at my toes, crooked inside my high heels. Joe Blink was wearing black high-tops, which were lined up side by side, but Jimmy Cannon's feet were tapping around and bumping into mine every second. All that clapping started sounding like rain, so I closed my eyes and pretended I was outside under a tree, listening to it.

Then someone yelled, "Way to go, Eeebs," which made my eyes pop open and watch that whole midget line of Perrys, plus the teepee of M, stand up and cheer for him.

The burning line of sun was all the way over to Jessie Cartwright now, who kept scooting over so close to Jimmy Cannon's shade that finally he said, "Hey, cut it out," which made Ms. Frane say, "*Shh.*" Finally, the last eighth grader shook Principal Parker's hand and walked back to his seat. But right when you thought we could leave, Principal Parker clapped straight into the microphone and started talking about "students who stand out" and "students who go the extra mile to get there." The burning sun was on Jimmy Cannon's knee now, and the next place it would go was on mine. I prayed there were only a few students who took that extra mile, but Principal Parker kept calling up practically every eighth grader and their brother, except for Eeebs, who was just lucky to get out of middle school *period.*

When the sun had finally sailed onto my left knee, Principal Parker wiped his forehead and took a deep breath, which sounded like a hailstorm when he let it out into the microphone. "Now today, ladies and gentlemen," he said, clutching the sides of the podium with both hands. "There is someone amongst you whose attitude and genuine courage just begs to be singled out, even though they are not graduating today."

The burning sun moved onto my right knee now. If you stared at it, it went nowhere, but if you looked up and listened to Principal Parker's voice saying—"This young lady simply has not slowed down, despite what we can only imagine has been a terrible time for both her and her family"—then looked back down again, it would have moved an inch.

I thought I heard my name.

I looked up. That burning line might as well have been inside my brain. Everyone, including Johnny Berman, was staring at me.

Principal Parker said, "Apron Bramhall" again, and Joe Blink elbowed me right in the ribs. All the people in the bleachers, even M, were clapping. Ms. Frane yelled for me to stand, so I did.

The Bs moved their feet for me to get by, but when I got to Albie Albertson something tripped me, and my hands slammed into the floor, and then my knees and my chin. Or maybe my chin then my knees, I couldn't tell, because all I could hear after that were cotton balls in my ears and Ms. Frane saying, "Apron, are you all right?" Someone pulled me up by the arms and there was a tinny taste in my mouth. Ms. Frane said, "She's bleeding" and told Albie Abertson to go get the nurse. There wasn't one eyeball in there that wasn't staring at me now, and it was quiet enough to hear a pin drop. Until Rennie said, "She's *such* a klutz."

Then, even two broken legs wouldn't have stopped me from walking over and getting my award. I wiped my mouth with the back of my stinging hand. People started clapping all over again and Principal Parker covered his microphone and said, "Are you sure you're okay, Apron?" I nodded. He handed me a gold and wooden plaque with the Falmouth Middle School sign on it, and shook my hand. I looked him square in the eye and said, "Thank you," and tried not to look up at M, but couldn't help it, and for a second, just a tiny second, I felt like running up and hiding behind her.

Albie Alberston got into a lot of trouble for tripping me, whether he meant to do it or not. But he didn't get detention because no one was going to stay late on the last day of school to give it to him. Instead, he got a warning and had to say, "Sorry for tripping you, Apron" really politely. I said, "It's okay," nicely back, because Ms. Frane was standing there with two parents and it turns out my award was for Best Attitude. So even though I was holding some ice on my chin that was so cold it felt like my face was on fire, I had to keep smiling. But the truth was dawning on me; I really *was* a klutz. I didn't remember being one before, but now it seemed like every step I took, I ended up on my face.

M found me in the gym while everyone else except me and the school nurse were having refreshments on the field. She leaned down to hug me so the nurse could watch. "Oh congratulations, Aprons," she said loudly. And I had to admit it was pretty lucky she had come.

But then the truth hit me harder than the gym floor.

"Did you know I was getting this?" I asked into her ear.

"Ucch," she whispered. "Why else would your father have made me come to this?"

I dropped my award and pushed her off of me. She screamed something all wrong in English and pulled her knee up. The school nurse thought she was going into labor, so she ran over and tried to get her to sit. And when she finally did, you could see M's little toe had already started to turn black and blue.

30

Cumulus nimbus
Rain clouds

M's baby toe might or might not be broken. That was what Myra Bennington's father said, leaning over her foot with a plastic cup of lemonade and a *Congratulations* napkin filled with cookies in his hand. Either way, she was going to have to keep it taped onto the next toe and wear one of those flat wooden shoes with Velcro flaps.

The school nurse had asked one of the sixth graders to go outside and see if there was a doctor, while M's face got wetter and redder, her bubble body turned sideways so she could keep her whole leg across some chairs. She was definitely in pain, even with the ice bag for my chin on her toe. My chin was still throbbing, but no one seemed to remember that now.

"The problem," Dr. Bennington said walking over to a chair and putting his cup and cookies down next to my plaque. "Is that you can't get an X ray anyway. You're expecting, right?"

M looked at me with her eyes so puffed out it was hard for her to squeeze her forehead together. "Pregnant," I told her. Then to Dr. Bennington, I said, "She's from Brazil."

"Ah," he nodded. Then he started talking to her like she was Helen Keller instead of just un-American. "*So, unfortunately, all you can do is keep it taped and stay off of it.*"

"For how longs?" she asked.

Dr. Bennington tipped his head, "I'd say, ooh, six to eight weeks. Just go by the pain. But a woman in your condition, ah, a *pregnant* woman, is going to take longer to heal. Your body just cares about the baby now."

M clenched her teeth when he said that.

Dr. Bennington must have seen her look too, because he started talking to me instead: Could someone come pick us up? Could someone find her crutches? Could someone get her one of those flat wooden shoes?

"I can call my grandmother?"

What I *couldn't* do was call my dad. Not in the middle of finals week.

"All right then," Dr. Bennington nodded, sitting down next to M's foot. "Nurse, can she use a phone?"

After the school nurse and I walked into the gym teachers' office and I pretended to laugh at the joke she made about how *me and my mom were quite a pair*—first I fall flat on my face and then she breaks her toe, ha ha—I dialed Grandma Bramhall's number.

After three rings, the answering machine picked up.

"Greetings," her voice said, with no hint of a shake. "I am not home right now. If this is that nice insurance man, I was calling with regards as to whether or not cruises are a part of my plan." She was probably out shopping for a bikini.

"No luck?" the school nurse asked, looking up from her magazine—tan, happy people all over the place.

I shook my head. "My grandmother's going on a cruise."

"Oh. That's nice," she said, but we both knew that I didn't know what to do next.

The nurse went back to reading.

I hesitated for a minute. But it was the only other person I could think of.

"Scent Appeal," Mike answered.

"Hi," I said.

"Oh hey, Apron. Listen, I'm just finishing up with a customer. Yes, that's a Casablanca, ma'am."

"Mike," I said, sounding different, because right away he said, "What's wrong?"

"I broke M's toe."

"What?"

I told him the whole story and didn't even stop when he whispered, "Yes, irises come in white, too," until I finished telling him how Dr. Bennington said it might or might not be broken.

"I used to think Chad was a klutz," he said. "But you take the cake."

"Okay," I said. "But I can't call my dad, he's giving finals right now. You'd have to be dead to interrupt him."

Mike sighed and I held my breath.

I hadn't actually come out and asked him to pick us up, so when he said, "All right, give me twenty minutes, I gotta go dig out my old crutches," I knew with every last drop of blood and every bone in my body that Mike was at least *related* to Jesus.

"Thanks, Mike," I said. "You're saving me."

"Then we're even."

"Do you remember how to get here?"

"What do you mean? Of course I do. I was just there this morning, dropping off the flowers."

"What?"

"Yeah. I told you. Your teacher got all the graduation flowers from us."

"No, you didn't." I couldn't believe it. "And you didn't even ask me to help set up?"

"Oh, we didn't set anything up. The head of the decorating committee wanted to do that herself, Mrs. Something-or-Rather. I can't remember now. So I just dropped the flowers off."

"Wait. This Mrs.? Did she have one big tight curl?"

"Yeah," Mike chuckled. "She did."

"That was Mrs. Perry. Rennie's mom."

"Oooh."

"Was Rennie there, too?"

"Nope. Just Mrs. Perry. See you in a bit," Mike said and hung up.

31

Iuguolo lemma per pietas.
Kill M with kindness.

It took a long time to get M into the Scent Appeal van.

First, Mike had to find us in the gym. M was still sitting with her leg up, sipping the lemonade I had gone out to get for her and I was waiting in the eighth-grade section, as far away from Dr. Bennington and the other leftover parents as I could without seeming rude. I smelled Mike and Chad's flowers. We would have done a much better job arranging them than Mrs. Perry had. On the soccer field, I had found Mrs. Perry and told her M wouldn't need a ride back now after all. My friend Mike was going to take her. I waited for her to recognize the name, but she just smiled and said, "Okay, honey," and, "Congratulations on the award," then checked on her curl and went back to talking.

When Mike finally walked in with some crutches under his arm, I jumped up and ran over to him.

"Hey, Apron," he said giving me a tight hug. His hair was back to being all around his face again and he was wearing his same old blue jeans and a white T-shirt, with a swipe of pollen on his left sleeve. I wished Johnny Berman had seen us. He might have thought Mike was my boyfriend. "You must be in big trouble," he whispered.

"Not yet," I said. "My dad still doesn't know."

"Looks pretty good in here," he said, glancing around at the flowers. "So where's the evil M?"

He didn't need my help finding her, though. We just both started walking toward the chairs and pretty soon the parents moved out of the way and there she was, her face slumped down so low her cheeks practically touched her chin.

Until she saw Mike.

Then all of a sudden, her face slid back up. She didn't exactly smile, but you could tell she was thinking about it.

"Well, *hello*," Mike said taking her hand and kissing the back of it. "You must be Marguerite."

"Yes," M said, shifting herself straighter. She smiled like the lady on *Dynasty*, but the bad one, with the black hair. Even though Mike had been standing next to me in church when she walked by and hissed, clearly M didn't remember him.

Mike brought the crutches out from behind his back with his other hand and said, "Your chariot awaits, Madame," then bowed to her.

M smiled. Even though her toe was purple and her bump was huge and I was about to get grounded forever, I smiled too. If you didn't know the whole story, you might think that Mike was asking M to marry him and giving her a set of crutches for a promise.

Dr. Bennington poked his head down in between them and said, "Hi there, are you Margie's husband."

"No," Mike said shaking his head low. "Alas, we all can't be."

M must have understood that Shakespeare, because she laughed quickly, throwing her head back.

"Okay," Dr. Bennington said. "I told her she needs to keep the toes taped together. She should be looked at by a doctor at some point, but for now, she needs to keep it up and iced."

"Thanks, doctor, can she come to your office tomorrow?"

"Oh no," Dr. Bennington chuckled. "I'm an oncologist, not a podiatrist."

My skin unzipped. Those were the worst kinds of doctors. They never saved anyone.

I tugged on Mike's shoulder and said, "Come on." The last thing I needed was for Rennie to walk in and start batting her eyelashes at him.

When M saw me do that, she lost her smile, but it came right back on as soon as Mike leaned down to help her up, hooking his hands under each of her arms. M kept her foot lifted and Mike reached back for the crutches and slid them into her underarms. "Perfect," Mike said. "Gorgeous *and* tall. Are you a supermodel?"

M giggled. Turns out she knew *that* word, too.

Mike said, "Apron, can you get Marguerite's shoe?" Then they both ignored me and started hobbling out the door, so I stashed my award for Best Attitude under my arm and hooked my finger under the smelly black strap.

I heard M say, "Are you one of Apron's teachers?" when I came around the corner with my bike.

"No," Mike answered. "Just a friend."

That put a skip in my step, until I saw Rennie and her family walking the same way as us toward the parking lot.

At first Rennie didn't see Mike, or M, or me walking my bike. But when she turned to say something to her mother, her face lit up. "Hey!" she said waving to Mike. "Mike! Mike Weller!" and came running over.

Mike stopped and smiled, keeping a hand on M so she wouldn't fall over. "Hey, Rennie," he said.

Her face turned neon pink, you could tell she was flattered he remembered her name.

When Mr. and Mrs. Perry saw the three of us standing there, they started toward us too, dragging Eeebs along.

"Mom and Dad, this is the Jesus, remember?"

Mr. Perry said, "Oh, of course. Pleased to meet you," and held out his hand. Then he nudged Eeebs to do the same. "This is my son, Ebert."

"Nice to meet you," Eeebs grumbled, shaking Mike's hand.

But Mrs. Perry crossed her arms. "Weren't you the one who delivered the flowers this morning?"

"Yes," Mike answered. "That was me."

"So how do you know Margie and Apron?" she asked through her tight mouth, looking over to me, standing on the other side of M.

"From Scent Appeal," I answered, staring at Rennie. "That's how we first became friends."

"You're Mike of the *gays*?" M asked, pulling her shoulder away from him. Her top lip was touching her pointy nose now.

Mr. Perry looked down, but Mrs. Perry kept staring at him with her arms crossed, and Eeebs looked horrified. I started to say something, but Mike's glance told me not to. Then he turned to M and lifted up a smile like it was the heaviest thing in the world. "The very same," he nodded.

M just stared, but Mrs. Perry uncrossed her arms and raised her eyebrows and said, "Well, I will say, you people certainly know your flowers." And with that, she steered Eeebs away.

"*And* you have a great voice," Rennie added, before following her mother.

"Yes," Mr. Perry agreed. "We enjoyed the play."

"Thanks," Mike said. "Glad you could come."

Mr. Perry lifted his hand in a wave and when he turned away with the rest of his family, we all saw it: Mrs. Perry leaning into Eeebs's ear to whisper something, and Eeebs quickly wiping his hand on his pants. The one he had used to shake Mike's hand.

I looked at Mike, still hanging on to that smile, but barely. "I hate those people," I said through my teeth.

Mike dipped his head at me and said as sad as the bluebird sings, "Then the cycle continues, doesn't it?"

Shame knocked the wind out of me. Not just for how much I hated the Perrys now, but for how much Mike didn't.

M broke the moment with a cluck. "Such the waste," she said, starting on her crutches again, oblivious to what Eeebs and Mrs. Perry had just done. "You are too handsome for the boys."

Mike grinned for real this time and started walking with her. "Well, if I had met you a little *earlier* things might have turned out differently."

M looked at him with a big smile as a blush broke out on her face. And for the first time ever, I wanted to hug her.

At the Scent Appeal van, I put my kickstand down and held the crutches while Mike helped M into the front seat, angling her so that she could still keep her foot up.

"You'll have to sit in the back, Apron," Mike said after he shut M's door.

I sat on my knees, my bike on one side of me and twelve bunches of yellow lilies on the other. And then we drove out the school driveway, M and Mike looking straight ahead, and me staring out the back window, watching my school get smaller and smaller, seventh grade gone forever.

32
Modus operandi
My new m.o.

Things went back to bad after Mike left. I begged him to take me to Scent Appeal with him. But he said, no—that I couldn't leave M all alone up there on my dad's bed watching TV with a bag of peas on her toe. And he had a lot of work to do. Chad was having a hard day and so far he hadn't even gotten off the couch. They had one retirement party and two bat mitzvahs to decorate this weekend.

"What about Toby, can he help?" I asked, the two of us walking down the porch stairs together, my feet finally free. I had small red dents across both ankles where my straps had been strangling me.

"He went back to cutting hair," Mike said jumping off the last stair and turning around to me, still a few steps up. The two of us were the same height now. In the bright afternoon sun you could see tiny wrinkles on his cheeks. "Toby was just helping us out for a while. Money's kind of tight, with Chad's medicine costing so much and all. Anyway, you'll be all right."

But I must have looked like the inside of my stomach, because Mike said, "Do you really think your dad is going to be that mad?"

I looked into his blueberry eyes and nodded.

"Jeepers," he said turning away and kicking a pebble under the van. "What does he expect? You're a kid. Goes with the territory, know what I mean?"

But all I knew was that I was a kid whose territory was about to get a whole lot smaller.

"Look, Apron, I really have to go check on Chad," he said turning back to me.

"Thanks for coming to get us, Mike."

"Don't worry about it," he said. Then he leaned into me so close that his hair brushed up against my cheek. "She's a would-be beauty queen contestant, Apron. If she gets on your case, just tell her she's never looked better. Kill her with kindness."

But even Mike didn't know the M that I knew.

After he climbed into the front seat of the van and closed his door, I jumped off the last stair and stepped up to his window to give him the high-five he was waiting for. But instead of slapping me back, he wrapped his fingers around my hand and held it.

"Was it awful, at the end, with your mom?"

"Yes."

Mike's blue eyes started melting. "Thanks," he said. Then he squeezed my hand and let go.

He started the engine and I stepped back and watched him back out. After the van turned around, he rolled down the passenger window and said, "Hey, I keep forgetting to bring you your report card. We signed for it at the conference. Ms. Frane says you're a killer writer, you know. She's entering your poem in some contest, did she tell you? That's why you didn't get it back."

I had noticed my free verse poem wasn't in my last homework pack, but figured Ms. Frane probably didn't have time to read them anyway. That's something only kids with parents who teach know; half the time your homework doesn't even get read, just graded.

Mike waved one last time and drove off. I waited until every single piece of dirt in our road had settled back down again before I turned and climbed the porch stairs.

↗   ↗   ↗

I spent the whole afternoon tiptoeing around and cleaning things up. My plan was ruined now. M couldn't look lazy with a broken toe.

Twice, I brought up frozen peas, lemonade, and Chips Ahoy! and left them all on her bed. Both times when I carried them in, she was on the phone talking all wrong in English with a very bad look on her face. The only word I could figure out was *horrivel* because it was the same in Latin. She never said thank you or no thank you, she only ignored me or rolled her eyes.

But one time, she screamed my name so loudly that even The Boss stopped twitching. Lately, I had been making an obstacle course for him around my room. I liked to figure out where he was going to go before he did, but most of the time he went straight under my bed and pooped. My room had started smelling really bad now, and I knew it was only a matter of time before my dad came in and figured things out.

When M screamed, though, he ran under my dresser. I cornered him, dropped him back inside his cage, and went to go see what M wanted, me twitching as much as The Boss.

"I have to use the bathroom," she said. "Get those things." She pointed to her crutches, lying up against the bed, close enough for her to reach.

"*Crutches*," I said, trying to do her a favor but getting sneered at instead. After she got herself up on one foot, I held my breath and tried to slide my hands under her arms like Mike had. But as soon as my hands hit her big boobs, she whacked them away. "I can do this," she said sliding the crutches under there herself and then clunking down the hall into the bathroom.

I looked at my mom's closet. The door was shut tight. If I had broken M's toe last week, my dad would never have saved her closet for me.

"Aprons!"

"What?"

"Come in to here."

I told myself not to be scared. But it turned out, I should have been. Because when I got into the bathroom, M was standing in front of the toilet with her pants down, and her big white underpants stretched across her bump.

"Hold these things," she said handing me the crutches. I must have looked as afraid as I felt because then she added, "Please."

After I took them from her, she started wiggling down those underpants. I turned around and found my freckled self staring back at me in the mirror. I didn't even know that kids with freckles could have circles under their eyes, but there they were, sort of greasy, in a deep shade of red.

M's pee shot out so hard it sounded like a water gun spraying into the toilet. I tried not to breathe. After it went to drip, she sighed and said, "I know that you hates that I am here, Aprons."

My heart ground to a stop and those eyes of mine bugged back at me.

I didn't know what to say, so I said, "It's okay. You have to be here, because of the baby."

She didn't say anything for a beat. Then she said, "Well. You know, Aprons, you could go to live with your grandmother."

Two other eyes were looking back at me in the mirror now, but these ones were mean and M's. Instead of being afraid this time, something in my brain snapped and I watched my own smile rise up. "I already tried that," I told her. "She said no."

She looked away first.

"Give those things now," she ordered me, nodding to the crutches that were still in my hand. I watched her wiggle the crutches under her arms.

"Hey. Were you ever in a beauty pageant?"

She stopped. I got ready for her to shoot darts out her eyes at me, but she didn't.

"Because I bet you would have won. You're pretty enough."

Her face wanted to lighten up, you could tell. But instead, she hobbled out the door. So I stood there, listening to her peg it back down the hallway. When she got to my dad's room, I turned back to the mirror and winked at the power of me.

Mike was right. And I had a new m.o.

33

Silentium
Silence

**My dad's car came down the dirt road right as The
Boss found the piece of guinea pig food I planted for
him in my shoe.** We were playing on my bed now, listening to the clock radio, but softly in case M screamed
my name again.

Downstairs, my dad didn't say anything for a few
minutes. Then he yelled, "Hello? Is anyone home?"
and M said, "Up here."

I waited until my dad had climbed the stairs before I
began counting backward, starting at twenty. The Boss
was already tucked back away in his cage and I sat on
the side of my bed with my back straight and my sneakers touching the floor, ready to go.

On *fifteen* I heard from his bedroom: "What *now*
for Christ's sweet sake?" And by *eleven* I heard: "Why
didn't you tell them to interrupt me?" and by *five* he
was calling my name out like a list, louder and louder
each time.

When the door opened there I was, already looking
at him. His hair was sticking out a little here and there
and he kept shaking his head almost as fast as Grandma Bramhall. "What the *hell* happened, Apron?"

I opened my mouth but nothing came out.

"You broke Margie's toe and you're not going to explain yourself?" He was holding my doorknob so tightly his knuckles were turning white.

"It was an accident Dad," I said finally, choppy. "*Errare humanum est?*"

It didn't work. "To error is human" doesn't count when you break someone's toe, I guess.

My dad pushed his lips out like a duck and kept shaking his head, looking at me up and down, from my sneakers to the top of my head, then back down again.

"I dropped my award on her by *mistake,* Dad. Ask anyone. *Anyone.*"

"I have no idea how to deal with you anymore. I have no idea how to deal with *any* of you anymore."

"Are you going to send me off to live with Grandma Bramhall?"

"Oh," he chuckled too hard. "I get it. No, Apron. Sorry. The last thing she needs is a troublemaker living with her."

I stared at him, my eyes filling with every fun time he and I had ever had together, so long ago now they were nothing but amoebas, ready to slide down my cheeks and drop off to nowhere.

"And what is that smell in here?"

I shrugged but he glanced at my open closet and walked over to it. The Boss smiled up at him with a twitch.

"He goes tomorrow."

"But—"

"*Tomorrow.*" Then in a softer voice he said, "I'll take him to a shelter."

He shut the door and I lay down on my bed. I didn't go down for dinner, and no one called me to, either.

34

Omne trium perfectum.
Everything that comes in threes is perfect.

In the morning, I broke my eyes open and looked at my clock radio. It said 7:59. I threw off my covers and hurried over to check on The Boss. He looked asleep for a second, but then he started up with the twitching. I was going to have to sneak him out this morning. Guinea pig shelters didn't exist and we both knew it.

Down in the kitchen, there were two coffee cups in the sink and a note on my lobster that said *Took Margie to doctor. Back later.* I stood there to make sure no one was playing a trick on me. "Hello?" I called out, but nobody answered. "*Shit!*" I yelled, but still nobody answered, so it was definitely all clear.

I ran back upstairs and got dressed, then grabbed The Boss and his cage, plus my Avon lady money and my white tennis hat. In the kitchen I took a bag of guinea pig food and a Pop-Tart and shoved them both in my backpack next to my Latin dictionary.

Then I heard the phone ring.

There were a few people I wanted it to be: Mike, Chad, my mom, or Grandma Bramhall, and only two people I didn't: my dad or M.

I picked up the receiver just before the new answering machine could get it.

"Apron," my dad said. "Looks like you're getting a sister after all."

"Did you hear me, Apron?" my dad asked. And then told me *again* that it looked like I was getting a little sister and didn't I have *anything* to say about that?

Finally I said, "Okay."

My dad told me that he was tired of my attitude. Not *once* had he asked me what I won my award for, and now there was a whole school of people who knew me better than he did. He told me they would be back sometime later and hung up.

But when they came home, The Boss and I wouldn't be here.

Outside it was foggy and most of it was low to the ground, which meant that later it would get hot, hot. A mosquito buzzed past me but stopped when it noticed I was alive. I slapped it fast and flicked it off my palm, then walked down the porch stairs, banging The Boss's cage on my knee every few steps.

Mr. Orso's car was glistening from a recent hose-down. I thought about asking him for a ride again, but after twice it's a habit. So I started walking up our dirt road instead.

Another mosquito got my leg, and when I leaned down to slap it, everything spilled out of my backpack, including the coffee can of sea glass I had collected a few days ago. I put The Boss down while I picked it all up and watched him jerk his head around. "I know it looks fun," I said realizing he'd never seen the outside before. "But you'd be toast in a minute."

Mrs. Weller's orange love bug was in the drive-way. I thought about knocking on her door and asking her to hide The Boss for a while, but she could barely remember to feed Nutter and he could *bark*, so I kept going.

Trees were rustling above me, which wasn't going to last long, they just hadn't heard the weather yet. Sweat was already lining up on my forehead. I was glad I had my hat.

By the time I got to the bus stop on Route 88 I was soaked.

I tried to get The Boss to suck water from his tube while we waited, but he looked too stunned now to even twitch. Finally, the bus with the same old lit-up *Portla d* sign on it stopped in front of us.

"Excuse me," I asked the big bus driver. "Does this still go to Bramhall Street?" I hoped she wouldn't notice the cage.

"Beats me, honey," she said, her eyebrows going in two different directions.

I looked down. But then I heard, "Hah! Course it does. Hop on." And when I looked back up, the bus lady was holding out a schedule for me and stretching her huge cheeks into a pile of smile. I held up The Boss, but she said, "Just keep it in the cage."

Only two other people were on the bus. One of them was white, but both of them were old. I sat in the single seat right behind the bus driver, where my dad told me I *had* to sit when I used to take it before. I was only allowed to take this bus because it went directly to Bramhall Street. Then, it was always cold and the windows were shut tight. But now, the top windows were pulled down into different size slits.

I looked at the messy graffiti in front of me. Then I made sure the lady bus driver was busy watching the road and took out a pen from my backpack and wrote:

Apron and Mike and Chad
Omne trium perfectum

When I stepped off the bus, half the Maine Medical Center was lit up by the sun, but the other half was
still dark with shade. There was a banner hanging down
over the entrance that said BLOOD DRIVE TODAY.
But what it should have said was: SAY GOOD-BYE,
because that's all you ever really did in there.

"And never go in there," I told The Boss. "*Everyone's* toast in that place."

At Scent Appeal, the broken window was the same
mess of trash bags and tape. I turned the doorknob,
but it was locked, even though the sign said *Hours: 9:00
to 6:00* every day except Monday, which said *Closed*. I
knocked on the door and tried the handle again, then
peeked in the window. No lights were on. A teenager
with ratty jeans and purple hair walked by in the reflection. I stepped back, trying to decide what to do now.

Then I noticed the Scent Appeal van parked across
the street. I put The Boss down and stepped into the
road and yelled up at their window loud enough for the
pigeons to take off. When a car honked at me, I jumped
onto the sidewalk.

I was about to step into the street again when Mike
pulled open the front door, the sun hitting him square
in the face.

He had dark circles under his eyes and the same
clothes he had on yesterday—the swipe of pollen still
on his left sleeve. Seeing him like that, my stomach felt
like I just ate some of M's oatmeal.

"Sorry," he said, his eyelids folded over like tiny piles of laundry. "We're closed."

My heart fell overboard.

"Mike?" I said. "It's *me*, Apron?"

His eyes widened. "Apron?"

I nodded.

He rested his forehead on the corner of the door. "Didn't see you under the hat."

I ripped it off.

"Why are you closed?"

"Bad night," he said picking his head up. "Sorry, Apron, I think you should go home."

I started to say no, when something fell upstairs. Mike turned and was gone.

I picked up The Boss and closed the door behind me. Then I put the cage down on the counter, threw my backpack off, and followed Mike up the stairs. Until I heard something that made me stop. From inside the apartment, Chad was moaning and Mike was saying, "Okay, Chad, hold on, hold on."

I peered around the corner. Mike was sitting on his knees holding Chad lying on the floor, rocking him slowly, a pile of wetness around them. Chad's head was resting inside Mike's elbow and he was quiet now, while Mike stroked his hair. Chunky piles splattered all the way up Mike's arm and next to them an IV stand had tipped over.

I stepped in carefully and when Mike saw me, he nodded and kept saying, "It's okay. I got you," over and over. I fell to my knees. Then I put my hand on Chad's sweaty back and the three of us sat like that, rocking, until Chad picked his head up and looked at me, the chunky wetness wiped clean off his mouth.

He screamed.

I took my hand off him and backed away.

"Get her away from me!" Chad yelled, pointing at me like I was a ghost, or something worse.

Ice water poured down my arms. Mike took Chad's face inside his hands, but Chad kept trying to turn again, to look at the monster of me.

"It's Apron," Mike said, his voice serious but sad about it. "Chad. Look at me. It's Apron. The nurse left already, okay? It's *Apron*."

Mike let go of Chad's head, and Chad turned his wide eyes to me.

"See," Mike said. "Apron." He was rocking Chad again, his voice back down to calm. "Apron who tells you the jokes. Apron who's your friend."

Slowly, slowly, like fog lifting from the grass, Chad's eyes softened. I stayed there, not saying a word, waiting for him to find me again.

"Okay?" Mike asked carefully.

Chad's mouth twitched. "Apron," he whispered. "*Look ma no hands.*"

I nodded.

"That's it, Chad," Mike said. "Welcome back."

35

Radix lecti
Couch potato

While Mike gave Chad a bath, I cleaned up. I found the bucket and gloves and mop and got to work. It wasn't as easy as *Juan Busboy* made it seem, though.

Then I stayed with Chad while Mike took a shower.

"Why do cows wear bells?" I asked him. He was propped up on one end of the couch while I was propped up on the other, his feet in black socks almost touching mine in nothing. It was one of the only pieces of furniture left around here, this long couch. The tables for the lamps were gone now. So were the lamps.

"Hmm," Chad hesitated, speaking slower than he normally did. "To get to the other side?" This had been his same guess every single time so far.

"No. Come on."

"To be the chicken?"

"No!"

"Pass the soap radio?"

"Their horns don't work."

One side of Chad's mouth smiled, but the other side was too tired. "Hey, Apron," he said looking at me, his brown eyes swimming inside two big caves. I stared down at his black socks. "Will you tell these jokes to Mike some day? He pretends to be an old guy, but really, he's just a kid like you and me."

"Okay," I said quietly, trying not to keep thinking what I was thinking, that Chad looked like he was a great-grandfather now.

"And Apron," he said. "Read him our poem too. Promise?"

I didn't answer.

He kicked me gently on my foot. "Apron?"

I looked at him. "Okay, I will."

He dropped his head back.

"Chad, I know this is a weird question. But. Have you ever noticed that Mike looks a lot like—I know it's impossible—but it's kind of weird, how much he looks like him."

"Who, Apron?" Chad sounded bothered, the way he used to.

"Like the real Jesus. Like he could practically be related to him." My cheeks burned. It was such a stupid thing to say.

But Chad smiled at the ceiling. "You know something, maybe he is. That would make sense."

"What?"

"Why he's such a saint." He picked his head up to grin at me. "I bet it's on his mother's side, though. His dad's gotta be related to Reagan. That's the only possible explanation for *that* man."

Another smile cracked out of him, which turned into a chuckle and a coughing fit. And then the bathroom door opened and Mike appeared, clean and dressed, but not looking much better.

"So," Mike said. "I'm going to get started down there." He flipped his wet hair and turned around to the kitchen. The IV stand was against the wall where I put it, and the bag was still halfway full. There was a big piece of tape at the end with the needle, but Mike had yelled at me when I bent down to pick it up. "Don't touch that part, Apron," he said. And even Chad looked worried. So I let it drag all the way across the floor without touching it once.

"Can I get you anything, Chad?" Mike asked, turning back to us. Over his shoulder the oven clock read 12:07. Lunch time.

"A new body would be nice."

"Okay," Mike said distracted. "Bang on the floor if you need me. Come on, Apron, I think Chad's going to sleep for a while." Mike disappeared down the stairs and I stood.

"Sweet dreams, Chad." I hoped he wouldn't forget me the next time he woke up.

Before I was all the way down the stairs, I heard Mike say, "What the heck is this thing?"

"Oh," I said hurrying down the rest. "That's The Boss. Sorry."

"The *boss*?"

"Yeah," I said. "M's trying to kill him."

Mike turned to me with a question mark on his forehead. "Huh?"

So I explained that he was mine, but now he had to go, which is why I had come. "I was wondering if I could put him up for adoption here, maybe one of your customers might want him?"

Mike looked back at the cage. "Sure, I guess. What's the boss mean?"

"The foxiest singer *ever*?"

Mike chuckled. "I get it. Yeah, he is pretty foxy." Which was a little weird, my dad would never have said that about Bruce Springsteen. For a second I wished I were at home.

"Does he sing, this Boss?"

"I don't think so," I said. "But he twitches." Mike laughed and told me I could put a sign on his cage and leave him on the counter. Then he opened the cash register, pulled out some money and slid it into his pocket. "All right," he said starting for the door.

"Wait," I pointed to all the flowers. "What about these? Want me to wrap them up?"

"Oh," Mike stopped. "Right, yeah. I said we had some jobs this weekend. We had to let them go. We can't do outside jobs anymore." His eyes shifted toward the stairs.

"No more weddings?"

Mike shook his head. "Chad can't go anywhere and I don't want him staying alone for long. Right now I'm just trying to make enough money to pay back some debt and buy Chad as many, as much medicine as we can, to keep him comfortable." Mike's blueberry eyes floated away when he said this.

"I can stay with him."

Mike looked at me. "I don't know, Apron. Where's your dad? Does he know you're here?"

I almost told him yes. "No," I said.

Mike sighed and threw his hands down. "I can't get rid of you, can I?"

Outside, trees screamed. I could hear them now in the dead silence. Mike didn't want me here.

But then his smile started slow and ended fast. "All right," he said. "I'll be back as soon as I can. And thanks, Apron. I'm sure you have a trillion other things you'd rather be doing."

I stared him square in the blueberries. "No, I don't."

"Okay," he nodded. "But don't you think you should call your dad at least?"

"He's with M, finding out that she's having a girl."

"Really?"

"Yeah."

Mike sighed. "Ah, life. Isn't it strange? You finally find your way out of it, and then before you know it, you have to turn around and climb right back in again."

I had no idea what he was talking about.

"Okay, you're in charge," Mike said moving fast again. "I should be back soon. But if anything happens, if Chad gets really sick again, you can call Maine Medical. I'll write down the number for you."

Mike started walking behind the counter, until I said the number out loud. "How did you know that?" he stopped.

"I used to practically live there, remember?"

36

Aspirat primo Fortuna labori.
Fortune smiles upon our first effort.

I couldn't look at him when I taped the sign onto his cage. *Guinea Pig for Adoption. Very quiet and doesn't smell.* But I could hear him twitching away like normal.

I went upstairs to check on Chad. He was sleeping on the couch, snoring a little, and even when I dropped the picture of him and Mike skiing on some snowy mountain together, he didn't open his eyes. I leaned against the wall and watched him breathe for a while, trying to tell myself not to go into their bedroom.

But one quick peek couldn't hurt anything.

It looked like a regular bedroom. There was a brown dresser with a bottle of Nivea cream on it next to some frames, plus a big unmade bed with dark blue sheets and two tables on either side, one with a book and one with a lamp. So far, gay people had bedrooms that looked just like my dad's: messy and too dark. It smelled different in Mike and Chad's room though, thicker with something. Love, maybe. At my mom's funeral, Reverend Hunter said that love is hard work and we pay a big price for it. But Mike and Chad's kind seemed to be free. While everyone else was paying too much.

Back in the living room, Chad was lying in the same position, breathing fine. So I went downstairs to get *The Long Winter* and see what Laura Ingalls Wilder had been up to lately.

But when I got there I looked at the cruddy taped-up window. If that didn't stop people from coming in, the rotting smell would. Maybe if things got cleaned up around here, I decided, Mike could make the money he needed for Chad without having to leave him alone anymore.

I picked through a bucket of pink gerberas. Most of them were flopped over with missing petals, but a few of them seemed okay. On the floor beside them was a bucket of tulips that looked a little better but smelled just as bad, like Mrs. Weller's kitchen with a hint of poison. I picked up both and brought them to the back.

I took out the flowers and poured the murk down the sink. It smelled so dangerous I had to close my mouth not to taste it. I piled the stems and cut off the brown. Then I did the same with the rest of the buckets. Once, there was a bang against the window. I ducked behind the counter, waiting for another rock to fly through. But when it happened again, it was more of a knock. I stood and saw a nose and some hands smooshed up against the door. *Sorry, we're closed* I mouthed to a man that looked like my dad but without the red hair and freckles. He pulled a face and left, and I got back to the flowers.

When every flower that could be saved was, I poured the goop into the garbage and stared at the huge pile I had now. Usually there were tubs of the same ones everywhere, with only a few mixed bouquets on the counter. Unsold bouquets cost them a lot of money and most people just wanted a bunch of the same kind anyway. But there wasn't enough of each flower left to fill a bucket. I thought about going upstairs to ask Chad what to do, but didn't want him to forget who I was and start screaming again.

So I got down some glass vases and filled them with water.

I found some wire in the cabinet and used it to stand up the floppier flowers. Then I started arranging them, poking some into this vase and adding some to that. Pretty soon, everything started smelling happy again.

I heard Chad coughing up there, but then he would get quiet again. And a few times the phone rang. I didn't know if I was allowed to get it though, so I waited for the answering machine to click on. My empty stomach kept calling me, too, trying to find out if anything would be dropping in for a visit soon. Mike still wasn't back yet by the time I finished the last vase. Or by the time I cleaned the sink and swept the floor either.

I stood back and stared at the flowers. The truth was if you didn't know it was me who had done the arranging, you might have guessed it was Chad. Something was still missing though, and then I remembered the straw ribbons with the little *Scent Appeal* tags. Outside, I heard a car door slam. Mike had to be getting back soon and I wanted everything to be perfect when he did.

I searched through the drawers until I found the square tags with holes punched out in the corner. Then I found the ribbon and got to work tying them around each vase. They were probably meant to have the same old *Happy Anniversary*s or *Sorry for your loss*es that everyone else put on them. The least I could do was spice them up with a little Latin.

Sea glass fell out of my backpack when I pulled out my dictionary. I picked the pieces up and poured them into one of the vases. It looked even better than I thought it would. So I used all the sea glass I had, enough to cover the bottom of half the vases, and started flipping through the dictionary.

I wrote *Vis consilii epers mole ruit sua* on the front of the first tag, and on the inside I put the translation: *Force lacking judgment collapses under its own weight*. And in case they still didn't get it, I wrote *Sorry! I'm just a big dummy*.

On the next tag I wrote *Eheu! Fugaces labuntur annii!* on the outside. Inside I wrote *Alas! The fleeting years slip by. Happy Birthday, Oldie!*

Magnus ab integro saeculorum nascitur ordo was the closest thing I could find for a new baby. *The mighty cycle of the ages begins its turn anew – Congratulations on your New Baby. I hope it likes it here*.

I ran out of vases before I ran out of quotes. And just as I finished the last tag, the doorknob jiggled and there was Mike's face up against the glass.

He opened the door with his key before I could get there.

"What happened in here?" he said, his eyes darting around. "I have a *truckload* of new flowers out there."

My freckles burned. I looked down. "Oh. I—"

"Are these the *old* ones?" he interrupted, looking at me like my dad did sometimes: sorry I was still a kid.

"Some of them were okay," I shrugged.

He walked across the room and picked up a vase of pink and yellow tulips with two roses and three irises. "Did you bring the sea glass?"

I nodded.

Then he looked at the tag. *"Frons est animi janua.* What's that supposed to mean?"

"It's on the inside."

Mike read it and shook his head. *"The forehead is the door to the Mind – So don't let anything fall out! Happy Graduation?"*

"I can cut them off," I said, walking toward him.

But Mike smiled. "Are you kidding? These are fabulous. Did you show these to Chad?" He walked up to me smelling like plant soil mixed in with a toasted bagel.

"He's still sleeping."

"He's going to love these," Mike said looking at the tag again.

I smiled back, not even trying to hide my teeth. "Really?"

"Are you kidding?" he said again. "You just earned yourself Employee of the Month." Then he laughed and put his hand on top of my red and squeezed it.

I blinked at him and said, "Thanks." But I didn't tell him how that was the best thing I had ever won, even better than Best Attitude. "Thanks," I said again, bringing up my shoulders like it was nothing.

"I'm going to go and check on him. Did you get anything to eat?"

"No," I said. "I'm fine."

But Mike threw me a bag from Portland Bagels with a warm soft lump in there. So I winked at The Boss, sat down on the couch and pulled out that chocolate chip bagel, my eyes hopping from vase to vase, smiling.

When I was finished, an old lady with a yellow cat on a leash walked in through the open door.

"Sorry, we're closed," I said smooshing my paper bag together and standing.

"Stay, Oliver," she said to the cat, who sat back on its legs like a dog.

"Sorry, we're closed," I said again, trying to be nice about it.

"Yes, it is," she said. "A little hot though."

I nodded. The lady shuffled around, bending over to inspect the flowers and holding up one of the tags. "Oh nuts. Are these already sold?" she asked. I shook my head. "No."

"Goody," she smiled, looking at a tag that said *Adulescenita Deferbui,* on the outside and *The Fires of Youth have Cooled – But you're still looking foxy!*

She placed her hand on her heart. "How clever."

"Thanks," I said.

I watched her shuffle around, reading tags and smelling flowers, laughing every time or smiling nice— what flowers were supposed to make you do.

"I'll take this one," she said picking up a vase of mostly white zinnias with a card that read: *Alea Iacta Est. The Die is Cast – Good Luck!*

She walked to the counter, but Oliver and I stayed where we were, watching.

"How much did you say?" she asked, her pocketbook hanging off her arm.

I widened my eyes and looked down at the cat. "I'll have to ask Mike."

"Twenty-nine?" She pulled out three brand new ten-dollar bills and put them flat on the counter next to The Boss. I thought about asking her if she might like a guinea pig, but Oliver didn't look like he wanted a playmate. "I remember when flowers cost fifty cents," she said. "But these are so nifty. I'm going to have to catch up on my Latin."

I smiled. "I'm Employee of the Month."

"Good for you. Keep the change then." She picked up the vase and walked back to her cat.

"Do you need some help with that?" I asked.

"Not me, honey," she said. "*Veni, Vidi, Vici!*" she pumped her hand over her head. Then she walked out the door and turned toward Bramhall Street.

After she left, I swiped up the money and ran, two steps at a time, to Mike and Chad. I waited at the top of the stairs until I heard quiet talking, then peeked in.

Chad was sitting up on the couch and Mike was sitting next to him, holding his hand. When they saw me, though, Mike dropped it.

"Look," I said, waving the money at them. "I sold some flowers."

They snuck a look at each other, like they had been talking about me before I got there. Like I should have charged more.

"I didn't know how much they cost. Sorry. This lady just gave me twenty-nine and let me keep the rest as a tip."

"What did I tell you," Mike said, turning to Chad, who nodded weakly. "Apron," he said, back to me. "Chad and I were just sitting here wondering if maybe you'd want to help out around here this summer. It's okay, if you can't, if you have camp or something. But even if you wanted to come in once in a while, we would, well we could really use your help. One of us would always be here, so we'd never leave you alone. And we'd pay you, of course."

I looked back and forth between the two of them. "You mean like a summer *job*?"

Mike nodded with his eyebrows raised and Chad said, "Do you think your dad's going to let you?" I lifted my eyebrows too. Then we all stayed like that, looking at each other and wondering.

37

Homonyms
Words that have the same sound but different meaning.

Chad and Mike had more friends than you might think. I found this out later, after we finished unloading the new flowers and two ladies with short hair and thick legs walked in and gave Mike a hug. "You're friends with *girls*?" I asked after Patty and Trisha went up the stairs to see Chad.

"As long as they're gay, too," Mike said, picking up my backpack and whipping his hair over his shoulder. He was taking me home. I told him it was okay, I could take the bus. But he said no, and then that if I really wanted to help out around here this summer, he was going to have to ask my dad himself.

But I was still staring at him when he said, "What? I'm just *kidding*. Whoa. Of course we're friends with girls. We're friends with you, aren't we?"

I nodded all the way out the door behind him.

When we were both in the van, Mike started pulling out of the parking space, and I stared at the dashboard. "How come you want to be gay?"

"Nobody *wants* to be gay, Apron," Mike answered checking his rearview mirror. "You just come out that way."

I didn't say anything.

"What?" Mike said looking over at me, and then back to the road, and then at me again. "It's okay. You can ask me whatever you want."

"So. How do you *know*?" I *did* stare at Jenny Pratt a lot. She was the meanest girl in school, but she was also the prettiest.

Mike chuckled and shrugged, but when he saw my face he shook his head and got serious again. "Okay. Think of a boy and a girl in your class. Tell me their names."

"Jenny," I said. "And, yuck. No one."

"Oh, come on. How are we going to find out then? Just name a boy, any boy."

I looked over at Mike's perfect profile. *Mike Weller,* I wanted to say. But I breathed in a mountain of air instead and turned back to the dashboard. "Seth Chambers." I was done with Johnny Berman.

"Good." He turned to me. "Now, if you had to, and I mean *had* to, like somebody said they would lock you in your room without food or water until you kissed one of them, Jenny or Seth, which one would you pick?"

I smiled at the world whizzing by outside my window and thought of kissing Seth Chambers right in front of Rennie and Jenny Pratt.

"Which one?" Mike asked again.

"Seth Chambers."

"There. You're not gay. Sorry."

"Yay," I said clapping like I just won something.

Mike didn't say anything, but later, when we were turning down our dirt road, I realized that if I had won, that meant Mike had lost.

↗   ↗   ↗

M was resting, my dad said, when Mike and I walked in quietly and startled him, sitting in his office with the door wide open. Mike had parked in Mrs. Weller's driveway behind her love bug, then run in quickly to tell her he would be coming back in a minute, but needed to ask my dad something first.

"Hi Mr. Bramhall," Mike said from my dad's doorway.

"Hi Mike," my dad said in a voice he used for his students, deep and full of facts. "How's Millie?"

"She seems okay today, thanks."

I waited for my dad to ask about Chad, but he didn't. Instead, he said, "Where've you been, Apron?"

Right then I knew I was in trouble. My dad sat back with his arms crossed and stared at me.

"Getting The Boss out of here like you told me to. He's up for adoption at Mike and Chad's. I took the bus," I told the floor.

Mike turned to me, then back to my dad. "I'm sorry, Mr. Bramhall. I should have made her call you. I had a bit of an emergency and by the time I got back—"

"Back?" my dad said, standing up.

"She wasn't alone. I didn't leave Apron by herself—"

I looked at Mike quicker than I should have. And then saw that my dad had watched me do that.

"Who'd you leave her *with*?" my dad asked.

"My friend, Chad," Mike answered.

"Chad?" my dad repeated, walking around his desk, getting bigger right before our very eyes. "Your friend with AIDS?"

I turned to Mike. All this time I thought it was cancer, like my mom.

Mike looked at me, then back to my dad. "Yes," he said.

"And you think *that's* smart?" My dad stared at Mike without blinking.

"Okay," Mike nodded, backing up. "Got it."

"Wait!" I said.

My dad shushed me. "Margie's *sleeping*."

Mike turned and walked out the door.

"Dad," I pleaded. "Can I work at Scent Appeal this summer? I'll take the bus. I don't need anyone to drive me or pick me up, and I'll call you if I'm going to be late, I promise." The words spilled out of my mouth faster than I could plan them. "Please?"

"A *job*?" my dad chuckled, next to me now. "Are you kidding, Apron? You have plenty of jobs to do right here."

Something inside my chest snapped. There was no way I was going to be stuck with M ordering me around all summer. I grabbed a pile of paper from his desk and threw it on the ground. "You have *no idea* how much she hates me, Dad" I yelled. Then it hit me. "Actually, maybe you do, and you just don't care."

I spun away and started after Mike. But behind me, my dad said, "Hold it. You're not going anywhere, young lady!" So I turned toward the stairs just as the screen door slammed.

38

Malus bonum ubi se simulat, tunc est pessimus.
A bad man is worst of all when he pretends to be a good
one.

M didn't want a girl.

I knew because she leaned her bad mood into my lobster and told me. "It is why I am so sick, because she is the girl. If she were a boy, I would be better." She said this while my dad was outside checking on a screen that was ripped.

I smiled *oh well*, and got up for some milk. I had already cleaned all the pans, even before serving the potatoes and hamburger meat I fried up. I told my dad I wasn't going to be eating meat anymore, but my dad said, "Well, you can still cook it," and left the package on the counter for me.

Then he said, because *that's* what I was going to be doing this summer, *chores*. And then maybe, when M could walk again without having to clunk around in her wooden shoe—it took her a whole phrase on the *Wheel of Fortune* to get down the stairs for dinner—I *might* be able to start doing things like a regular kid again. That was when he went to look at the ripped screen and M leaned over into my lobster.

After Mike left, I hadn't planned on coming out of my room, ever. But my dad knocked on my door and told me if I didn't get downstairs and start helping with the dinner, he was going to make me clean out the entire garage. And *that* was just the beginning.

"At least she will not be lazy like you," M said touching her bump.

I sat down with my milk and looked her straight in the eye, trying to find some nice words to kill her with, but before I could, my dad walked back inside slapping his neck. "Damn mosquitoes. That screen's fine. I don't know how they're getting in."

Neither of us had touched our dinners, but my dad didn't notice until he sat down and picked up his fork.

"What's going on? Apron? I asked you a question."

"*Malus bonum ubi se simulat, tunc est pessimist,*" I told him. Then I snuck a look at my palm, where I had written it. "*Pessimus,*" I corrected myself. A bad man is worst of all when he pretends to be a good one.

My dad tightened his mouth. He glanced at M to see what her reaction was, but when he saw it was the same old blank one, he looked back at me. I wanted to tell him that it wasn't too late. M could leave and take that little whatever with her, but I hadn't looked that sentence up yet.

"*Vos have orator satis,*" he ordered me in a dark growl.

But he was wrong—I *hadn't* said enough.

"Dad," I said praying, my two hands smashed together in front of me. "Dad. You don't *get* it. She doesn't *want* a baby girl. She doesn't want a *baby*. She hits it."

M's face went stark white and her eyes flickered back and forth so fast she looked like a TV channel that lost its picture. My dad shook his head at me, mad tucked into every wrinkle. "Apron. I don't want to see you for the rest of the night. Go to your room."

I stood. Yesterday, my *Save the Seals* pamphlets had finally arrived. The baby seal sprawled out next to its bloody stump of a mother on the cover had a better chance of surviving than me around here now.

I spun away, but before I walked out, I turned back and saw M's face, still as white as a ghost.

When it got dark, I sat under my window and looked at the stars. Some of them were shiny, but most of them were dim: here one blink, gone another. I used to love looking at the stars, but now they looked old and used, like they should be swept up and thrown away.

Later, I tiptoed down the hall to the bathroom. My dad's door was shut, but downstairs I heard him talking. At first I thought it was to M, probably eating a whole tub of ice cream while he rubbed her back, but then I heard him say, "You sure, Dr. Timmons? There's no chance she can get it?"

39

Non si male nunc et olim sic erit.
Heaviness may endure for a night, but joy cometh in the
morning.

In the morning, when I woke up for the hundredth time since I had first fallen asleep, it was finally seven o'clock. All night long I had nightmares about M holding me down in murky water while my dad and Mike played four square outside on our newly paved driveway. And every time I woke up, dripping in sweat and lifting my head for air, I tried to keep myself awake so I wouldn't have to go back to sleep and wake up again, remembering how my dad wouldn't let me work at Scent Appeal.

But morning was here to stay, you could tell by the birds.

I walked over to the mirror and right when I lifted my pajama top up to check on my progress down there, the door opened and my dad stuck his head in.

I pulled my top down. My dad blinked and disappeared, shutting the door quickly. A few seconds later, he knocked.

"Come in," I said trying to sound like he hadn't just seen me naked.

"Apron," my dad said sitting on my bed. He looked like he had been up all night. His hair was going this way and that, and he had on the same green pants and dark blue polo shirt he had been wearing yesterday.

"What?" I asked.

"I've been thinking," he said wiggling his toes, cracking them around. "I've been thinking that maybe helping your friend Mike this summer would be a good idea." He looked at me after he said it, but I clenched my teeth and told my heartbeat to knock it off, there were two sides to every story.

"Why? What does she need now, free flowers?"

My dad sighed, exhausted. Then he clasped his hands on the back of his neck and looked up. His elbows pointed at me. "Isn't there any way we can all get along?"

I looked at the floor, at his toes that had jumped on rocks and kicked in the ocean when he was still that freckle-faced boy in Grandma Bramhall's picture.

My dad stood.

"So. If you help around here before you leave in the morning, and help with dinner when you get back, well, we can try it. All right?"

I shrugged again. But secretly, every single amoeba sliding around in my stomach was blowing on party horns now. It might be an M-less summer after all.

"Okay?"

"Okay."

He put his hand on my doorknob. "And no sharing their cups or using their forks," he said pointing at me with his other hand. "I don't care what Dr. Timmons says. I mean it, Apron."

Before he turned to walk out, I stepped forward. "Dad?" I asked quietly. "Does this mean Mike has it too?"

My dad shook his head and said, "I don't know, Apron. It might."

My heart dropped like an ice cube.

My dad started to leave but then stopped. "Did anyone take The Boss?"

"Not yet."

"Great," he said. "So you can still visit him then?"

I nodded.

"Great," he said again and closed the door.

I dropped back down on my bed. Mike looked completely healthy, except for his crooked teeth. I thought about crawling under my sheets and pulling them over me for the rest of my life. But the truth was, it gets hot under there and I already knew that sooner or later you have to come up for air.

So I finished getting dressed. I had a job to get to.

On the way downstairs, I heard my dad mumbling something serious in his room. If he was talking to the doctor again, this time I wanted to hear it. I tiptoed closer, and peeked in, M was sitting on the bed with her back turned to him. He lifted his hand to her cheek, but she stiffened and turned farther away. Then my dad dropped his hand. Maybe I wasn't the only one M hated around here now.

40

Si hoc comprehendere potes, grati
as age magistro Latinae.
If you can read this, thank a Latin teacher.

The Scent Appeal door was unlocked. And when I opened it, Toby wheeled out from around the counter. He was dressed in all white again, with his knees still too close together.

"Hey, kid," he said.

"Where are Mike and Chad?" The air seemed heavier than it should.

"Mexico."

My chin dropped. "Mexico?"

"Oh hey, *little* Mexico."

"Where's that?"

"Down around there some place." Toby waved his hand behind me, toward the street. "I don't know exactly myself. They'll be back by lunchtime and I'll be here with you until then. Mike's orders."

"Okay," I said, trying not to sound disappointed. Toby always made something in me hurt.

I walked up to The Boss. "Hey, little guy." He smiled and twitched.

"I see we have a new friend," Toby smiled. "Why are you getting rid of him if he doesn't smell?"

"I have to," I said putting my backpack behind the counter, glancing around at all the new flowers Mike had brought in yesterday, still wrapped in newspaper. "Someone's trying to kill him."

"Then it's a good thing I know *kar-ra-te!*" he said, slicing the air with his hands.

I looked down at Toby's legs before I could tell myself not to, and then looked away before I could tell myself not to do that, either.

"Oh, you'd be surprised," he said smiling up at me, "of what I can do." And without any warning, he spun around on one wheel.

"Wow. How'd you do that?"

"Practice."

I smiled, but then hesitated and pointed to the window. "Hey, Toby. They're not going to fix it, are they?"

"Probably just get busted again if they did. That was the third time."

"*What?*"

I didn't want them to be gay anymore. I didn't want people like Mrs. Perry to make a face and step away from them; I didn't want Mike to shuffle his feet and clear frogs out of his throat whenever he talked to my dad; and I didn't want Chad to go around making fun of himself so nobody else could. And most of all, I didn't want them to have AIDS.

"Yup," Toby sighed. He had curly dark stubble on his chin and extra dark brown eyes. And his teeth were as white as his shirt.

"Why don't they ever do anything back? Like throw rocks at *them?*"

He frowned. "Those two?" I shook my head with him. Chad might act mad a lot, but he wasn't the violent type, and Mike wouldn't hurt a fly.

"Listen, little lady, the people who do this kind of thing think if we rub up against them, they'll catch it. But there ain't no catching what we got," he smirked. It was the same thing Mike had said. "Either you *is* or you isn't. And if you're lucky, you *isn't.*" Toby's extra-brown eyes softened. "Life's hard enough."

He looked at me while I thought about this: Being gay wasn't any different than having freckles. Either you had them, or you didn't. And if you're lucky, you didn't.

"Well, I came out with *these*," I said pointing to my cheeks.

Toby's face broke into a smile wide enough for me to see every single one of his teeth.

"You're all right," he nodded.

"Thanks."

"Come on, let's get the show rolling. Mike says we gotta do exactly what you did yesterday. Said he made a bucket of dough in one afternoon."

"Really?" It must have been true. There were only a few of my arrangements left.

"Yeah. Said some lady with a cat came in and *bought* the joint. Had a big bridge game or something."

"Was the cat on a leash?" I asked looking down at Toby.

"Don't know. Now the only thing you *ain't* in charge of is the cash register, okay? That's my gig." I pretended to be mad. "Hey, man, better to be the beauty than the beast, trust me."

I shrugged, but I knew he was just being nice. People with red hair and freckles never play the beauty.

"Do you know any Latin?" I asked him.

"Nope."

"You'd be surprised," I said, unzipping my backpack and handing him the dictionary, "of what you might know."

And that was how we started: me at the sink, cutting and piling, and Toby in his wheelchair, reading Latin phrases and taking notes.

"Hey, how about this: *Amor Tussisque non celantur?*" I waited for him to tell me the translation, but when I looked at him, he just stared back at me.

"Toby, I'm not *fluent.*"

"Oh. Mike said you were, like, a genius."

I told him my dad was, not me.

"*Love and a cough cannot be concealed.*"

I thought for a moment. "*Get Better Soon!*"

"Right on," Toby smiled, writing it down.

And pretty soon we had a list of good ones, and a list of pretty good ones in case we got desperate. When we were done, I caught Toby staring at my hair. I put my hand up to brush down the frizz, but Toby said, "You know, I could layer it a bit, calm it down a little." So I nodded and he smiled.

I sat on the coffee table while Toby got the scissors. Then he wheeled up to me and started snipping. Red commas fell around my feet, lying there like Ms. Frane's corrections. When he was done, Toby pushed back and said, "Go see," pointing to the bathroom for *Employees Only.*

I closed my eyes and turned on the light. Then I flipped open my eyes and sucked in a quick breath. I was still red and freckled with a Ping-Pong ball of a face, but I looked so much older—like my mom had died a long time ago now. I raised an eyebrow and watched it fall again. My mom was never going to see this new me. She was never going to see my shirt sprout, or my ears pierced, or even the braces that my dad said he would get me someday when he could swing it. I ran my fingers through my new hair and then I turned off the light and stepped outside.

41

Amor caecus est.
Love is blind.

By noon, when Chad and Mike walked in, the store was filled with bouquets. We had already sold six, plus two people said they would be coming back later.

Mike held Chad by the arm when they walked in together, slowly. Chad was wearing dark sunglasses, but he still looked bad. He was so skinny now his pants were hanging off of him and the bones in his face made angles that weren't supposed to be there. After Mike sat him down on the couch, Chad lay his head back and said, "Howdy, girlfriends, it looks fab," without even taking his glasses off, or looking around. "In fact," he said. "It's the best I've ever seen it look in here. Except for last Christmas when we had the petal party, remember Mike?"

But Mike had gone back outside. "Mike?" he said again.

"He's outside," I told him.

Chad picked up his head. "What do you know about that? Well, anyway. Remember how we dumped petals everywhere to look like snow?"

"I do, man," Toby said. "It was a white Christmas all right."

"A white Christmas. Yep, it was."

I kept hoping Chad would say something about my new hair. But he didn't. Toby and I looked at each other for a second, thinking the same thing, that Chad's voice was different—forced and too loud.

Chad looked down at his hands. I thought I saw a new black splotch on one of them before he stuffed them both down his pockets. I turned away and started sifting through some willows.

"So how you feelin', guy?" Toby asked in a softer voice, wheeling closer to Chad.

"Pretty good for a dead guy," Chad said, smiling with half his mouth and shrugging.

Toby snuck a quick look at me, then leaned in closer to Chad and put his hand on his knee. "How was Mexico, man? You get what you need?" Toby said this very quietly, but I could still hear it.

Chad nodded. "Proud new member of the Hemlock Society," he said, all the meanness gone now. "Yeah."

Toby looked down and no one looked at me, still poking at those willows, twisting them in between my finger and thumb, anything to look busy. I couldn't imagine Chad being a member of any society, at least not like the ones Mrs. Perry was in.

"When are you going to let me turn you into that blond sun-kissed surfer boy?" Toby asked Chad, trying to lighten the mood. "Today? I got time right now."

Chad dropped his head back against the couch. You could see his adam's apple pop out, except it looked like a tennis ball. "I have three pieces of hair left, Toby, which one do you want blond?"

Toby's shoulders slackened and I picked up the bucket of willows and moved it to the other side of the table for no reason.

"All right then," Toby said loudly this time. "I'm off. I have bangs to pay and people to trim."

"Thanks, Tobes," Chad mumbled, sinking down deeper into the couch.

"No problemo. That kid's a great boss. She understands the little people."

I smiled at Toby, thinking about Grandma Bramhall's little people.

Toby winked at me and I waved, then he rolled himself out the door. I wished he didn't have to leave and I wished Mike would come back. It seemed like all Chad wanted to do was sleep right there in the flower store, not exactly good for business.

I walked back behind the counter as quietly as I could and started writing out more Latin phrases on tags. Every time I looked up at Chad, he was sitting there, breathing quietly. Someone opened the door, and I started to say hello in a semi-whisper so they wouldn't wake Chad, but when I looked up it was Mike, holding a bag from Portland Bagels, that lobster claw pinching the bagel.

Mike looked over at Chad and then stopped.

"Chad?" he said, a little panicked, dropping down next to him. "You okay? Want some bagel?"

Chad groaned and sat up. "No," he said. "Do I have to?"

"One bite."

Mike fished around in the paper bag for the bagel and I walked toward them with some of the new tags. Maybe, if Chad was sitting up and eating, he might want me to read a few of them. I sat down on the coffee table, waiting. Mike winked at me and broke off a tiny piece of bagel and put it in Chad's open triangle mouth, just another mother bird feeding her baby.

"Good Chad," Mike said. "Eat slow." Which was exactly what Chad was doing, chewing so slowly it looked like he might fall asleep in between each one. Chad should have had an IV, I realized. But an IV cost a lot more than a bagel.

Mike dug his hand in the bag for more, but Chad pushed it away. "No more," he said.

Mike sighed. "All right, but later." Then he turned toward me, putting a smile on. "How'd it go this morning?"

"What?" Chad said before I could answer. "Was I not *there* with you, all morning? Was I not *there* with you and the *vajos*?"

Mike turned back to Chad. "I was talking to Apron, Chad," he said softly.

"She's gone," Chad said looking right at me.

My skin stung. Something wrong was in the air.

Chad kept looking straight at me. Then he pushed his sunglasses on top of his head and blinked. I looked at Mike and then back at Chad, waiting to see if I should say anything.

"Apron?" Chad said.

Mike nodded at me slightly.

"Yeah?" My tongue was bark.

"Oh," Chad said squeezing his eyes tight and opening them wide again. "There you are. I didn't see you before."

Mike stood and Chad put his sunglasses back on. "Let's get you to bed, Chad," Mike said, scooping him up like a new bride.

"Bye, Apron," Chad said, waving to the corner of the table.

"Bye, Chad," I said. But I didn't stand up. I stayed there sipping in that wrong air, until it filled my lungs with knowing that something bad was about to happen.

♐ ♐ ♐

"He's going blind," Mike explained when he came downstairs, after the old man wearing red Nantucket pants like Mr. Perry's had walked out the door with his new bouquet of loose French tulips and a tag that read, *Qui me amat, amat et canem muem – Love me, Love my Dog.*

"Blind?" I asked. "*Blind* blind, like you can't see blind?"

"Yes," Mike said, dinging open the cash register and pulling out some money. "It's what happens in the final stages."

I stared at Mike. Then handed him the eighteen dollars the old man had just given me. "Thanks," Mike said.

"How long?" I asked quietly.

"A few weeks," Mike said, looking down, counting out money.

"A few weeks? He's only got a few *weeks*?"

"Oh," Mike said looking up at me. "To *see*. I thought you meant how long does he have left to see."

I kept staring at Mike, trying not to say it.

"To live?" he asked, reading my mind. "Nobody knows. Sometimes people can live like this for months."

"Months?"

"Not years," he said, taking my hand and folding some money into it.

I kept my hand out, exactly where he had left it. "But what are you supposed to do now? I mean, how are you supposed to act normal?"

Mike looked at me, his blueberry eyes searching. "I don't know, Apron," he said. "I was hoping you could tell me."

And then, just like that, I understood what my real job was this summer, and it had nothing to do with flowers.

42
Conlige suspectos semper habitos.
Round up the usual suspects.

Walking down our dirt road, the evening fog had already rolled in and the only thing making any noise was Mr. Orso's lawn mower and a few of his barks when the mower turned off. I waved to him, and he waved back. I tried not to think about how Chad couldn't see me doing that now. Helen Keller said that when you lose one sense, another one grows stronger. But by the time Chad learned how to hear me waving, it would be too late.

Mrs. Weller's orange love bug wasn't in the driveway and her rose bushes were starting to look scraggly: there were missing petals everywhere. Cold fog blew on me when I turned into our driveway and saw my dad's car in the garage. It felt good to be cold. So I stood at the bottom of the porch stairs and took in a long deep breath, then held it in there like oven cleaner.

In the sky, seagulls were coming out of nowhere, doing a fly-by and then disappearing again. It didn't smell like low tide yet, which meant I would have to go down to get more sea glass later, after I had done all the chores for M.

I made sure the screen door didn't slam when I walked into the house. The last thing I wanted was for people to start ordering me around before I could get some food. The Portland Bagel Mike gave me had worn out hours ago.

When I walked into the kitchen, there was fog in it. I looked to the back door, but it was shut.

And then I saw the window next to it was shattered.

My heart started beating backward. The window had jagged pieces sticking up like shark's teeth and behind it on the back staircase you could see the top of a kitchen chair. I heard footsteps outside. Blood drained into my feet and I couldn't move. Those footsteps kept getting closer, two more steps and I would be kidnapped, or worse.

"Apron," my dad said sticking his head in between the shark's teeth. "Be careful."

"Dad, what happened?"

He pulled his head out and opened the door.

"Well, it's okay now," he said, dragging in a big garbage can from outside.

"Did we get robbed?"

"No," he said, too calmly. "Just a little argument, it's over now."

"With who?" I said. "Did they try to steal your book?"

"With *whom*. And no, Apron," my dad said, turning to the broken window and carefully pulling the glass teeth out one by one, then dropping them into the garbage can. "No one tried to steal anything. Margie and I, we just had a little . . ."

M, I thought grinding my teeth. "Did you kill her?"

"What?" my dad said turning back to me. "No, Apron. Just a chair, went through the window. Margie's upstairs."

"You threw a chair?" The blood started leaving me again. My dad never used to punch people or throw chairs. I stepped back a little.

"Well, one of us did. Let's just leave it at that."

My dad went back to pulling teeth. But I stood there, grinding mine. "Dad," I said. "Did she hurt the baby?"

He cocked his head sideways, staring at me, not answering.

Finally he said, "No. Why would she do that?"

I shook my head and stepped forward to help him. There was a lot of cleaning up to do around here, and my dad wasn't going to be able to do it alone.

43

Diis aliter visum.
The gods decided otherwise.

This was what happened now: I woke up and had breakfast with my dad and his newspaper head, then walked up our dirt road and took the bus to Scent Appeal.

Sometimes I got my normal seat, and sometimes I had to peek over other people's heads to see my graffiti. The lady bus driver was usually there, except on Tuesdays, and maybe Mondays, but I wouldn't know because on Mondays, Scent Appeal was closed. On those days, I helped Mrs. Weller with her rose bushes.

It wasn't as hard as it looked, cutting those old buds. Some of the petals floated away before I even clipped them. Mrs. Weller still bled here and there, sometimes she might scrape her ankle against a leaf and have to go lie down, and one time she got another nosebleed. But other than that, she was very happy that I was helping her and kept trying to give me fifty cents. But I told her no, flowers were my profession now and I needed all the practice I could get. She bought me my own rose bush as a thank you, which we planted in my mom's old garden. "I see you've got your mother's green thumb," my dad said one day, puffing on his cigar and squatting down to pull out some weeds.

My dad tried to tell M she couldn't go out with her friends at night anymore. She was still in her wooden shoe, but she could waddle around as fast as she wanted to now. When he told her this, M threw a fork at him. "They're all wild, Margie," he argued. "Too wild for a pregnant woman." But she just stormed off, clunking her way down the porch stairs and meeting up with her friends anyway.

One night, I made them tofu pasta. M said it was the most disgusting thing she had ever seen, but my dad said, "Hey, not bad."

"Try some, Margie," my dad said. But we both knew she wouldn't. She had stopped eating. Her doctor said as long as she kept drinking water, she didn't need as much food as you might think. But M looked like a scarecrow that ate a mixing bowl now.

"Where do you think you're going tonight with those girls?" my dad asked, putting down his fork and crossing his arms.

"Just to go and to see the movie," M said, looking pale. "I am still allowed to do that, Dennis," she said flatly, but with a pinch of a question in it.

"Eat something then," my dad said picking up his fork and taking another bite.

"I cannot eat that, Dennis," M said, pushing her plate away.

My dad looked at me. And I stopped chewing. Then they both watched me slide that plate off the tap-dancing lobster.

"Apron, can you make some without the tofu then?" my dad asked.

I nodded. *A good chef is prepared to be creative should a particular ingredient become unavailable.* That was what it said in *Quick Cooks:150 Easy Recipes for Busy People.*

And I *was* busy now. Usually I got home from Scent Appeal just in time to head down to the beach before the mosquitoes started showing up in truckloads. Mosquitoes don't like to buzz down past the high-tide mark so the lower the tide, the more blood you could keep. I had started putting periwinkles at the bottom of my vases, too. Stargazers and lily of the valley looked great with them down there, but a few flowers, like tuberoses, didn't.

"Thanks, Apron," my dad said after I brought some regular pasta back to the table. M didn't thank anything.

"Eat it," my dad told her, crossing his arms again and staring at her plate.

Lately my dad had been talking to M like that. I would have gulped that pasta down in one bite if he talked to me that way. But M wasn't even scared. She just blew air through her lips and said, "Horrivel."

"Fine, Margie," my dad said, giving up. "When Holly was pregnant she ate everything but the kitchen table."

"She did?" I asked proudly.

My dad lifted his eyebrows and nodded. "She never felt better," he said, twirling his pasta and taking another bite, not seeing M roll her eyes.

A little later, when I was cleaning up, dirt crunched on our driveway. I listened to M's wooden shoe clobber down the stairs and my dad's voice meet her at the bottom.

"Who's picking you up?" he asked.

"Suzanna," M said like she had told him that a thousand times already. It turned out that Suzanna was the other nurse at the church the day I knocked the shake out of Grandma Bramhall. She was going back to Brazil at the end of the summer. There was no Mr. American Right for her, I guess.

"Damn it, Margie," I heard my dad say. "You're pregnant. You can't be parading around with those girls all night."

"I tell you we are just going to the movies, Dennis," M said, but she wasn't sounding mean enough to be telling the truth, and my dad and I knew it.

I kicked at the bottom of the broom to knock the dirt off and emptied the dustpan into the trash. My dad said something I couldn't hear and M said something back, fast and hot.

"Twenty weeks, Margie, you waited twenty God damn weeks to tell me. You had plenty of time to change your mind, so don't give me any more of *that* bullshit."

M yelled something then clobbered off down the porch stairs. My dad went back into his office and slammed the door. I stood there listening to Suzanna's car back out and take M up to Route 88, and on to who knows where.

Almost six hours after M had left for the movies, lights moved across my window shade and tires crackled down the dirt road and stopped in front of Mrs. Weller's house. A door shut quietly and then the car started backing up, never even pulling into our driveway. Way up the road, I heard the door shut again, hard this time. My punched-in stomach said it was the middle of the night before my clock did. A few minutes later, you could hear slow careful clobbers coming up the stairs and turning down the hall into my dad's room. He wasn't there, though. I had heard him earlier go into the little whatever's room and lie down on the bed in there.

44

Spectemur agendo.
Let us be judged by our acts.

**I was reading the *Fancy Facts* on the back of my
new cereal box when the phone rang.**

"Hi, dearie," Grandma Bramhall said.

"Hi," I said relieved. Every time the phone rang, I
worried it was Mike calling with bad news. Chad had
been pretty much the same since he started going blind:
some days he came down to the shop and wanted me
to tell him a few jokes, and one day he came down so
quietly I hadn't even heard him. I found him squinting
over me while I read *The Little Town on the Prairie* behind the counter. *The Long Winter* was finally over and
Laura was practically all grown up, whether she liked
it or not. It was my least favorite book in the series. I
waited for Chad to laugh at me and ask why I was reading a baby book. But instead he asked me to come sit
on the couch and read it to him. They were his favorite
books, too.

"I had to read them with a flashlight under my covers so my parents wouldn't see," he said smiling down
around my belly button, the two of us sitting so close I
could see my legs were thicker than his now.

So the next day I brought in my old, soft Book One
and that was what we did, Chad and me. There were
nine books in the Laura Ingalls Wilder series and I

wanted to get through all of them before the end of summer. Which was why I worried every time the phone rang.

"How's the boy?" Grandma Bramhall asked. My dad had told her last week that I was working at Scent Appeal for Mrs. Weller's nephew and his sick friend, Chad.

Grandma Bramhall waved her hand down and said, "I know all about it, Dennis. Millie never knows when to shut that trap of hers."

She also knew about the Latin tags because it turns out the lady with the cat on the leash was hosting their bridge group one night. And when Grandma Bramhall read the tags, she asked what color hair the girl who sold them to her had and knew it was me.

"Chad was okay yesterday," I told her.

"Good," she said. "Listen, dearie, do you think that father of yours would like to come to a pre–Fourth of July party tonight, before Mr. John and I set sail tomorrow? It's a last-minute thing, but you never know what might happen to us out there."

Grandma Bramhall had started talking like this, like they were heading out to sail through the Bermuda Triangle instead of staying on a cruise ship that was bigger than my school. It was starting to drive my dad crazy too. "Look, Mom," he said. "Correct me if I'm wrong, but it's a *cruise ship* and the only sail you'll be setting is when you're three sheets to the wind."

"Don't be sassy," Grandma Bramhall said. My dad smiled though, for the first time since M had clobbered back up the stairs that morning saying, "No way, will I to sit at dinner with that mother of yours and listen to her tell me how to serve you all the day, Dennis."

"A pre–Fourth of July *pool* party?" I asked hopefully. Already, it was hot and humid and Grandma Bramhall's pool was the perfect solution.

"Of course," she said.

"I'll tell him."

"All right, and oh, do you think *she's* going to feel
up to coming?"

I said I didn't know. My dad had told Grandma
Bramhall that M was having a hard pregnancy and that
her broken toe wasn't helping matters. He didn't tell
her about the smashed window or the fork throwing,
though.

"No matter," Grandma Bramhall sighed. "Six
sharp."

After I hung up, I swung my backpack on, heavy
with six bags of bleached rocks that I was going to try
in the vases this morning and some more food for The
Boss. No one had adopted him yet. But Chad and I had
started playing with him upstairs in their apartment.
We made a collar for him out of my Swatch watch
and tried to walk him on a piece of string. It took a
few nudges for The Boss to get moving, but then he
got good enough to take out onto the sidewalk. When
Mike caught us he got really mad, though, and told us
we were scaring customers away. We kept doing it anyway, whenever Mike was gone.

Usually it was fun when people stopped to watch
us, until Johnny Berman and two of his skateboard
friends zoomed by. Johnny did a double take when he
saw me and flipped up his board.

"Hey, Apron," he said. "What are you doing?" He
was even cuter with blonder hair and a tan.

"Nothing," I told him. I glanced over at Chad to see how sick he was looking just then. He had his sunglasses on at least.

Chad tugged on The Boss's leash. "We're training him for the *David Letterman Show*."

As soon as Johnny got a good look at Chad, his face pulled up and he stepped back. The truth was: Chad looked like a skeleton. He had on his same jeans, but his belt was cinched so tight it almost went around him twice. And the black splotches on his neck were impossible to hide. Another one had come out on his forehead.

Johnny looked at me and then back at Chad, before throwing down his skateboard and jumping on again. "Cool. See ya."

After he zoomed away, Chad stopped and tipped his head at me.

"Sorry."

"For what?" I leaned over to fix The Boss's Swatch watch collar.

"For being seen with me. I'm guessing my good looks have started to fade a little," he smiled his gray, cracked lips. "Not exactly good for the popularity meter."

He was right. But I stood and looked him square in the sunglasses. "He's just a stupid boy from my class. He's in Special Ed, I think. And besides, you don't have to do anything for some people to hate you."

Chad held out The Boss's leash for me, and when I took it, he took my hand too. I squeezed it tight, black splotches and all, as we walked back into Scent Appeal.

Now, I left a note for my dad on his lobster. *Grandma Bramhall tonight 6 pm party,* and walked outside.

The heat hit me like a ton of bricks. My hair was still looking fancy and layered, though. When my dad first noticed it, he nodded and said, "You're growing up, all right."

When I got to Scent Appeal, the door was open but the lights were off. Usually this meant Mike had gone out to get more flowers or something for Chad. Mike said today would be a busy one. We'd probably have to stay open late because people would be running in at the last minute to buy flowers for their Fourth of July parties, and if that happened, don't worry, he'd drive me home. Mike had even bought a bag of tiny American flags, which I stuck into all the vases yesterday even though Chad said he'd rather have his fingernails peeled off than celebrate Reagan's crusty right-winged America. The *real* Boss was mad at President Reagan, too, for singing "Born in the USA" without permission. The story was on the cover of my dad's newspaper. Even when Bruce Springsteen looks mad, he's still a fox.

I got busy with the flowers in tubs that Mike left for me every morning. Then I found the largest vase with the biggest opening, and dropped a bleached rock into it. A long crack spread across the bottom. I didn't know how much a vase cost, but it had to be worth at least a couple of Chad's pills. Every day, Mike made him take about ten. I felt guilty, but there was nothing I could do to save it. So I put it in the trash and sprinkled the rest of the bleached rocks around the tables and lobster traps instead.

Twenty minutes before we opened, an orange danger cone dropped into my stomach. Mike still wasn't back yet and I hadn't heard anything upstairs at all. I went up quietly to check on Chad. But when I opened the door, he wasn't on the couch. Or in the bedroom. Or anywhere else in the apartment.

45

Nemo hic adest illius nominis.
There is no one here by that name.

I ran so fast to Maine Medical Center that standing in the hallway in front of the check-in reception-
ist I thought a fly was crawling down my arm, but it
turned out to be a drip of sweat instead.

"Chad," I panted.

"Chad who, honey?" the fat lady behind the counter asked. She didn't remember me. In all the times I'd
been here for my mom.

"I don't know," I said. "Chad, somebody. He's really sick."

"That's not all that unique around here, doll. What's
his last name?"

"I don't *know*," I said. "Weller, I think."

The lady said, "Hmmmm," the whole time her eyes
searched the list.

"Sorry, I can't find a Chad Weller anywhere. I can't
help you."

My eyes burned. "He's got AIDS."

The noise around me stopped and the fat lady said,
"Hold on," and picked up her phone. Next to me, a
man and a woman stood staring.

"Fifth floor," she said, hanging up. "But you're not
going to be allowed inside. He's in quarantine."

I was already inside the elevator before she finished talking. A nurse with a food tray walked in after me and smiled. I studied her until I was sure she wasn't a friend of M's, then I looked down. She got off on the fourth floor, the sick kid floor, which was why I had never seen her before.

When the elevator doors opened again, there was another set of doors staring back at me. I stepped out and pulled them open.

Inside was so quiet you could hear the rug growing. No one was anywhere. Even the nurse station was empty. I walked by it and headed left, toward the *No Admittance – Contagious Area* sign. I came to another set of doors, but these were locked. Everywhere you went in this place, there were doors and floors keeping you away from the people you loved.

I stepped back and leaned against the wall, and when I did, the doors swung open. I ran through them and slammed into a nurse.

"Whoa, can I help you?" she asked, her hair was hidden inside a blue paper hat and a mask was down around her neck.

"Chad," I said. "He has AIDS. Is he here?"

"All right," she said taking me by the shoulder and leading me out the door again.

She sat me down in a chair across from the nurse desk and pulled up another one for herself. "Are you related to Chad?" I could tell she had brown hair under there somewhere, the same color as her eyebrows, and she had blue eyes, but not blueberry ones like Mike.

"No," I said nodding.

"No or yes?"

"No, I'm not, but I'm really good friends with him. And Mike. Is he okay?"

Her face stayed the same. "You can't go in there, um, what's your name?"

"Apron," I said.

"Apron?"

I nodded once and clamped my lips together. No way was I going to start on that.

"Okay, Apron," she said. "I can get Mike for you, if you want."

"Yes, please."

I followed her back to the doors, where she stopped and said, "No. You have to stay here." So I watched her disappear.

After a century, those doors pushed open and Mike walked out, blinking and looking around like he forgot where he was. I stood and we met half way. He hugged me hard, but I hugged him harder. "Hey," he said. He smelled like plastic tubes.

"Hey," I said. We both stepped back a little. "Is he okay?"

Mike shook his head. "He had a seizure. I thought he was just coughing."

I was about to say something when the elevator dinged and the door opened. Toby wheeled himself out with two men walking next to him on either side. Both of them looked like Chad used to: bald and bouncy.

"Hey, little lady," Toby said wheeling over and reaching up to me for a hug.

I leaned down into him. "Hi."

The man with blonder hair said, "Any change?" And Mike shook his head.

"Apron," Mike said. "This is Marcus and Chris, good friends of ours."

I shook their hands and told them it was nice to meet them.

"Can we go in?" Marcus asked. His voice was high and light.

"I think so," Mike said. "Hold on." He walked back to the door and pushed the button I had leaned up against. When it opened, he disappeared inside.

"So guys," Toby said, smiling up at me. "This is the little lady I was telling you about. The one that watches over the shop now." He winked at me and the other two nodded. "Right," Chris said. He had a deeper voice, but his eyes didn't stop on me for long. Finally, Mike and the nurse walked out together.

"Let's go," the nurse said waving us in. I waited for Toby to go first, then followed Chris and Marcus. But the nurse stepped in front of me. "You have to be eighteen," she said, not looking sorry about it this time.

I turned back to Mike. For a second it looked like he was going to leave me and head in through the doors anyway. But then he nodded at the nurse and stayed. "Listen, Apron," he said. "She's not kidding. It's a rule. I'll call you later. I promise, okay?"

"But," I said, "But, what if he—"

Mike shook his head and stepped closer to me. "We're going to wait until he's out of pain, and then take him home," he said quietly. "He doesn't want to die in here. I promise. I'll call you." Then he hugged me again and disappeared through the doors.

I ran to the elevator and pushed the button over and over until a man and a boy were standing in front of me. The man was wearing a blue *Maineiac* hat and the little boy was holding his hand. They would never remember me from the night my dad told me M was pregnant. They had walked by me then, outside on the stairs waiting for my dad and M, watching the burning sunset crash into the hospital, before I knew about Mike and Chad. Before I knew about a lot of things.

I stepped inside with them and turned around quickly. I had to get home and find a picture for Chad before it was too late.

46
Potes currere sed te occulere non potes.
You can run, but you can't hide.

My dad's car wasn't there, but M was in the kitchen; you could hear her talking. I shut the screen door without letting it click and listened.

"Yes," I heard her say, frustrated. "That's what I said."

With everything else that was changing, you could always count on M and her bad mood now. I stood there, my tongue begging me to get some lemonade. I had waited at the bus stop for twenty minutes before the next *Falmouth* bus came.

M was becoming even more bothered. "Yes, I said that. Do you speak *English*?"

I started toward the kitchen. When I got there, M was leaning over the counter with her back to me, the phone squeezed into her neck.

I went to the icebox and opened the door. "Yes, that is all," she said. I grabbed the lemonade and turned around. She was staring at me with her hand on her bump. I knew she was going to warn me not to drink out of the container, but she didn't. She just flipped her face onto happy. "Hello, Aprons."

"Hi," I answered. My tongue was so dry I could barely get the word out. And her bump was so big now she had to stand crooked.

"This was my friend on the phone," she said.

"Okay." I undid the lid. There wasn't much left in it anyway.

She stretched her mouth into a straight smile. "Yes, and then how are Mike and his boyfriend today?"

My stomach tugged at me. She had never asked me that before. "Fine." I swished the lemonade around gently to mix it up.

"You know what I think," M asked evenly.

I brought the bottle to my lips.

"I think you are such sad ugly girl you can only have gay boys for friends."

A yellow wave flew out and onto my T-shirt. Then I heard my dad's voice. It was loud and furious, the name that he yelled. But it wasn't mine. "Don't you talk to my daughter like that," he said. "*Ever.*"

For a second it looked like M might faint. "Dennis," she said. "I didn't see—"

"Neither did I," my dad said from the doorway, looking at me before looking back at M. I could feel the cold lemonade on my neck.

"Apron," my dad said still looking at M. "Get in the car. Your grandmother's turned it into an afternoon pool party. We're late."

I left the lemonade by the stove and heard my dad say, "You're coming too, Margie, let's go." M said something back, but my dad said, "From now on, you'll do what I say."

But she didn't. I waited in the back of the car for so long that my T-shirt started cracking from the dried sugar. Finally, my dad came down the porch stairs and got into the car. "It's better anyway," he said. "Just let her cool off for a while."

I didn't say anything. When my dad's eyes caught mine in the rearview mirror, he sighed and said, "She didn't mean it, Apron. It's just her hormones talking."

Mr. John was at the pool party too, in his blue swim trunks. He liked to do cannon balls, they were his specialty, even though they weren't very good—too wide and messy.

Grandma Bramhall had a red sarong with little mirrors on the bottom wrapped around her. I tried to find my reflection in there when she sat down next to me on the lounge chair and said, "Why don't you go in with Mr. John? Show him your backflip."

But I shook my head and then another spray of water hit my ankles. When Mr. John popped his flattened hair up again, he said, "What was *that*?"

"A seven," I told him.

Mr. John punched the air with his fist and climbed up the ladder, blue trunks and gray hair clinging to him everywhere.

"Come on," Grandma Bramhall said nudging me with her elbow. "This could be the last time I ever see you do one."

I rolled my eyes, but smiled too, and then so did she.

"Grandma Bramhall?" I asked her quietly, the two of us watching Mr. John bounce on the diving board, getting ready. "Do you think that one day, like when I'm older, I might not be so ugly?"

"What?" she turned her shake to me. "What are you talking about?"

"Me," I said looking down at the blue veins crashing into each other on the back of her hand. "Me and my ugly freckles."

"Apron," she said. "You watch. Someday you're going to love those freckles."

"No I'm not."

Mr. John leapt through the air after that, feet flailing and his back arched too far away from his knees: his worst one yet.

After both of our ankles got splashed again, Grandma Bramhall picked up my chin and said, "You are as beautiful as your mom was," and then kissed my cheek with hers.

I looked down at the mirrors in her sarong again, tiny little pieces of blue sky in them. "Thanks," I said quietly.

"You're welcome," Grandma Bramhall said squeezing my hand.

"How was that?" Mr. John yelled, popping up and dog paddling toward us.

I snuck a look at Grandma Bramhall. "A ten," I said.

"Yes!" Mr. John yelled, raising both fists this time and sinking back into the water.

Grandma Bramhall and I had to suck in our cheeks not to laugh. "See how beautiful you are, Apron?"

It was like me telling Grandma Bramhall that her shake was beautiful. Except right then, smiling like that, she and her shake really *were* beautiful.

I looked back down at Mr. John, swimming toward us again. "An *amateur* ten," I said, unwrapping my towel and standing up. "Now let me show you how the pros do it."

$\nearrow$ $\quad$ $\nearrow$ $\quad$ $\nearrow$

During dinner, when steamed clams were every-where except on my plate, which only had Tater Tots—I was pretty sure clams had parents—I got up twice to call Scent Appeal. No answer either time, which meant they were still at the hospital.

"What's going on?" my dad asked the first time he found me in Grandma Bramhall's kitchen with her phone in my ear.

"Chad," I said like a fact.

"Oh," my dad nodded, reaching into Grandma Bramhall's icebox and pulling out another beer. "Did something happen?"

So I told him. I wanted to tell him in the car on the way over, but he didn't want to talk, you could tell. But now, my dad leaned against the icebox and listened with worried eyes the whole time I told him about Chad and the hospital and his seizure. I made sure to leave out the part about nobody being at Scent Appeal this morning.

"You know, though," my dad said, twisting open his beer but not drinking it yet. "They're right, Apron. Minors can't go into quarantine areas. Unless they're family."

I looked down.

"Listen," he said. "I'm sorry for Chad. But you didn't think he was going to make it, did you?"

I looked up at him.

"Hey," he said. "It's not like what your mom had, kiddo. No one ever makes it through what Chad's got. At least not yet, anyway."

He started toward me, but I turned away and picked up the phone again. "Let me know if they need anything, okay?" he said walking to the door, but then stopping. "Hey, has she seen any little people in here lately?"

I shrugged, even though right before dinner Grandma Bramhall told me she had seen one of them mopping her floor last night when she came down for milk. And she showed me the mop leaning against the back door to prove it.

✗ ✗ ✗

I still hadn't talked to Mike or Chad by the time we were in the car saying good-bye for the seven hundredth time already. My dad was counting. There were things to remember though, in case the unthinkable happened. There were cousins who lived in Detroit and old furniture being lent out that was "quite valuable, you know."

When we finally pulled into our garage, my dad went straight upstairs to see M. And I went straight into the kitchen. Still, no one answered at Scent Appeal. My dad walked in, his face looking bad again. "Is she in *here*?" he asked, opening the pantry door and looking around before heading toward the back porch. M must not have been out there either, though. "Where the hell did she go this time?" I heard him say.

In the kitchen again, he rubbed his eyes and looked at the phone. "Off to bed now, Apron."

"But Dad, if the phone rings, and it's Mike, will you *please* get me? *Please?* Even if it's the middle of the night?"

He said all right.

"Thanks," I said. Then, without even thinking about it, I took a few steps toward him. I never kissed him goodnight anymore, but suddenly I forgot that. Before I got to him though, he spun around on his heels and headed over to the icebox, his forehead pinched in worry.

In the living room, I stopped at the bookshelf and slipped the frame into my backpack.

I had to be ready at any given notice.

47

Frater, ave atque vale.
Brother, hello and good-bye.

The air smelled like worms. I thought I had heard Suzanna's car crunching down the dirt road sometime in the middle of the night. But now I remembered it was just the rain, sometimes pounding hard and sometimes tapping light.

It was already eight o'clock. I flipped over my covers and ran down the stairs and into the kitchen. I looked for a note that said Mike had called, but there wasn't one. Not on my lobster, or on my cereal box or anywhere else. So I picked up the phone. They didn't have an answering machine anymore. Just when I was about to hang up, Mike said, "Hello?"

"Mike, it's me, Apron. Are you back?"

"Hi, Apron," Mike said way too slowly, "I was waiting to call you."

My stomach slipped out of me. "You *promised*," I said, leaning into the wall.

"Apron," Mike cut me off. "He's here. Chad's here, but he—it's going to be his last day today."

"How do you know?"

Mike laughed, so quick and sharp it could have been a hiccup. "It's the Fourth of July. He wants to go out with a bang."

"I'm coming right now," I told him. Then before I hung up, I said, "Tell him to wait for me okay? I have something to give him."

"I'll tell him, Apron. He's been asking for you."

I ran out of the kitchen and up the stairs and straight into my dad in the hallway. He looked yellow, he was so tired, and his red hair was flat on one side and sticking out on the other. "Oh," he said, "I thought you were Margie."

"Dad. I talked to Mike. I have to go see Chad."

My dad still wasn't listening, though. He peeked his head into the little whatever's room and said, "Is she downstairs?"

"I don't know," I said slipping by him and going into the bathroom. I whipped my toothbrush around and fluffed up my red layers. Then I ran back into my room and got dressed: jean shorts and a turquoise Indian shirt. After that, I grabbed my raincoat and slid into my flip-flops, only slowing down to put on my backpack.

Downstairs, my dad was still standing around like he was lost, this time in the middle of the kitchen. He opened the back door and peered down the staircase. "She didn't come home," he said, like I couldn't believe it either.

"Dad, I really—"

"Hold *on* a minute."

He shut the door and turned around again, thinking. I tried to look worried while I tapped my feet and glanced at the clock on the oven. I might still be able to make the early bus if I left right now. "She probably stayed at Suzanna's," I said. And then I remembered: the buses weren't running. It was the Fourth of July.

"Dad! There aren't any buses today. Can you take me? Please?"

My dad turned his zombie face to me and shook it. "She didn't come back last night, Apron. I have to wait here. What if she tries to call?"

"Dad?" I said, my jaw so tight it could break. "You said to let you know if they needed anything. They need *me*. Chad's been asking for me."

But my dad just turned his red head back to the phone and picked it up. Someone slapped me in the heart. I stood there watching him get ready to dial, then stop. "I don't know it," he said spinning around and staring at me with the same lost look. "I don't even know Suzanna's number."

"Dad," my voice was squeezed so high it came out my ears. "I need to see him before it's too late. Like Mom."

Finally, he listened. He put the phone back on the hook and started walking to the door. "Let's go."

And we were already down the porch stairs and halfway to the car by the time the screen door slammed behind us.

48

Di te incolumem custodiant.
May the gods guard your safety.

My dad's face stayed tight the whole time we drove. The only noise came from the windshield wipers: the steady swish and then the fast squeaky pull to get them moving again.

We found a place to park right in front of Scent Appeal. The street was practically empty and so wet that I couldn't make it onto the sidewalk without stepping into a greasy puddle first. "I'm coming in with you," my dad said shutting his door, drops of rain plopping onto his shirt. I was going to say no, he didn't need to, but changed my mind when I saw his face.

He was looking at the picture frame I was carrying. "Is that—?" I heard him say. But I slipped it into my backpack and hurried up to the door, which was unlocked just like yesterday.

Inside the lights were off and all my vases were scattered around.

"Would they be up there?" my dad asked behind me.

I nodded, and he started up the stairs first.

I prayed there wouldn't be anything contagious-looking in their apartment, even a cup. My dad took the stairs two at a time and stopped at the top to wait for me, making himself a wall so I could go in first.

The living room was empty and dark and so was their bedroom.

"Looks like they're gone," my dad said.

We were too late. Again. I grabbed onto the wall.

Until I heard, "You're here."

I spun around so fast my backpack hit my dad's elbow. I looked at him to say sorry, but he held up his hand and nodded, *It's okay*. Then Mike walked toward us, out of the dark bedroom, his hair hanging loose all around him.

"Hi, Mr. Bramhall," he said, holding his hand out, but then pulling it back in again quickly and slipping it into his pocket.

But my dad said, "Hi, Mike," and held his hand out there until Mike took it. And then when they stood like that, shaking hands for longer than normal, you could see they were the exact same height.

When they dropped their hands, they turned to me.

"Thanks for letting Apron come over, it means a lot to her," my dad said.

"No," Mike said. "Thank you. It means a lot to Chad."

Mike smiled at me when he said that, and I smiled back.

"How's he doing?" my dad asked, his face ironed down into a worry now.

"Well, he's not in as much pain."

My dad nodded. "So what time are you thinking, then?"

Mike blinked at my dad. "Tonight," he answered, putting both hands in his pockets this time. "Definitely sometime tonight."

"To pick Apron up, I mean," my dad said quickly. "What time should I pick Apron up? An hour?"

"Yuh." Mike pulled his hands out of his pocket, his face flush. "Sounds good."

My dad turned to go down the stairs, but stopped at the top. For a second, I thought he might ask me if I wanted him to stay. But instead he said, "Can I bring you boys anything when I get back?"

"No. Thank you, Mr. Bramhall. We're all set," Mike answered.

So my dad waved once and disappeared.

Mike stood up straighter and looked at me. His blueberry eyes were cloudy. "Okay. You ready, kiddo?"

I nodded and slid off my backpack. Mike took my raincoat and hung it over a kitchen chair, and then I picked up my backpack again and followed him into the bedroom.

49

Anima vagula
Little soul flitting away

At first it looked like the bed was empty. But Mike walked up to it and pulled out a hand. "Hey," he said.

The sheets moved slightly.

"Apron's here."

The sheets moved faster.

"Calm down," Mike said. "She's not going anywhere."

A head slid up against the bed board, and there was Chad, looking awful, his cheeks glued on the wrong way and his black splotches looking blacker. I turned my eyes away, into Mike. And then he knew too, that I wished I hadn't come.

"It's okay," he mouthed, shaking his head. "He can't see you."

"I heard that," Chad said in the same grumpy voice he used to have, when his eyes were real.

"Hi," I said. I didn't recognize my own voice.

"Get over here, Apron. I've been waiting for you." Just saying that much got him out of breath. I looked at Mike. He nodded once and then we traded places.

"What's the difference between a woman from Maine and a moose?" Chad asked slowly, his eyes turned exactly the right way into mine, but not moving at all.

"I don't know," I said, but barely. It was hard to talk. "What?"

"About ten pounds," he tried to laugh but coughed. His teeth looked too big for his face now. He tapped the mattress with his finger. "That's the best one yet. Don't forget it, promise?"

I looked at Mike to see if it was okay to smile, to see if he was smiling too, like the old days when we told jokes and made bouquets and danced together.

"Don't look at *him*," Chad said reaching for my arm but missing it. "He won't remember it. He'll be bereft."

"Okay," I said. "I promise."

Then no one said anything and Chad's breath got longer right away.

"So," Mike said, a little too brightly. "Can I get you anything, Apron?'

"No, thank you."

"All right, well, I'm going to go down and wait for Toby. You can sit, Apron, if you'd like."

When I looked at Mike, I thought he would be nodding to the bed, but he was looking at one of their kitchen chairs against the wall.

"Okay," I said turning to get it, sliding it closer to Chad.

"Hey, Mikey," Chad called out in the loudest voice he had left.

"Yeah?" Mike stopped and turned around.

"You and me. Later." He patted the bed and winked.

Mike grinned and shook his head, then walked out the door. I stood for a moment, wondering if Chad had forgotten I was there.

But he hadn't because he said, "Apron, sit down, already."

I slid my backpack off and sat. Chad looked pinker all of sudden, like we might be wrong and he would be good as new by tomorrow. But then he coughed so hard it sounded like things were breaking inside of him. "Are you okay?" I asked.

He nodded like it hurt. "Fine."

I looked out the door for Mike, but he was gone. So I leaned down into my backpack and unzipped it. The noise made Chad's eyes move fast.

"What's that?" he asked.

"A picture of my mom," I said, opening his ice-cold hand and putting the frame in it gently.

"But Apron," Chad said. "I can't see."

"I know. But it's not for now. It's for when you get there, so you can find her."

Chad tapped his finger on my mom's cheek. "Does she look like you?"

I thought about it hard enough for Chad to take in another long breath. "A little bit," I said.

"Not quite as pretty?"

"Well," I said. "You'll have to see for yourself."

Chad raised his eyebrows. "I'll find her, Apron. I promise. If you promise me something, too."

I nodded, but then remembered he couldn't see me. "What?"

"Don't stay sad. Remember our poem. What it means. Promise?"

"Chad," I said. "Does Mike have it, too?"

He moved his finger over my mom's chin. "We don't know. He doesn't want to find out yet." His voice cracked.

My eyes stung hard and fast. And Chad knew it. He tried to smile again.

"Hey, can I tell your mom the Woman from Maine joke? It wouldn't offend her, would it?"

"You can tell her," I said, forcing my throat to work. "She's going to love that one."

"Apron," Chad said, sounding a little nervous. "I've been wondering. Do you think you and me would have been friends, if, you know, we were in seventh grade together?"

I thought about it for a second. I thought about Rennie and Jenny Pratt making fun of Chad, his swishy way of walking down the halls, and Johnny Berman and Sherman Howl writing *faggot* on the top of his desk and picking him last for dodge ball. And I thought about how, if I ignored them all and decided to be friends with Chad anyway, he would have been my only one.

"Yes," I nodded. "We'd be friends."

"Yup," Chad said smiling as far as his cracked lips would let him. "That's what I think, too."

We both nodded in quiet smiles. Then Chad closed his eyes and folded his arms around my mom's picture. I looked out the door, but didn't see Mike, and didn't know if Chad was supposed to be alone now. So I reached down into my backpack again and pulled out *The Little Town on the Prairie* and started reading to him quietly, while his breathing turned long and smooth, and my mom floated up and down on top of him.

Laura Ingalls Wilder should have been in class with us, too. With friends like us, she never would have had to put up with Nelly Olsens or Jenny Pratts. With friends like us, she never would have had to feel bad about wearing her same dress every single day of her life. "Hey, Chad," I said. "I bet Laura would have been friends with us, too. Don't you?" I grinned and lifted my eyes off the page to look at him.

He didn't answer me though. And my mom wasn't moving up and down anymore, either.

The book fell when I stood.

I shivered, but my throat closed so tight I couldn't scream for Mike. Chad was completely still. I tried not to blink in case I missed the flash or the bell or whatever it was that tells you a person is really dead. But nothing happened. Just more and more nothing.

"Chad," I whispered. "Chad," I said again. "Is it scary?"

His face stayed the same, not smiling but not sad, either. Just thinking. Maybe even about being in seventh grade with me.

Footsteps came up the stairs. "Mike," I yelled. Except it came out in a croak.

I waved at Chad and walked out the door.

The kitchen was empty and so was the living room. Blood dropped out of my head so fast I had to squeeze my eyes closed. When I opened them again, Mike popped up from behind the kitchen counter, a new paper towel roll in his hands.

"Hey," he said. "Toby's still not here. Did the phone ring at all?"

I didn't answer.

"Apron?"

I didn't answer again. And then I didn't have to.

Mike's arms fell to his side and the paper towels landed with a soft thud. I walked around the counter and straight into his white T-shirt. Then we stood like that, him holding my red head, and me listening to the part of his chest where his heart used to be.

↗ ↗ ↗

Chad's quiet look was still there. I watched Mike's fingers carefully circle around Chad's mouth and chin and then move back up to Chad's forehead and start down his cheeks all over again.

"I'm sorry it was me in here."

Mike nodded and didn't say anything.

But then he looked at me. "Maybe they want it that way," he said, his voice crackling. "So we can't stop them." And I thought about it. Maybe they did.

"He really loved you, Apron," Mike said, and now there were strings of wetness in his mouth.

He took his hand off of Chad. Then he flashed his broken blueberry eyes at me and said, "I'm going to lie down with him for a minute, okay? Will you be all right out there by yourself?"

I nodded. I bent down and picked up my book and my backpack. I looked down at Chad one more time and saw in between his hands my mom's face peeking out, smiling. Maybe she was laughing at the moose joke right now, the two of them sitting together, late for nothing. I gave them both a small wave and shut the door behind me.

In the living room, I sat on the couch and stared at the picture of Mike and Chad in the sailboat together, laughing so hard you could tell they were going to have to come up for air sometime soon.

And a little later, when my dad climbed the stairs, he stood in the doorway for a second, then looked past me to the bedroom door, still closed. I started to stand, but he walked over to me first and sat down.

"Chad's dead," I said, my eyes burning all over again.

My dad didn't say anything. He just sighed and wrapped his arms around me and pulled me in close. He smelled different than Mike and my head sank deeper into his chest. Then we rocked back and forth a little, and he started singing *It's okay, it's okay* over and over—the way my mom did, but a little off-key. I didn't even know he knew that song.

50

In Hoc Salut.
In Him is Salvation.

For three days in a row I stayed in my room, mostly reading Books Seven and Eight, all about Laura Ingalls Wilder's happy golden years, which after all that scalping and starving she deserved. Mike called me the day after Chad died to tell me he was going to be cremated. He also told me there was a going-away party next week, for both of them. Mike was moving back to St. Pete.

"What?" I asked dropping onto the floor, forgetting about the lemonade I was sneaking upstairs. Everyone was always leaving Maine. *Vacationland* was on all Maine license plates, even ours.

"What about Scent Appeal, and everything?"

"I need to go home." His voice was deeper now. "To see my parents before—"

But he stopped right there.

"Before what?" I asked, picking up an old piece of cereal and rolling it around in my fingers. I felt meanness covering me like a warm blanket. Mike still had me and his other friends and even Mrs. Weller to think of.

"Before it's too late for me, Apron. To get to know them again."

I dropped my forehead into my knees. *We pay a big price for it*, Reverend Hunter said. And I was almost out of money.

"So do you want to come?"

"What?" I picked my head up. My eyes started darting around. "I mean, yeah. Sure. I'll have to ask my dad, though." I tried not to sound too excited, but there was plenty of summer left for me to go on a trip and Florida wasn't that far and M certainly wouldn't miss me.

"I hope he'll come, too. Tell him the party will just be a few hours."

Mustard squeezed into my stomach. There I was again: a road to nowhere.

I threw the crusty piece of cereal back under the counter. "I'll tell my dad, but he's not going anywhere. Not until M comes back."

"Where'd she go?"

"Nobody knows."

"What? What's going on?"

I told him that we hadn't seen her since the night before Chad died. That my dad had even figured out where Suzanna's house was, but she wasn't there and neither was Suzanna. And even though Nurse Silvia had no idea where they were, she knew Suzanna took the long weekend off because she looked it up in the nurse schedule.

"Oh, man," Mike said. "How's your dad doing?"

"Not really talking," I said. But I didn't tell him that I wasn't either.

"I'm sorry, Apron. Tell him thanks for the food, though. I just finished ordering it, right before I called."

"What food?"

"Portland Bagels," Mike said. "He had a very gener-
ous gift certificate sent over with a note that said to use
it for Chad's reception. He's obviously been through
this before. It's really thoughtful of him, Apron."

I felt my heart blink on for the first time since Chad
died.

"I'll see you Monday?" Mike asked.

I told him yes and we hung up.

Then I picked up that old piece of cereal and threw
it into the trash.

On Saturday morning, after my dad drove off to
search for M—*Maybe she's wandering around Shop &
Save, Apron*—I biked to St. James Church.

When I got there, I left my bike in the rack and
walked past the Mary with her baby and his chipped
toe. I stood at the huge front doors, trying to hear if
anyone was dying or getting married in there. But it
was quiet.

Inside it smelled like the same old soggy hope that
it always did. Mike and Chad's decorations were long
gone. But the Jesus on the rug was right there, his hands
and feet bleeding.

I walked down the aisle, stopped at the third row
and slid in. Then I looked up at Jesus. Anywhere you
went, he had his eyes on you. I put my hands together
and bent my forehead into them and asked for things.
"Please, God," I said. "Please have Chad find my
mom. Please have Mike not feel so bad. Please save

those baby seals." But I couldn't make myself ask for the last thing.

So I dropped my hands and sat back. Jesus and I just stared at each other. *Apron*, he said finally. *It's time.*

I looked away, but then clapped my hands together, leaned forward, and dropped my head into them again. "And please have my dad find M."

When I sat back, I heard a door open. From up at the altar, Reverend Hunter said, "Apron. Is that you?"

I nodded. There was no hiding behind this hair, even if it was shorter now.

He started walking down the stairs toward me. "I was pleased to hear everything turned out all right with your grandmother."

"She's fine," I said.

"And you got home with those boys?" he asked, stopping at my pew.

I shrugged. "Chad died."

"Oh dear," Reverend Hunter said. And the bees came. I tried to stop the stinging, but there were too many of them.

"May I?" he asked sliding in next to me. I scooted down, letting those drips fall, not even trying to wipe them away. Reverend Hunter clasped his hands in his lap. He smelled like Dunkin' Donuts.

"You know how you said that it costs a lot to love someone?" I asked quietly.

He looked at me confused for a moment, but then said, "The price we pay. Yes."

"Well, it seems like God charges some people more."

"You mean like you and your father?"

I wiped my nose. "And Mike and Chad. They loved each other the best. Better than anyone else around here. And people hated them."

Reverend Hunter glanced up at the altar. I thought I saw him nod to Jesus before he looked down at his hands again. "I don't know, Apron. The fact is, tolerance is something we could all use more of." He looked at me with a small smile. "And sometimes it takes a child to remind us of that."

"I'm not a child anymore," I said, clenching my teeth more than I meant to.

He dropped his eyes off me. "Yes. I know that, too. You've had to grow up much faster than most of your friends."

I wanted to tell him that I didn't have any friends now. Chad and Mike were my last ones. But instead, I looked up.

"Why didn't he ever save anyone, Reverend Hunter?"

"Jesus?"

I nodded.

"Well he saves all of us, every day, Apron. You, me, your mother, Chad."

"No, he doesn't. He couldn't even save himself."

"Oh, but he did," Reverend Hunter said, his voice getting smooth and preachy. "He overcame his fear. By not resisting death, he showed us how to overcome our own fears and choose the opposite."

"What's that?"

"Love. The opposite of fear is love, and every minute of every day, we choose between the two."

It was kind of the same as my free verse poem.

"So how come we always have to see him up there? Stuck like that."

"Oh, he came down, Apron," Reverend Hunter said sounding worried that I didn't know that.

I looked over at him.

"Yes," he nodded at me. "Look at all these pictures of Jesus back in Heaven." Reverend Hunter gestured around to the stained glass windows, some high and some low.

"You mean that's him *after*?" I squinted at the pictures of Jesus with rosy cheeks and thorny crowns, smiling and holding his hands out to people, offering things.

"Yes, Apron," Reverend Hunter said, surprised. "Maybe you could ask your grandmother to bring you to Sunday School. We have an excellent one you know, for chil-, *young ladies* just your age."

He looked at his watch and stood.

"Come next weekend, Apron. We'll talk about it more. I'm sorry about your friend. And your mother, of course."

I waved and watched him go, then went back to looking around at all the Jesuses up on the walls and inside those windows—everywhere. And each one of them looking just like Mike.

51

Soror
Sister

The rain started after I had biked all the way up to Route 88 and back, twice. Chad and Mike's going-away party was tomorrow and M still wasn't home.

I put on my raincoat and walked down to the rocks to watch Sea Glass Cave disappear under the high tide right before my eyes. Every once in a while, it smelled like seaweed left out of the icebox for too long. I picked up a few clam shells on the way back, which I had started putting around my new rose bush.

I was laying down the thirteenth one, upside down so they looked like white stones, when I heard the phone ring. I stood, but stopped when the ring cut off. My dad had been at his lobster reading the paper the last time I saw him.

And then, just when I took a step back to count how many more shells I was going to need to finish the circle, the screen door slammed shut.

"Apron," my dad said at the top of the porch stairs. "We have to go."

"Where?" I asked looking up at him, drops of rain stinging my eyes.

"To the hospital. Margie's in labor."

I looked at the unfinished circle and tried to think. She wasn't having that little whatever until the end of

September. I looked up at my dad. "But I'm not even back in school yet."

"I know. But something's happened and I need you."

I waited for him to tell me *why* he needed me. But he didn't. Instead he said, "Now, Apron," and started down the stairs. Light raindrops landed on top of his red head and stayed there like tiny bubbles. "*Right now.*"

Things moved fast when we got into the hospital. My dad led me straight into the elevator. Everywhere, people were walking fast, squeaking loudly on the wet floor. The elevator was full of people, all of them taller than me, except one: a little boy with no hair, and no raincoat on either.

I smiled at the boy, but he was too busy speeding his plastic lobster boat up and down the wall. So I hoped he had Nurse Silvia for a nurse and looked away.

When the elevator stopped on the seventh floor, my dad nudged me and we stepped off. I pulled my hood down and looked around, but my dad was already walking.

I ran after him until we came to a set of doors that I had never seen before. *Maternity* it said on the wall. All this time, I hadn't realized that babies were being born right above my mom. Maybe, if I had listened hard enough, I might have heard a cry.

My dad pulled open the door and we walked in. Pictures of babies in duck shirts and fancy hats, smiling big and wet, were everywhere. In between them, the walls were painted with storks, bags hanging from their beaks. After a few more corners, my dad walked to the nurse station and leaned over it, whispering to a nurse back there.

"Apron," someone said from the other side of the room. Nurse Silvia. She wasn't in her nurse uniform, just some plain black pants and a light brown shirt. She stood and walked over to me. I hadn't seen her since M's wedding day.

"Hi," she said. Her lips were shellacked with brown lip gloss.

"Hi."

Two men were sitting together a few seats down reading magazines and another man was lying across a row of chairs with a sweater over his head. I looked at my dad. His arms were moving around while he talked. Then he groaned and stepped back and a nurse with gray hair stood up. I didn't recognize her. "She doesn't want you in there, Mr. Bramhall. I'm sorry," the nurse said with her arms crossed.

"It's *my* baby," my dad said.

"I understand that, Mr. Bramhall," the nurse said dropping her arms. "We're trying to help you *keep* that baby of yours."

My dad stood still for a second, but then took off to the right, around the nurse station and in through some doors. I started running after him, but Nurse Silvia grabbed my arm. "You can't go back there," she said.

I turned my burning face to her. "Why, because I'm a *kid?*"

"No," she said looking at me with her soft brown eyes. "She doesn't want anyone in there, not even your father." Nurse Silvia spoke English so much better than M that I had to keep reminding myself she was from Brazil.

"What happened?" I asked.

Nurse Silvia looked over to the door where my dad had disappeared and then back to me. "They need to get the baby out right away."

"Why?"

"Come," Nurse Silvia said waving me toward the chairs where she had been sitting. They were just as scratchy as they had been before, one floor down.

She started from the beginning, quietly, so no one else would hear: M had been away with Suzanna, visiting one of their nurse friends in Vermont who was going to rotate with Suzanna at the end of the month.

"Are you leaving, too?" For some reason I didn't want her to say yes.

"I'm not sure yet," she said looking down. I looked down, too. You could tell there used to be bright orange and yellow half-circles woven into the rug once, but now they were mostly just different colors of gray, faded like Mrs. Weller's slippers.

But anyway, Nurse Silvia said, this morning, Suzanna heard a crash and a moan and when she went to check on M, she found her on the floor holding her bump, a chair knocked over next to her on the floor.

"A moan?" I asked, pulling away from her. "Like a cat?"

"I don't know that, Apron," Nurse Silvia said.

But I did.

"All I know," she continued, "is that Marguerite told Suzanna she had tripped over a chair on the way to the bathroom, but was fine. Then driving home,

Marguerite started cramping and by the time they got back to Portland, Marguerite couldn't even sit up so Suzanna brought her here. And now she needs to have the baby right away."

"How did my dad find out?"

Nurse Silvia crossed her legs and looked down at her lap. "I called him."

I smiled at her, but she didn't see me.

And then my dad came back out through those doors with another nurse, this one short and fat, but nicer looking than the gray-haired one. They stopped and Nurse Silvia and I both turned in our seats to watch them.

"Because, Mr. Bramhall. It's too risky. The baby's already in distress," the nurse said. She wasn't as nice as she looked.

"But it's my *right*."

The two men looked up from their magazines when he said that. And then listened while the nurse told him that, no, actually, it *wasn't* his right.

"Look," she said. "I understand your position, Mr. Bramhall. But you're *not* coming in. Doctor's orders."

The nurse turned and disappeared through the doors again. My dad stayed looking at the wall, clenching his teeth. I locked down my stomach because whenever his freckles popped out like that, something was going to happen.

As fast as lightning, my dad slammed his fist against the wall hard enough for a picture of a pudgy face with a wet smile to fall off and crash on the rug. Nurse Silvia squeaked in her seat next to me. And out the corner of my eye, I saw that sleeping man's head spring up, the sweater halfway off his face. But I stayed exactly where

I was. Even after my dad dropped his forehead onto the wall and breathed and then picked up that frame and hung it up again, I didn't move a muscle. Not even the tiniest ones that were connected to my blink.

After he turned away from the picture, he put the hand he used to slam the wall with in his pocket and looked over at us. He took a few steps, then stopped. "I'm going to take a walk around the block," he said, to all of us—even the two men sitting together and the one man sitting up with the sweater on his chest now. He nodded a *stay put* look to me. I nodded back.

↗   ↗   ↗

A little later, after the two magazine-reading men had been waved in through the doors by a happy blond nurse, and Nurse Silvia had gone down to Pediatrics before her shift started and brought me back a puzzle to work on, my dad returned with his newspaper and some french fries and a lemonade for me.

"Anyone come out for us?" he asked, looking down at me on the floor, sitting in a middle split with almost the whole world between my legs. Hawaii and most of Russia were missing and when I figured out where Brazil was, I threw those pieces back into the box. "No," I shook my head, watching him sit. I thought I was still too sad about Chad to eat, but after the first speck of salt exploded onto my tongue, I didn't stop chewing until the paper box was empty.

Finally, when my legs felt like they had grown roots, the nice-looking mean nurse came out of the doors and walked up to us.

"The procedure is over," she said.

My dad let the newspaper fall off his lap when he stood. "Can I see her?" he asked, extra nicely this time.

"No," the nurse said, turning. "Not yet. But I'll come back when you can."

My dad took a step closer to her. "Is she going to make it?"

The nurse glanced back at him. "You'll have to talk to the doctor, Mr. Bramhall."

"*Please*," my dad groaned from his chest, the way Nutter begged when Mrs. Weller tried to make him sleep in his doghouse. "Is she going to *make* it?"

The nurse stopped and turned around to face him, "Fifty-fifty," she said quietly. Then she disappeared through the doors again.

My dad squeezed his head in his palms, then shook out the hand he had hit the wall with and sat down again, stepping on top of the newspaper when he did, ripping it. That sleeping man had left for a while but was back now, lying in the same spot with the sweater back over his face.

"Dad," I said carefully. "What's going on?"

"I don't know, Apron. These nurses won't tell me anything." He slumped back.

"Is M?" I said, but stopped. Then I took a deep breath and started all over again. "Is *Margie* going to be all right?" Her name tasted like sour milk.

My dad looked at me with his forehead squeezed together. "Margie?" he said sitting up. "It's the baby we're talking about. She's ten weeks early, Apron. She's a preemie."

"A preemie?" I pulled my knees up, destroying all of Africa.

"Yes," he said, looking away and staring at something. "I sat right there, too," he said pointing to the man with the sweater across his head. "When they came out to tell me about you."

I looked over and smiled. "Really? You sat there the whole time?"

"They wouldn't let the husbands in back then. I told your mother I was going to pay one of the nurses twenty bucks to videotape it for me." He smiled, thinking about it. "She told me she'd cram the thing down my neck if I did."

My dad got lost in his remembering and I didn't want to interrupt it.

I looked down at the world again, like the way God must do every day when he wakes up and looks out his window. From here, it seemed like all you really needed to do was stay on the green parts not to drown. You couldn't see all the other millions of places just waiting for you to fall in.

After a few more moments, I lifted myself up next to my dad. And we sat like that, the blood finding its way back into my legs, while outside, the sky flashed.

It took a while for the thunder to come, but when it did, the bangs were so loud it sounded like someone's room was blowing up above us. Outside the window, if you watched long enough, you could see the whole sky light up before the next crash. My dad didn't look up once, though, so I watched it alone.

52

Fac ut vivas.
Get a life.

A doctor was standing above us. For a few blinks, I thought he was one of Chad's friends. But then he said, "Dennis?"

"Yuh," my dad answered, rubbing his eyes and standing. We had both been asleep for a while, you could tell by the sour ball in my stomach.

"You can see her now."

"Great," my dad nodded, looking at me then back to the doctor. "Can my daughter come, too?"

I knew what that doctor was going to say. But he said, "yes," instead.

When I stood, my legs were so wobbly my dad had to grab my arm. We walked like that through the doors. It smelled like Band-Aids mixed in with chicken broth in the hallway. Doors were lined along the walls, all of them shut with *Delivery* written across them. But further down there was another one that said *Pediatric ICU* with a long window after it. The doctor stopped in front of it, tapping his finger lightly on the glass.

"Over there," he pointed. "In that incubator."

My dad and I put our hands up to the window but there were so many incubators in there, we couldn't tell which one he was pointing to.

"Which one?" my dad asked.

The doctor tapped on the window harder this time and a thin nurse looked up. Her face changed when she saw it was the doctor, pointing and waving. He dropped his hands, but my dad and I kept ours flat on the glass. We watched the nurse walk over to an incubator by the wall and start wheeling it closer, through the baby traffic, until she stopped below us. Then she turned the whole thing around.

Under the blanket, there was a bump the same size as a loaf of banana bread, with a purple teardrop for a nose and two puffy wrinkles for eyes.

"Three pounds, two ounces," the doctor said. "She's stabilized."

"Stabilized," my dad repeated quietly. "She looks all right, right?"

She looked like she was made out of play dough.

"She's okay, Dennis. Better than she should be really. Abrupt deliveries don't always end up like this. We got lucky."

But I didn't even know what they were talking about. *Lucky.* That purple banana bread of a baby had tubes sticking out of it everywhere. I stepped back.

The doctor told us to go home now, there was no need to stay.

My dad turned to him and said, "What about Margie?"

"She's fine, Dennis. Tired, but fine. And still not talking."

My dad shook his head.

"I've seen it before," the doctor said. "From a steering wheel. The mother was driving and she wasn't wearing her seatbelt."

"Did the baby make it?" my dad asked. Way in the distance I heard another crash in the sky.

The doctor looked at me and then him. "For a little while," he said.

I stared down at the old gray half-moons on the rug. The doctor told us again that we might as well go home. My dad sighed, "Thanks, Doctor," but stuck his hands up on the glass again.

The doctor started to walk away. Until my dad said, "Hey. Look at that," quietly, like he might be watching a butterfly land on a petal.

The doctor turned back to the glass and I stepped forward again. The nurse had lifted up the pink cap slightly, and underneath it there was a flash, a tiny taste, of red.

53

Tempus fugit.
Time flies.

**In the morning, when I opened my eyes, a long
triangle of sun was covering most of my bookshelf
again.** The thunder and lightning from last night were
gone. I closed my heavy eyelids. I missed Chad in the
same way that I missed my mom now: always.

I turned to my clock radio. 11:09.

I threw off my sheets. I had a good-bye party to get
to. I pulled on my Avon lady dress and slid into my
flip-flops.

In the mirror, my tired eyes looked like Grandma
Bramhall's, small and hidden inside a few piles of skin.
My new layers of red were all over the place; one side
was curled under my ear like Mrs. Perry's, and the other side was sticking out in a J. But of all the things that
were staring back at me, it was the dress that looked the
worst.

So I pulled it off, walked over to the trash and
dropped it in there, forever. I put on blue jeans and a
white T-shirt, instead. Except for the layers of red and
my freckles every second, I might look like a smaller
version of Mike.

My dad's door was wide open and his room was
full of sun. Last night, after we finally climbed up our
porch stairs, I was so tired it felt like I was walking

underwater in Grandma Bramhall's pool. My dad looked just as tired but said he had some things to take care of before he went to bed. "See you in the morning, Apron," he said.

But now, downstairs, I didn't see him anywhere. And I had forty-five minutes to get to the party.

"Dad!" I yelled through the screen door, but the only thing that answered was a seagull and Mr. Orso's lawn mower somewhere on the other side of his house. And when I stepped outside, I saw my dad's car was gone. I ran down those stairs and over to Mrs. Weller's lawn, but her orange love bug wasn't in her driveway either.

So I ran back up our porch stairs and into the kitchen. My dad hadn't even left a note. I tried not to, but my skin prickled with it anyway: he was probably with M and the little whatever—his new family, all made up and happy at the hospital. I looked at the clock and pulled out the bus schedule. Another one was coming in seven minutes.

I ran so fast up our dirt road that even the chipmunks couldn't keep up with me. A few times, I twisted my ankle on some rocks that I hadn't seen coming, but I didn't stop, I just put my chin down and pumped my arms and legs faster.

At Route 88, I took a right and kept running. A few seconds later, my hair blew up and the bus flew past me. I waved my hands and screamed at the top of my lungs, but it just kept getting smaller and smaller in front of me. And when I took in another burning breath, I had to slow down.

Until way up ahead at the bus stop, I watched the back lights flash red.

I clenched my teeth and picked up speed again. My lungs felt like they were pulling in glue instead of air. A red pickup truck like the one Mike used to have sped by me and then veered around the bus, which was still waiting at the empty stop. I pumped my arms harder. But just as I got close enough to yell for the bus driver again, the red lights went out and the bus started moving forward again.

I threw my hands up in the air. Then I screamed so loud that even God up there, sitting by his pool, could have heard me. "*Stop!*"

But it didn't.

I bent over and tried to catch my breath.

Brakes screeched. When I looked up, the bus *had* stopped. I started running again.

When I got to it, I stood panting in front of the door, which stayed closed. I knocked on it and finally the bus driver lady noticed me and opened it.

"Hey, Raggedy Annie," she said. "Are you all right?"

I opened my mouth to say yes and thank you, but nothing came out except air.

"Hey, did I just drive past you back there?"

I nodded. She waved me in. "I didn't recognize you with your fancy new hair*do*."

When I went to put the money in her meter, my hand stopped above it.

"Forget something?"

"Yes," I panted. I didn't have any money. I sighed and looked down toward the back of the bus. Five people were looking back at me, and two people weren't.

"I won't tell anyone if you won't," she whispered.

"Thank you," I said. "Thank you for stopping."

"Don't thank me, honey," she said pointing to the front window. "Thank him." Out there, that red pickup truck had stopped in the middle of the road. It didn't just look like Mike's old truck, it *was* Mike's old truck, the ORD UCK still on the back. It was tilted down to one side now, with a gray-haired man standing next to it. "I wouldn't have seen you at all if that guy hadn't blown a tire."

I glanced up at the sky. Maybe God had been watching after all. But then the bus driver lady told me to go sit down, so I did.

It wasn't the same bus. The graffiti was different. But still, I watched the world whiz by and got my breathing back down to normal.

↗   ↗   ↗

At Scent Appeal, the door was open and the window was fixed. Nothing was written across it now so you could see people inside. Chad's friends, Marcus and Chris, were there and so were Patty and Trisha. But I had never seen the rest of the people standing around, talking loudly. Most of my flower arrangements were standing tall, though.

"Sorry, love, they're closed," a man with bright yellow pants said when I walked in.

"I'm here to see Mike," I told him quietly and kept going.

It was way too hot. I had to dodge clear plastic cups with tiny umbrellas sticking out of them with every step. It was weird, to think that Mike and Chad had so many friends. When I bumped into one man, he turned around and I saw he was wearing blue eye shadow and red lipstick. "Ooo, honey," he said pulling his drink up to his shoulder. "Watch the punch." Then he turned back to another man wearing earrings. Inside the sea of people, there wasn't one Mike.

When I got to the counter, The Boss was gone. He wasn't by the cash register either. Or by the sink. I squeezed my way through more people to the apartment door, but it was locked. Then I stood there, hot and dizzy and short. No one had told me about The Boss. No one had told me. I didn't even get to say good-bye.

I leaned back against the door. After all that running, my legs felt like someone had poured sand into them now. And the more I looked around, the more I wanted to leave.

I squeezed my way up to Marcus or Chris, I couldn't remember which one was which, standing in a circle of people, laughing. "Excuse me," I said.

"Oh hey, kid," whichever one it was said.

"Do you know where Mike is?"

"Yeah," he said turning to another man, who come to think of it, *did* look familiar. I couldn't remember where I knew him from though. "Didn't Mike say he had to go somewhere?"

"The theater?" the man said. And then I remembered who he was: Judas.

I took a step back, said thanks quietly, and turned away from them.

At the door, I looked back at all those people I didn't know and thought about how small your heart is but how big of a space it takes up. And how, even though you can't see it, that heart space grows so quietly across a room or up some stairs into someone else's living room, that even if you never step foot in it again, the air in there is changed forever.

No one even noticed me leave.

54
Lacrima Christi
Tears of Christ

Outside, the sidewalk was silent compared to the party going on inside. I looked in the window one more time, but still no Mike. So I started walking.

Just when I reached the corner, honks happened and then the Scent Appeal van stopped next to me.

Mike leaned over Toby in the passenger seat. "Hey," he said. "Where you going?" His hair was loose around his shoulders and even though he looked tired, his eyes were back to being blueberries again. Toby, in a light striped shirt, put his hand up for a high-five.

"Hi," I said, giving it to him. "You guys weren't inside, so I was going to the hospital. M's there. We found her, *them*," I said, my voice dropping at the end.

Mike's face lifted into a question mark. "The baby? She had the baby?"

I nodded.

"Why?" Mike asked.

"That's what girls do, man," Toby said, hitting Mike in the shoulder.

"Why *now*" Mike said ignoring Toby. "I thought you said September."

"I did."

"Is everybody okay?"

This time, I knew who he was really talking about, so I said, "Fifty-fifty."

Toby lost his smile. "Uh-oh," he said.

"I'm going to park," Mike said.

I nodded and listened to voices filter out of the party while Mike backed the Scent Appeal van into its spot. After a moment, he opened the back door and pulled out Toby's wheelchair, then pushed it around to the passenger side and gently lifted Toby out.

After Mike laid him in his chair, Toby winked at me and wheeled himself into Scent Appeal. But Mike leaned into the van and came out with a manila envelope. Then he walked over to me. "Aren't you coming in?" he asked.

I shook my red. "No." I looked away from him, over toward the noise. Mike looked over, too. "A bit much, I know. You sure?"

I nodded. "Mike, what happened to The Boss? He wasn't in there."

"Oh," Mike said. "Someone adopted him, finally."

"Who?"

"A man, who came in."

"What was he like? Was he nice?"

"Seemed it," Mike said, shrugging.

I swallowed and nodded, anything to stop the bees. Mike leaned into me. "Hey. That's good news, though. It's what you wanted, right?"

"Right," I said. Then I glanced over his shoulder. "I'll come back tomorrow. I'm going to go see if I can help my dad. He needs me." I stood up straighter and looked at Mike when I said that. He noticed and smiled.

"But Apron," he said clearing his throat, his smile gone. "I'm leaving tonight."

The bees swarmed. "No," I said. "You can't."

Mike glanced up at the sky and bit his lip.

"Chad and I had a lot of friends, Apron, but nobody like you," he said. "You're different. You'll see, when you're all grown up. You'll see that you're not like everyone else. You're the bravest girl I know, Apron."

I shook my head. "All anyone ever does is *leave*."

Mike lifted my chin. "Hey," he said. "Not everyone's leaving. Your dad's not going anywhere and he needs you, remember?"

"No he doesn't," I said, whipping my chin off his finger. "He's got M."

Mike smiled. "Exactly." Then he started imitating her, big and panicked. "Oh to be the poopies inside of the diapers, Aprons! Oh that is the crying that needs of the milk!"

And I couldn't help it, a smile crept up.

"Guess what?" I said. "I think she's going to have red hair. Like me."

"You see? *She's* the one who really needs you. You're a big sister now."

All this time I had been thinking about having a sister, I had never thought about *being* one.

"Hey," I said, standing taller. "Do you, maybe, want to come see her?"

He nodded. "I would love to."

"Really? Let's go then." I said it quickly, before he could change his mind.

But he didn't move. He looked down at me and said, "I can't, Apron. I can't go in there, just in case." I must have looked confused. "You know, germs and stuff."

Someone yelled Mike's name and he started to turn his head, then stopped.

"And I should stay here. Someone needs to chaper-one those animals." He lifted his lips up into a smile. "Okay?"

I nodded. He opened his arms and I walked in. "Hey," he said. "I'll write you okay? And here." He dropped his hug and handed me the manila envelope. "You left your book."

I pulled little pieces of air into my lungs and took it. Mike pointed at it. "Your last week's pay is in there, too."

Inside there was some money and *The Little Town on the Prairie*. I looked up at Mike. "But I don't get it. How did you know that was going to be his last day?"

Mike sighed. "They say when you go blind, it's the beginning of the end. Nothing can save you. And Chad refused to be a burden." Mike shook his head and looked away. "I shouldn't be telling you this. It's big stuff. It was better planned, that's all."

High tide spilled over my lashes.

Mike wiped both of my wet cheeks with his thumbs. But standing like that, with the sun behind him and his blond hair blowing slightly, even his own mother would have thought he was the real Jesus.

"Mike?" I said looking into his blueberries. "Chad and I decided—" I couldn't say it.

"What?"

"That you must be related to Jesus." I said it quick-ly, but it still sounded dumb. So I shrugged. "But only on your mother's side. He said your dad's related to President Reagan." He blinked at me confused. But then he shook his head and laughed the way he used to, tipping his head back up to the sky. And when he looked down at me again, his eyes were wet. "Chad never could keep a secret."

"God, I miss him," Mike said. "And you," he pulled me into another hard hug. "I am going to miss you, Apron."

"Me too," I said. Then he told me again that he would write and I promised I would write him back.

Someone turned the music up inside Scent Appeal and a car driving by stopped. "Hey," a teenage girl with a cigarette hanging out of her mouth yelled to us. "What is that place?"

"A beauty salon," Mike said stepping back from me. "For men only."

"That stinks," the girl said, driving off.

"It is?" I asked.

"Yeah, it's Toby's place now." Mike looked at it proudly. "*Fringe Benefits.*"

"Maybe my dad will come in."

Mike laughed. Then a man with a bright yellow crewcut popped his head out the door. "Mike, you coming? We're waiting to start the toasts."

"Okay, be right there," Mike said. He turned back to me and put his hand on my shoulder. "You sure you don't want to come in, Apron?"

"I'm sure." I looked down at my envelope. "I should go find my dad."

"Hey, hold on a minute," he said turning and running into the party.

I took in a deep breath, and then exhaled my lie. My dad didn't need me anymore. He and M were probably holding hands, staring down at their perfect purple banana bread baby. I felt a wrong note ping in my heart. In the waiting room, Nurse Silvia told me the same thing that my dad did about hormones talking: how they can be crying one minute, telling my dad to go away, and then happy as a clam the next, begging my dad to come back. But the only kinds of hormones M had were mean ones. Thinking about the rest of my long hot summer with her made my head tingle.

Mike walked back out carrying one of my flower arrangements: orange roses with baby's breath. "Give these to M," he said smiling.

I took it from him and said thanks, but didn't read the tag because I already knew what it said. "Still looks pretty good," I shrugged, turning the vase around and fluffing the flowers up a bit.

The music turned off behind him.

"Okay," he said standing up straight and breathing in with his eyes closed. "I can do this." Then he looked back down, but I knew he wasn't talking about saying good-bye to me anymore. He was talking about saying good-bye to Chad. And when he stepped up to hug me again, all I could smell were roses.

"See you," he said squeezing me hard. "Catch you on the rebound."

"See you," I said. But I was fresh out of phrases.

We turned away from each other at the same time, the space between us getting longer, until it looked like we hadn't even been standing together in the first place. But we had, and it was there: another heart layer on top of that sidewalk, changing it forever.

55
Fortuna dies natalis
Happy Birthday

The seventh floor was as quiet as it had been yesterday. There was a different nurse behind the counter now, still gray haired but with a much nicer smile, and that picture of the baby my dad had knocked off looked as wet and happy as the others.

"Excuse me," I said, putting the roses down on the counter. "Can I please see the Bramhall baby?"

"Who did you say, honey?" the nurse asked, getting a list and reading through it. "Bramhall."

"I don't see any baby by that name here. You sure you have the right hospital?"

I sighed. "Bramhall," I said, spelling it. "Like the street?"

"No," she said shaking her head. "What's the first name? Maybe I have a typo."

I looked behind her. "I don't know."

The nurse picked one eyebrow up and then the phone. She turned away when she started talking, so I did too. There was only one person, a grandmother, sitting in the chairs now, knitting something square. I heard the nurse hang up and saw Nurse Silvia standing in the doorway. She was in a pink dress and her brown wavy hair was in a headband, instead of a bun. "Hi, Apron," she said holding the door open. Before I could say anything back, she winked at me and waved down low.

The other nurse was busy with some paperwork. I walked quickly over to Nurse Silvia, who took my arm and pulled me in.

We started walking fast.

"Your dad was just here, did you know that?" she whispered.

"Not really," I said.

We passed by the same shut doors with *Delivery* on them and stopped at the long window into the nursery. There were still a few glass cribs in the middle of the room, with blankets and tubes coming out everywhere, but others were lined up along the back wall now, no tubes anywhere, empty.

My stomach hit rock bottom and I looked up at Nurse Silvia and her brown lip gloss. *Fifty-fifty.*

Nurse Silvia tugged my arm. "Look," she said. "She's in that one."

I moved my eyes so fast everything went lopsided for a second.

Then we stood like that, Nurse Silvia and me, smiling.

"Can I see her up close again?" I asked.

Nurse Silvia looked over, surprised. "Did they let you do that before?"

"Yes," I said. "The doctor did."

She turned back to the glass for a moment. "Okay," she said. I thought she was going to tap on the window, but she turned and walked further down the hallway, then disappeared around a corner. I looked back in through the window, at the two nurses in there, both of them bending down into cribs.

I heard Nurse Silvia whisper my name. She was peeking around the corner. "Come on," she said waving me toward her. When I got there, she handed me a blue paper shower cap and a matching mask. "Here you go."

Before I could say anything, Nurse Silvia said, "Put those on." So I did, right away. Then she opened the door and pulled me in.

Inside, the air smelled so fragile you could break it with a sneeze. A few beeps were happening and everything was so bright and white it was hard not to squint.

Until you saw one of the purple banana breads up close—and then it was hard not to turn away. They shouldn't look like that.

Nurse Silvia stopped at the crib furthest from the window. There was a pink sign taped to the end of it now; *Baby da Costa* it said. I started to walk to the other side, but Nurse Silvia shook her head and turned the case around so I could keep my back to the window.

I wished she hadn't. Inside, you could see arms and legs so purple and skinny it looked like they should be in a nest instead of a crib. Hospital bracelets were around both ankles and a tube was stuck down her throat. Her chest was covered with tape, which had monitors on it too, and even though they were closed, you could tell her eyes were too big for her head, which was smaller than a tennis ball and completely covered up under her pink hat this time.

"There she is," Nurse Silvia said, smiling the way nurses do when they know too much.

"Is it still fifty-fifty?" I asked.

She looked at me carefully and nodded.

"When will they know?"

"Every day. Every day, she will go one way or the other."

I looked back down at that purple gumdrop of a hand. It wasn't enough of a chance, but it was something and I smiled.

Nurse Silvia smiled too. "Already in love with her, huh?" she said. I jerked my eyes away and thought about it. But there it was, that tiny heart space, already spreading out between us, my sister and me.

"Can I touch her?"

Nurse Silvia got nervous and looked around.

"Go wash your hands," she said pointing to a sink on the wall next to us. "Quickly."

I pressed some pink soap into my hand, then scrubbed carefully and rinsed off. I pulled a paper towel off too loudly, but when I glanced over my shoulder, those two nurses were still bent over the other cribs.

"Okay," Nurse Silvia nodded. I started to reach my hand in but stopped.

"What?" she whispered.

I lifted my hand and pulled the blue paper cap back a little, until a piece of my red fell out, then I reached my hand back inside the case. I slid my finger under some tubes and into her tiny purple hand. And just like that, like she had known it was me all along, she squeezed it.

I tried to shake the happiness out of me, I tried to remember that it was M's baby, but it wasn't working. I smiled down at that banana bread sister of mine and knew that Mike was right; she did need me. "Nice to meet you," I whispered. Then I felt another squeeze around my finger, light as air.

56

Alma matur
Nurturing mother

Back out in the hall, Nurse Silvia took the cap and mask and told me I better get going. My dad was probably home by now. I stopped for a second and looked her straight in the eye. "Thank you," I said. Then I hugged her. My first real hug with someone from Brazil.

"Okay," she said. "Go." Then she spun one way and I spun the other.

Halfway down the hall, I heard a thud against a wall. I turned back to Nurse Silvia, but she was gone. The *Delivery* doors were all closed and no nurses or doctors were anywhere. Except for one room, which was opened slightly. And then I heard someone mumbling something all wrong in English.

M.

If I hadn't just seen the baby, I would have wondered if maybe she'd thrown *her* against the wall.

I thought about knocking, telling her congratulations and that Mike had given me flowers for her, but then I changed my mind. It was bad enough to be around M when all those pregnant hormones were raging, who knew what would happen now that they were falling out. So I kept going and two steps later, there was M, her hair in a hurricane and her face so white she looked like her tan had dropped off.

"I asked for the nurse!" she yelled at me from the doorway. "The *nurse*, not you, Aprons."

I stepped back. "I was—"

"You were *spying*," she said.

I didn't know whether she meant I was spying on her, or her baby. So I shook my head and said, "Sorry."

She grabbed my arm and pulled me into the room. "Well then, *you* help me."

The room was small and hot and thick with mean. M was wearing a hospital gown, but underneath it she was in pants and a shirt. There was a bag on her bed and next to her, a plastic water pitcher with a bouquet of wild flowers; Queen Anne's Lace and yellow marigolds mixed in with some cat's tail from our garden.

"Cut this off," she said holding her wrist up and motioning to her hospital bracelet. *#13083.*

"I don't have any scissors," I said.

"There," she said, pointing toward where I had heard the thud, a pair of long silver scissors lying on the ground and a dent on the wall above them. She could have killed someone.

I picked up the scissors and walked back to her. M looked nervous suddenly, like I might turn them upside down and stab her instead. I slipped the scissors under her bracelet and snipped. She let the bracelet fall to the floor, then turned and sat down on the end of her bed, a flash of pain crossing her face when she did. No one ever told me how much it hurt to have a baby, but now they didn't need to. M put her face into her hands and started crying long deep sobs. I didn't know what to do.

I went to the door and looked down the hallway, but no one was there.

"Do you want me to call my dad?" I asked carefully, stepping back in, a little closer this time.

She didn't answer.

I swallowed and took another step. "Margie?"

Without lifting her head, she said, "I want you to get out."

And right then I was sure: M had been born with the mean gene.

It's the way we come out, Toby said. Maybe M being mean wasn't any different than Mike and Chad being gay, or me having freckles. Mean was just the way she came out. She hated me all right, but it was nothing personal.

I started for the door, then stopped and turned around. "She's really pretty," I said, smiling.

M lifted her head and glared at me. If you didn't know they were eyes, you might have thought they were ice cubes. Then, without looking at it, she reached for the vase of wildflowers and threw them at me.

The vase hit the wall and water and flowers splashed everywhere. M put her face back in her hands, but behind me I heard footsteps and the nice-looking mean nurse was standing next to me. "What happened?" she asked, like I was the one who did the throwing. But I couldn't have been. The flowers were spread out the wrong way and the nurse knew it.

"It's time for you to leave," she said, bending down to start cleaning the mess. I looked at M and turned away. But before I started out the door, I walked back and picked up the broken hospital bracelet. I slipped it into my pocket.

"*Habetis bona deum*?" the gray-haired nurse read out loud behind the nurses' station, holding the tag up from the orange roses still on the counter. "How are we supposed to figure out who these go to?"

"I don't know," a curly-haired nurse said, frowning over her shoulder. "Open it."

"*Have a nice day*?" the nurse read, confused. "*It could be your last?*"

The two nurses looked at each other and shrugged. I dipped my head low and walked by them.

57

Dulce domun
A sweet thing, home

It took a long time to get home.

It was a good thing Mike gave me that money, a *miracle* actually. Sitting in my seat behind the bus driver, I watched houses and buildings and cars zip by, too fast to see what was really going on inside any of them, but hoping for them all the same. Maybe that was the way God felt up there watching us zip around down here, too fast to really see every one of us, but hoping for us just the same.

My dad's car was in the garage. "Dad?" I yelled, again and again, walking through the living room, the back porch, and all the way up the stairs.

I stopped in front of his bedroom door and listened. It was quiet. And when I walked in, it was empty. His bed was only messy on one side, the way it used to be before M. The shades were up, but the sun had passed by a long time ago, you could tell by the cool smell of sheets. Some of M's beauty supplies were fallen over, making their usual mess, but not as many as there used to be. And then I saw that my mom's closet door was open.

I hadn't been in there since Reverend Hunter's key fell out of my pocket, not with M and her blue toe sprawled out on the bed all day. It shouldn't have been open. I clenched my teeth and walked toward it, then stopped.

Something sniffed.

I stepped back and got ready for a rat or a chipmunk to run out and crawl up my leg. That had happened before: a chipmunk in the kitchen. My mom didn't even yell, she just got a broom and swept it outside.

I didn't have a broom, but I did have a crutch. Both of them were still leaning up against the wall and right when I grabbed one, another sniff happened. My skin tingled, but I walked over and pulled the door open.

And saw my dad's red head.

A croak spilled out of my mouth at the same time his head popped up. He was sitting on the floor with his knees pulled in and his arms wrapped around them, the bottom of my mom's velvet dress draped over one of his shoulders.

I wished it had been a chipmunk.

"Dad," I said dropping the crutch and kneeling down next to him. "Is it still fifty-fifty?"

My dad nodded slowly, like even that was too tiring. "She's okay," he said. "The same."

I closed my eyes, then snapped them open again. "What are you doing in here?"

"Advice," he said softly.

All this time, he had needed my mom's closet as much as me.

"On what?" I crawled in, leaning back against the scuffed up wall next to him.

My dad tapped his knee into mine and held up a folded piece of paper.

"It's the right thing," he said. "She was a mistake, anyway. Never should have happened."

My breath blacked out. I slid away from him. "She's not coming home?"

A tiny shake was all he needed to say.

That space between our hearts, my sister's brand-new one and my old banged-up one, cracked like the top layer of sand after a rainstorm.

"Who is she going to live with?"

"Someone in Europe, I think," he said tapping the paper. "At least that's what it says in here. "

From the outside, I could see M's way of writing all wrong in English. And across my dad's face, I saw it: that little boy in Grandma Bramhall's picture, as sad as the bluebird sings.

It was my fault.

I got to my knees. "I'll change, Dad. I swear. I'll keep everything clean; I can do all the cooking—"

"Stop it," my dad interrupted. "She's not going because of you, Apron. She's going because of *me.*" He sighed. "*Mea Culpa.*"

We both paused. I wanted to tell him that no, none of this was his fault. But the truth was, most of it was. He should have seen the real M a long time ago. And now, after everything she had made us go through, I was never even going to get that sister.

I looked at my dad. "*Errare humanum est,*" I put my hand on his arm and sat back.

He smirked at me. "Well I'm sure the house won't miss her. This place was a bigger mess with her *in* it. And now—with a baby around? Forget it. You and I are going to be busy enough."

I snapped my arm back. "Wait. We can keep her?"

"She's your sister. Of course we can keep her. Margie bought a one-way ticket for *herself.* She wouldn't even hold her own baby." His voice cracked when he said that, and something shivered inside my heart. I used to think the saddest thing had happened to me, but now I knew it had happened to my sister instead.

I got to my knees again. "I'll hold her all the time, Dad. I promise. She won't be sad. Ever."

"I know," he nodded calmly. "I know you will."

We smiled at each other for a second.

"Wow," I said, sitting back, a million thoughts going through my head.

"So what should we call her?"

I turned to him. "Hey. Why doesn't her nametag say Bramhall on it?"

He looked down at his fingers, tapping them together in a think. "Because we never actually got married," he said, a crooked smile growing on his face.

"What?"

"All right, I know. But there were no appointments at the courthouse that day, and we were going to have to wait weeks and I just couldn't listen . . ." He stopped talking and glanced over at my mouth, dropped wide open. "So I paid the desk clerk fifty bucks to marry us in a back room. He sounded legitimate enough."

"But you told me—"

"I know. Margie didn't know, either. Until after I heard her," my dad stopped for a second, "talking to you like that. Then I told her the truth."

I nodded, pretending not care what she called me.

"Dad," I said, swallowing hard. "Mr. Perry was in love with mom."

He glanced at me, but said nothing. Suddenly I wished I hadn't told him. He'd had enough bad news for one day. But then he nodded. "I know."

"You did? Is that why you punched him?"

"I punched him because he was right when he called me a terrible husband. I *was* a terrible husband for a little while. So he was right, and it made me mad."

I didn't get it. "But *he's* the bad husband. He kept a picture of Mom in his boat and bought her a Cyndi Lauper backpack. You would never have done anything like that to Mrs. Perry."

My dad let out a quick chuckle. "No," he said, "I wouldn't have." Then he hit my knee with his again. "But Apron," he said in a new voice. "Sometimes things get broken and people make mistakes. It's just what happens. And then, if you're lucky, they get fixed again, before it's too late." He paused. "Do you understand? And I never loved your mother any less for it."

I slid away from him. Suddenly there wasn't enough air in there.

My dad had watched me. "No one deserves to be lonely, kiddo," he said in a soft version of his serious voice. "That's what your mother always said. That's what she said when she asked me to look after Margie."

I blinked at my dad, but his face didn't change, it just stayed on serious.

"No she didn't!" I said shaking my head, furious. "She would *never* have done that to me." Except it was a lie, my mom used to like M, always talking to her about finding a husband so she could stay in Maine. She didn't know the real M any better than my dad did. "Mom hated M."

"Okay," he nodded away from my glare. "You know what Apron? I'm not good at this stuff. I don't know what I can tell you because sometimes I forget you're still a kid."

I clenched my crooked teeth. "I'm not a kid, Dad." But for the first time in as long as I could remember, I wished I were. Kids wouldn't be able to understand any of this. But I could.

My dad smiled. "You're right," he said, no more fight in his voice. "And we don't need to talk about this anymore, either."

We both dropped our heads back against the scuffed up wall after that. All those times my mom pushed over hangars or searched for her shoes were behind us now.

"I bet she's with Chad," I said quietly. "I gave him a picture of her, so he could find her."

My dad looked at me with his forehead wrinkled in. My face burned, embarrassed at how dumb I was for saying that. Embarrassed at how dumb I was for *doing* it.

"Just as a joke, I mean."

My dad didn't say anything for a little longer but then he nodded. "You know what? That was smart of you. I never would have thought to do that."

And I couldn't help it, I smiled.

He cleared his throat. "So what are we going to name her? That's what I was asking your mother. I'm waiting for her to get back to me."

"Dad," I said carefully, the words begging me not to say them. "Maybe we should call her Margie?"

He dropped his smile. "You wouldn't mind?"

I shook my head. And swallowed.

"Of course, we could always call her the Latin translation for it instead."

We shook on it. It wasn't quite as good as my name, but not everyone can be named Apron.

58

Nunc scio quid sit amor.
Now I know what love is.

The next morning after my dad and I ate pancakes at our lobsters, he went to change Daisy's last name to Bramhall and I got out the *Save the Seal* **pamphlets.** The bloody hot dog of a mother was still frozen in front of that sad baby seal, but behind them, there were other seals, some small and some big, some in the middle of a roll and some floating in the ocean, that needed to be saved, too.

It was already hot, the kind of day when you think the sun broke down up there and was going to laser beam you forever. When I went into the pantry to get a water bottle for my bike, something twitched.

The Boss was staring at me.

"Hey, little guy," I said, poking my finger into his cage.

He didn't look any different, but I could tell he was glad to be back.

Up in my room, I took M's broken hospital bracelet out of my pocket and slipped it into my drawer next to my mom's. Daisy might want it someday.

↗ ↗ ↗

Later, after my dad came back and I had delivered every single one of those pamphlets, my dad sat down with me on the porch stairs.

"Mike only told me it was a man who adopted him."

"A handsome man?" my dad asked.

"No," I smiled. Then after a beat I said, "But a nice one."

He chuckled. "Well, it was Mike's idea."

But he was lying and we both knew it.

"So how was the hospital, did you get to hold her hand, too?" I asked, both of us slapping at a fly that was suddenly trying to land.

"You got to hold her hand?" He turned to me, his eyebrows pulled up somewhere between sad and surprised, forgetting about that fly for a moment.

I pursed my lips together.

"Well," my dad said, slapping my back, and still missing. He wiggled his eyebrows at me. "Ask me again tomorrow."

I smiled a dare back, but noticed that down toward the ocean a line of fog was building up.

"Is she going to be okay, Dad?"

My dad stared at his hands, his fingers crossed over each other into a prayer. "I don't know," he said squeezing them once, then dropping them apart and taking my hand instead. I had forgotten how small mine were in his.

↗   ↗   ↗

We started going back to the cafeteria for dinner again. *Juan Busboy* was happy to see me, you could tell by the wink. One night at the soda stop, I turned around too fast and spilled my drink down someone's shirt. "Look out!" a girl yelled, dropping her tray.

We both jumped over curly noodles and tomato sauce.

"Sorry," I said lifting my head up to Annie Potts's face.

"Hey!" we said at the same time.

"You got your hair cut," she said.

"You got braces."

Right away, *Juan Busboy* came over with his bucket. "Sorry," I told him. We thought he would be mad, but he just winked and said, "No problem," and pretty soon it looked like nothing ever dropped in the first place.

"Where are you sitting?" Annie Potts asked.

I pointed to a corner inside the regular dining room. There was a picture of a red lobster above my dad's head now. I had just started getting good at drawing it. I only had one chance to get it right when I painted it on the table; a lobster holding a daisy.

"Want to sit with me?"

She nodded and her eyes fell to her empty tray. "But I'll have to go up and get some more money first," she said looking a little worried. "My parents are upstairs with my grandmother. She's getting out tomorrow."

I shook my head. "Let's go talk to Carlos," I said taking her by the arm. "It's okay, Barbara won't charge you again."

♐ ♐ ♐

After that, Annie Potts started coming to the cafeteria with us, but not to see her grandmother, to see Daisy. She wasn't a banana bread anymore and every day she got pinker and fatter. Lately, when she saw my big red head rising over her crib, her eyes lit up and she smiled. My dad nudged me with his elbow and said she was just having gas, but then he winked.

I had one week left before starting eighth grade, and three weeks before Daisy was coming home. My dad would be going back to teach full time after that, but Grandma Bramhall wasn't going anywhere ever again. *Especially* not on a cruise.

"It was like being stuck in a port-a-potty," she said, her pinched in forehead shaking. Then she told us how her room was the size of a walnut shell and the dining room had just that *one* chandelier from the brochure in it. Mr. John had a great time cannon balling into the pool the size of a coffee mug, but all he ever wanted to do was swim and she decided she was never traveling again, especially with him. "In fact," she said, a corner of her mouth pulling up. "Now that my car's in the shop, Mr. Orso says he would be more than happy to pick me up and take me anywhere I need to go."

Grandma Bramhall had rammed her car smack into Mr. Orso's car one day while he had been backing out of his driveway. Neither of them were hurt, but they stood for hours together talking and laughing, a whole lot of barking and shaking going on, even after the tow truck came and took Grandma Bramhall's car away.

"Or," my dad told Grandma Bramhall, looking up from pruning my rosebush, with some dirt smudged on his cheek. "You could make it easier on the poor guy and hang out here more often. I've heard you're pretty good with little people." We had been searching the classifieds every day. We didn't need a maid anymore. We needed a nanny.

Grandma Bramhall looked back and forth between us, faster than her head could shake. Then it started nodding up and down instead. We hired her on the spot.

59

Promitto
Promise

Eighth grade started out better than you might think. Johnny Berman wasn't in any of my classes this year and Rennie hadn't grown even a centimeter. She wasn't going to be friends with Jenny Pratt much longer, you could tell. She started slowing down when she walked by me and Annie Potts, playing handball by the swings, or just talking under the big maple tree, but I tried not to notice. Mr. Solo had paired us up for flashcard buddies though, so lately we had started talking again.

When I asked her if her mom was still cooking at 4:30, she said yes, but sometimes she and her dad and Eeebs snuck out to McDonalds before dinner these days. Mrs. Perry was going through an Indian phase right now. She asked me if I wanted to come with them sometime. I told her I would think about it, but that while Daisy was still there, I had dinner at the hospital with my dad.

One night at our new regular table, after I had drawn my tenth perfect lobster in a row, my dad crunched down his newspaper and stared at me.

"Apron," he said. "Did you enter a poetry contest?"

I shook my head, but he said, "Well, what's this then?"

My eyes stopped right below my dad's finger. Right where it said: *Falmouth Middle Schoolers Win Poetry Contest.*

"Oh yeah," I said. "Mike told me that Ms. Frane entered my free verse poem in something."

"Ms. Frane?" my dad said, looking confused. "Did Mike know Ms. Frane?"

I dropped my eyes to the floor. I thought about telling him that she must have been a regular customer at Scent Appeal, but told him the truth, instead.

My dad looked sad, just like I thought he would, but then he smiled and said, "Your aunt and uncle? Doesn't look like she believed you," and turned that newspaper around so I could see that Ms. Frane had kept Chad's name in, right next to mine.

I read it again.

What Love Means To Me
by
Apron Bramhall and Chad Weller

Love doesn't always mean rings and veils and walks down the aisle.
Sometimes love means broken windows and broken hearts,
And not being able to fix either.
And sometimes love means telling you,
There's no such thing as time in Heaven so don't rush to meet me.
Stay a while, and pick, girl, the roses.

"*Collige virgo Rosas.*" My dad looked up at me. "I forgot about that one. You should send this to Mike."

And I did.

Acknowledgments

First, thank you to Caroline Leavitt, who didn't just knock on doors for me, she blew them down. And to my parents, John and Jinxie, who taught me to see the story in everyone. Thanks to Blake, Hilary, and Curtis, those first stories; and to my exquisitely wonderful mother-in-law, Jane Hummer. Much love to my friends: Amy Olivares, Jessica Benjamin, Carrie Bell, and Tory Morton—all a girl really needs is one true friend and I got four. Thank you to Lou Aronica and Jennifer Unter, both of whom picked me out of their piles and started the career I'd been waiting so long for. Thank you to David Kessler and Jessie Sayward Bright for their expert eyes and colorful vision. Thank you to my stunning and sweet girls: Madison, Daisy, and Tatum—the *every* in my *thing*. And thank you to my beautiful and kind husband, Craig, real winner of "Best Attitude" and my favorite noun ever. And finally, thank you to Mike for being my friend.

About the Author

Jennifer Gooch Hummer received her B.A. in English from Kenyon College. She lives in Los Angeles and Maine with her husband, their three daughters, and their dog, Apple. *Girl Unmoored* is her first novel.

You can visit her website at jennifergoochhummer.com.